WANDOR'S VOYAGE

CALIBER BOOKS

Also from ROLAND J. GREEN

<u>WANDOR Series</u>
Wandor's Ride
Wandor's Journey
Wandor's Voyage
Wandor's Flight

<u>PEACE COMPANY Series</u>
Peace Company
These Green Foreign Hills
The Mountain Walks

<u>STARCRUISER SHENANDOAH Series</u>
Squadron Alert
Division of the Spoils
The Sum of Things
Vain Command
The Painful Field
Warriors for the Working Day

WANDOR'S VOYAGE
Book Three

For further information visit the Caliber Comics website:
www.calibercomics.com

Cover image by: Dubya2x

PROLOGUE

In the thirty-third year of the reign of King Nond II over the Kingdom of Benzos, Bertan Wandor, Master in the Order of Duelists, came to stand before the Guardian of the Mountain beneath Mount Pendwyr. And the Guardian of the Mountain, last of the Five-Crowned Kings, spoke to Bertan Wandor, and set him a testing, thus:

"Go and win Firehair the Maiden.

"Go and win the faith of Strong-Ax and Fear-No-Devil.

"Go and win aid from Cheloth of the Woods.

"Go and seek these—the Helm of Jagnar, the Ax of Yevoda, the Spear of Valkath, the Sword of Artcs, the Dragon-steed of Morkol.

"Go among all peoples and through all lands and against all who torment and distress men, wherever you find them barring your passage.

"Go then to the house of him you call father and take up the talisman and watch, while Mount Pendwyr splits with fire, and the hills and woods rise into the sky and are scattered to the sea.

"Go then at last forth to battle and smite those who come against you with all your strength and cunning.

"All such will be your testing. The road is long. The testing is great. May your strength be great also."

And the Guardian of the Mountain returned to the fires whence he came. And Wandor heard these words and rode forth.

Now in Benzos, Wandor was given a task by King Nond, for he won the trust of the king and of the king's strong right arm, Count Arlor. And Wandor was likewise given as servant a freedman of the Sea Folk named Berek, and he and Berek swore to each other the Sacred Oath of the Drunk Blood.

And Berek of the Sea Folk bore the War Name Strong-Ax.

Now in those days Duke Cragor, the Black Duke, sought Nond's throne and Nond's life, and wrought evil against all those who might uphold Nond to the uttermost limits of his own powers. And those powers were exceedingly great, for the Black Duke was a lord mighty in the land of Benzos, and in his service was the Master Sorcerer, Kaldmor the Dark.

In the Viceroyalty of the East, Cragor's hand lay heavy, save in the South Marches. There Baron Oman Delvor held strong for Kind Nond in honor and with power. And it was to the house of Baron Delvor that Wandor was sent to aid and strengthen that house in all possible ways.

But Cragor wished Wandor ill, and in the moment of Wandor's arrival in the Viceroyalty the sorceries of Kaldmor the Dark were unleashed against him. Yet he suffered not, for the Guardian of the Mountain appeared to Kaldmor, and all his sorcerous learning availed him naught, and defeat and humiliation were his lot.

So Wandor came safe to the Marches, and in the castle of Baron Delvor he met Gwynna Delvora, daughter to the baron and a woman of Power. And he found her altogether beautiful, yet he felt no desire for her.

Then came a night when the Earth Voices spoke, and Gwynna received Wandor as a woman receives a man.

And she was Firehair the Maiden.

And she told Wandor of yet another testing, at the hands of the terrible Yhangi, who rode far and wide across the Plains beyond the Silver Mountains.

So Wandor and Gwynna crossed the Silver Mountains. They did strong battle against the floods of the river Zephas, against hunger and cold, against the wild beasts of the Plains. And by the favor of the gods to the brave and by Gwynna's own Powers they won through to the Plainsmen and were received among them.

But Cragor was an unsleeping foe and wrought further ill against the Marches. His assassins struck down the seneschal of the Delvors, Sir Gar Stendor, and his hirelings and vassals made war against the Marches. But in this war Sir Gilas Lanor swore an oath with the Khindi, the dwellers in the forests of the Viceroyalty. They came forth to serve in the war and wrought much havoc among the servants of the Black Duke.

The spring came and with it the time of Wandor's testing before all the Yhangi. Wandor came forth to fight against Jos-Pran, War Chief of the Gray Mares, a man filled with pride and distrust. And he defeated Jos-Pran in three combats, yet Jos-Pran was not content.

So Wandor was bidden to ride the King Horse of all the Thangi. And this Wandor did, though none had done it before. And from that moment onward, the Yhangi swore to follow him and do his bidding.

He had great need of them, for in that spring Duke Cragor came against the Marches with a great army. But there was a need to open the South Pass of the Silver Mountains before the Plainsmen could pass to aid Baron Delvor. The Guardian of the Mountain answered this great need, for he made the earth move so that the South Pass lay open to the Plainsmen.

And in the end Cragor's army came to Delkum Pass in the Marches, and there Wandor met it and conquered it. For the Plainsmen came by the tens of thousands, and the *Red Seers* of the Plainsmen overcame Kaldmor's sorceries, and the greater part of Cragor's army perished altogether from the earth and went down into the House of Shadows. Yet Cragor and Kaldmor the Dark fled in good time from the field of Delkum Pass. Though their strength was for the moment shrunken, yet was their malice toward Nond and all who marched with Nond not diminished. And so they continued their labors for the fall of Nond, even while there was peace in the Viceroyalty for the space of about a year.

Now in the spring of the thirty-fourth year of the reign of Nond there was again war in the Viceroyalty of the East, as those who followed Duke Cragor strove against those who followed King Nond. Those who followed Nond had small advantage, for the Khindi who had aided them in the year past came not out from their forests.

In that same spring the Black Duke himself labored mightily to gather his strength against King Nond. He poured forth his gold into the pockets of mercenaries. He swore friendship with the Ponans of the north, and promised them yet more gold and lands which their fathers had lost to Benzos. He sent Kaldmor the Dark forth into the Hills, to seek out the new and greater Powers certain to be needed in the struggle.

In that spring there was also hunger in the land of Benzos. The hearts of men who held for King Nond grew faint, and in truth even the heart of the king himself was not at ease.

Now Kaldmor also labored mightily and to good purpose when he entered the Hills. It was given to him to reach out to Nem of long-dead Toshak, held terrible in the memories of men for the darkest of Powers. It was given to him to make a *limar* in the form of Master Nem, through which Nero's Powers could flow forth from the House of Shadows.

So there came a night when Kaldmor caused those Powers of Nem to flow forth, and the sorcery of Toshak made mighty signs in the sky, and the hearts of men sank in fear as ships sink in the storms of the sea. Cragor led forth those who followed him, and between one sunset and the next he became Master in Benzos.

Yet the Black Duke was not content, and with good reason. For on that same night there fled from Benzos King Nond and Count Arlor, aboard the ship of Captain Thargor called *Red Pearl*. And they sought the Ocean and the Viceroyalty of the East where Baron Delvor and Bertan Wandor held for the king.

Now the night when Kaldmor brought forth the sorcery of Toshak revealed much to the Lady Gwynna who was wife to Bertan Wandor. It seemed wise to seek new strength for the holding of the South Marches against the Black Duke. Yet there was no new strength to be found save that of the Khindi, who followed their own paths in their own forests.

Therefore Bertan Wandor and Jos-Pran of the Yhangi would ride south into the Blue Forest, and with the favor of the gods seek out the Helm of Jagnar. For in a time long past Jagnar the Forest King led those Khindi called forefathers against the Beast Magicians and warriors of the Empire of the Blue Forest. Beside Jagnar went Cheloth of the Woods, whose Powers had cast down Nem and all Toshak, and together they also cast down the Empire.

So Wandor and Jos-Pran rode forth into the Blue Forest while fear spread across the South Marches. Yet the gods smiled upon the seekers of the Helm of Jagnar, for they passed through the Blue Forest and the rivers that flowed there, among the unclean beasts of the air and the land and the water, to the city that had ruled the Empire. They entered into the city and found the Temple of the Dwarf God.

Bertan Wandor entered into the Temple of the Dwarf God in a proper spirit, so that the beasts and Powers guarding it did not slay him, and came to where Cheloth of the Woods lay. And in that moment Cheloth of the Woods awoke from his sleep of two thousand years, and gave to Bertan Wandor the Helm of Jagnar.

The gods smiled upon those who sought the Helm, yet they did not smile so greatly upon all who strove against the Black Duke and the evil he wrought. For mercenary soldiers of Master Besz, who served the duke, took the Lady Gwynna and bought her to Fors, and Baron Galkor cast her down into prison, though he would gladly have slain her. But he knew his master loved to give great pain and had terrible dreams of all that might be done to give the Lady Gwynna the hardest of deaths. So Galkor did not slay her for he was a faithful servant to the Black Duke.

And the gods frowned again, for though Nond and Arlor came safely across the Ocean to the Viceroyalty, they did not enter safely into the South Marches. Kaldmor again sent forth the Powers of Nem and cast Nond and Arlor down into sleep so that the men of Baron Galkor took them and brought them to Fors. And there was fear in the hearts of Nond and Arlor and Gwynna as they looked upon one another.

But Nond's hands were free, so he took up a sword and smote about him, and Count Arlor and the Lady Gwynna also fought, so that many men of Baron Galkor perished. And Arlor and Gwynna leaped from a high window into the waters of Fors Bay and swam safely to the shore. But more men of Baron Galkor came against King Nond, and they slew him, and the Guardian of the Mountain received his spirit.

Now Count Arlor and the Lady Gwynna rode south, and the Khindi took them and wished to burn Arlor as a sacrifice to Masutl the High Hunter. A watcher of Cheloth of the Woods came upon them, so that the Khindi were filled with fear. Yet Count Arlor felt no fear, and so earned from the Khindi a praise name.

And that praise name was Fear-No-Devil.

Then the Powers of Cheloth of the Woods and the Lady Gwynna made a showing, so all the Khindi saw that Bertan Wandor wore the Helm of Jagnar. Thus did Wandor gain the Khindi to the cause of King Nond, and now the strength of that cause was very great in the South Marches of the Viceroyalty of the East.

And Wandor came to the city of Yost with his new strength. By a cunning stratagem he entered into the city and took it and its citadel, so that King Nond's cause grew stronger still.

Now the winds of winter blew in the Viceroyalty, and men foresaw an end to war for that year. But the wisdom of Bertan Wandor in war was beyond that of other men, and he gathered his army and marched north upon the city of Fors.

And that which had the shape of King Nond walked by night upon the walls of Fors, and slew men in a horrible manner. The hearts of men there were filled with a fear colder than the winds, and in time the army of Baron Galkor was driven forth to do battle.

So it came to pass that the armies of Bertan Wandor and Baron Galkor met upon a field to the south of Fors. Great and terrible was the strife, and freely did Kaldmor the Dark use those foul Powers of Toshak which were now his. Yet the Powers of Cheloth of the Woods surpassed those which were Kaldmor's, and the valor and skill of those who followed Wandor likewise surpassed the valor and skill of those who followed Galkor, and so in time it was Wandor who gained the day.

The army of Wandor marched up to Fors and entered into the city. Kaldmor the Dark and Baron Galkor fled beyond the Ocean. And Count Arlor chose Bertan Wandor to be Viceroy in the East, for he now wore two Crowns and both the Yhangi and the Khindi followed where he led. So it seemed fitting to Wandor that he become Viceroy, and he entered upon his rule without great joy yet without fear.

Then there was peace in the Viceroyalty for the space of that winter. But in time spring came upon the Viceroyalty, and upon the Ocean that washed its shores. Across the waters of the Ocean the Sea Folk came to plunder and slay along the shores, for Duke Cragor had given gold to many of them, and hope of power to some among them who were ambitious. Still others among them had turned toward the Beast Cult of Yand Island, and sought favor from its Beast Wizards by taking from the Viceroyalty men and women for sacrifice to the Beasts.

So there was war once again in the Viceroyalty, and once again it seemed that the gods frowned upon Bertan Wandor and those who stood beside him against the Black Duke.

From *The Shorter Chronicle of Wandor*

CHAPTER 1

Darkness pressed upon the Ocean like a thick lid of black sea jade upon an immense bowl. Toward the east a thin streak of pale light crept along the horizon. The gods were lifting one edge of the lid, to peer down into the bowl and laugh at the antics of the creatures scuttling frantically about within it.

Daraun Son of Hymok stood in the prow of his seal ship *Mistwing* and shivered. He did not shiver from the chill dampness of the air or from the wind that blew out of the blackness around him. He had endured without shivering the cold and the winds of the gray seas on the edge of the ice where the HaroiLina hunted the whale and the walrus.

He shivered at his own creation, the image of the world as a bowl and men as tiny creatures placed in it for the amusement of the gods. It was not a badly conceived image. Indeed, putting it into a verse would certainly uphold his reputation as a bard. It would not so well uphold his reputation as a Captain, Warrior, and sturdy leader at sea and in battle, trusted and respected by many though not as yet honored with a War Name. He would put the image out of his mind for now and prepare his spirit for battle as he had already prepared his body.

He looked aft, and the two men at the steering oar looked back at him. Casting his eyes slightly upward he could make out the loom of the sails. Looking higher still, he could make out the blue lanterns burning on either side of the lookout platform on the mainmast.

Soon they would be taking down both sails and lanterns. As daylight spread across the Ocean, the five seal ships that followed in *Mistwing*'s wake would no longer need the lanterns to guide them. On shore, waking eyes would turn seaward, and the tall lateen sails could give needless warnings.

In the darkness amidships, contorted shapes began to move, gradually settling into the forms of men. Most were tall, their lean and sinewy bodies clothed only in trousers or breechclouts, their long hair caught up by a single bronze or silver ring. Daraun watched the awakening of his fighting men with peace in his soul from the knowledge of how well they would fight in this day's battle. He knew that he lacked a War Name and he thought he knew why, but he also knew that he had an honor equal to any War Name and of more use in battle—strong warriors would follow him.

"*Hai-yoh!*" he shouted. "Morning watch—prepare us for battle!" A dozen men sprang into action, seizing on the spider's web of ropes that controlled the two sails. High above, the two lanterns went out. The long varnished yards with their heavy sails of linen slid down the masts until they lay across the three gangways running fore and aft. The men fell on them, rolled them up, bound them as tightly as any sausage, then pushed them from the gangways down into the hold.

Now the men who'd been below while the sails came down began to scramble up on deck. They already wore battle gear—boots, leather or sheepskin trousers, and long tunics of heavy leather sewn with iron rings. In one hand each man carried his helmet—boiled leather for some, iron for those with wealth or good fortune in past battles. In the other hand each carried his chosen weapon—sword, spear, ax, or bow and quiver of arrows. Sharkskin soles scraped on wood and metal clanged on metal as the men finished arming themselves and took their places along the side gangways of *Mistwing*, each man behind his shield.

As the morning watch went below to arm themselves, Daraun looked across the water to the other five ships. They also had their sails down and their men bustling about on deck, all except Foyn's *Fang of Giyo*. But then Foyn was a sadly unskilled Captain, with no luck in attracting men able to do what he could not. He bore the War Name of Line-Cleaver in memory of a feat of mad, witless bravery done twenty years ago, but he had done little worth noting and nothing worth honoring since then. This had begun to oppress Foyn, making it wise to avoid him on future raids.

To be sure, Telek the Fatherless was sailing with Foyn, and all the deadly skills Telek had learned from the *mungans* of Chonga might be at Foyn's disposal. Whether Foyn would be able to profit from this, no man could say.

Now all the ships showed bare masts and decks crowded with armed men. Daraun remembered his own earlier raiding days, when it was rare for even two seal ships to sail in company and no man living had heard of more than four seeking battle together. The people who called themselves the HaroiLina—the Children of Haro, whose enemies had named them Sea Folk—traded in fleets for wealth. They raided alone, which was as it should be for men who wished to prove themselves and win the favor of Haro Sea Father.

This had changed, along with much else that when Daraun was young had seemed as changeless as the tides of the Ocean and the flight of the gulls on the wind. Now they raided less to win the favor of Haro than to win the favor and the gold of Cragor, the Black Duke, Royal Consort of Benzos, king of that mighty land in all but name. Now they raided not to prove their courage, but to burn and kill among Cragor's enemies and preferably to live to return home and receive their rewards.

So now the HaroiLina raided with five, six, or eight ships together, with three and four hundred fighting men. It did not matter that there was seldom enough booty to divide among such a host. Once it would have mattered greatly, for there were a hundred songs of murders and blood-feuds sprouting from quarrels over a golden bowl or a fair slave girl. It did not matter anymore, for a raider's rewards came not from the strength of his arm but from the Royal Treasury of Benzos.

These things were so, and Daraun could see no great chance that they would cease to be so, as long as Cragor ruled in Benzos. Certainly he could not change them by any skill or gift or power of his own. Therefore he would not try, and would put the matter out of his mind.

Some of what was new did worry him, whether or not he could

change it. There were those among the HaroiLina who now followed the Beast Wizards of Yand Island. Nor were these only the wretched and the outcast. Among them were no less than four men who had borne the Spear of Valkath as Speaker to the *Kym* of Captains.

Foyn was among those who had turned toward Yand. When Daraun was young, a man who whispered once what Foyn had said aloud a dozen times would have done well to escape exile or slavery for his blasphemy.

Yet perhaps what drove men to Yand Island and the Beast Cult was not so much evil as the fear that they could not endure otherwise. Much of the world looked the same as ever, but even the wisest among those who looked more carefully or listened to the tales from the lands to the south had their doubts.

It was said that the Powers of Toshak were loose again in the world, battling once more as they had battled long ago against the Powers of one called Cheloth of the Woods. It was said that the sorcerer who had called forth the Powers of Toshak served Duke Cragor and wielded those Powers in his cause. In reply Cheloth of the Woods had come forth from his two-thousand-year sleep at the call of Bertan Wandor, now Viceroy of the East and leader of Duke Cragor's enemies.

Bertan Wandor, Viceroy of the East, rider of the King Horse, wearer of the Helm of Jagnar, leader of the Yhangi of the Plains and the Khindi of the forests, proven warrior and captain, husband to Gwynna Delvora who commanded the sorceries of the Red Seers of the Yhangi. Bertan Wandor, who had sworn the HaroiLina's own Oath of the Drunk Blood with Berek, called Strong-Ax, son to Daraun's own brother.

It was the place of Berek that weighed most heavily on Daraun's spirit. He did not know or care much about Toshak or Cheloth. Only those old men and older Hearth Mothers who had nothing better to do than compare one scroll or song with another knew if the HaroiLina had come to their present home before, during, or after the great sorcerers' duel of two thousand years ago. In fact, some doubted that Haro Sea Father had in those days even taken on the seal's form in which he begot the first of the HaroiLina upon a human woman.

What was known was that there had been much terrible fighting among men. There would be still more for years to come. Berek stood in the middle of it all, sworn to fight at the side of Bertan Wandor and share his fate, whatever that might be.

Daraun's brother was dead, also his brother's other sons and his own son. The daughters of neither man had sons of an age to perform the rites over Daraun or stand beside him in battle or *Kym* meeting. Daraun stood alone, his back bare to any enemy who might wish to strike.

Nor was that all. Daraun led raiders of the HaroiLina against the Viceroyalty of the East, while Berek led defenders of the Viceroyalty against the raiders. They might come face to face, and then what? There was hardly any curse more terrible than that upon him who slew a brother or a brother's son, except that curse which would be upon Berek if he broke the Oath of the Drunk Blood to Bertan Wandor.

The forested hills of the Viceroyalty's coast were lifting their dark-green crests up over the eastern horizon. Soon watchers on those hills would be able to make out the raiders' ships, even with their masts bare and their dark hulls faint against the darker sea.

Daraun cupped both hands and shouted up to the lookout, "The battle standard!" A moment later a dark ball dropped over the side of the platform, stopped in mid-air, and broke open. A dark-red banner streamed out, a spear's length wide at the base and as long as three tall men. Without waiting to see the other ships break out their own banners, Daraun gave his next order. "To your places for rowing!"

His men were all past their first youth and their first battles, so there were no wild cheers. In silence they climbed below and sat down on the chests that served them for rowing benches. A wild clattering told of oars being unracked and thrust through leather-sealed oar holes. One by one the oars came forth like serpents from their holes and trailed in the water alongside. Daraun looked below again and met fifty pairs of eyes looking up at him. He signaled to his Second Captain, who stood aft beside the steersmen. The Second Captain raised his spear high then slammed the butt down on the deck with a dull *thunk*. The oars lifted and swayed in the air. The rising sun seemed to ignite each drop from them before it reached the sea.

Thunk—and the oars came down with a splash,

Thunk—and the oars swung back,

Thunk—and the oars rose again.

Thunk, thunk, thunk. Rhythm of spear-butt, rhythm of oars, rhythm of the splash of water at the bow—all rose together. *Mistwing* came about until the seal's head on her high-swept prow pointed directly at a distant hilltop. Then she began to move, and behind her the other five ships fell into a line that stretched out straight toward the enemy's shore.

CHAPTER 2

There was movement in the village, but only ashes blowing in the breeze and a scrap of cloth flapping from the end of a charred beam. There was sound, but only the faint pop of dying coals and the drone of flies around the bloody head of a young man who lay on his back in the village's single street. He lay with one hand cut off and the other clutched around a woodsman's ax. The villagers had fought the raiders, but they'd fought alone, with what came ready to hand.

In the end the village went up in flames, and the villagers went down into the House of Shadows or into the holds of the seal ships. The raiders were safely off-shore before the first of the Viceroy's soldiers appeared. By the time Wandor and Gwynna rode down the village street, the raiders had been gone half a day. Half a day of sea wind should have blown away the last of the death-smell the raiders left behind them, but it was not so. Wandor and Gwynna stayed in the village only long enough to see what had to be seen.

They rode up the trail from the shore, moving fast until they'd left the last of the burned houses behind them. As fast as they rode, the smell seemed to follow them like a stalking beast of prey. It seemed hours before Wandor could take a deep breath and smell nothing but pine trees and springtime earth and the salt wind blowing over them. He reined in his horse and Gwynna pulled hers to a stop beside him.

They'd come on far ahead of their escort, so they stopped to talk a while and let their horses breathe. Gwynna took off her hat and brushed the last few specks of gray-black ash off the long curling golden feather.

"Ugly," she said at last. "What makes it worse is that all we can do for them is to keep up our own strength and hope to avenge them someday. The Sea Folk are raiding the coast at will. We've already had a dozen raids this year since their ships took the Ocean, and we'll have fifty more before winter. They've discovered that they can put two hundred men ashore, burn a village, and be off beyond our reach between sunrise and sunset. Every time they do it, Cragor pours more gold into their hands, so their next raid is bigger and worse for us."

Wandor nodded. "And the Beast Wizards of Yand praise them for the victims they bring to feed the Beasts."

"That may not last forever," said Gwynna. "I have heard that the Hearth Mothers doubt the wisdom of this turning toward the Beast Cult. The *Red Seers* of the Yhangi keep a bond with the Hearth Mothers, so I have been able to learn this."

Wandor did not ask what sort of bond this might be. Nine chances out of ten, it was something drawn from the sorceries of the *Red Seers* and Hearth Mothers, Gwynna's own gifts, and the gods alone knew who or what else. He would take the bond's existence on faith, for he trusted Gwynna even in those moments when he could not deny that he somewhat feared her. He would not seek to know more, for the more he knew about such things the more small and helpless he felt before those forces that shook him like a pair of dice as they played their own games.

He could not let himself feel small and helpless. Otherwise he could barely wield his own human powers, any more than a Duelist with pulled wrist tendons could wield his sword. He had to retain command of himself and all those gifts and skills the gods had given him long before they called him to become something else. He owed it to all the people who followed him or trusted the strength and wisdom they thought he had. There were many of them, few of them caring about duels carried on by mighty powers far beyond their understanding. There would continue to be many of them even when he wore all Five Crowns. So that he could do what must be done for these people, Wandor would deny himself knowledge. This would not be the last act of self-denial his leadership would demand of him. He was certain of that. He was equally certain that some of the self-denials yet to come would be far more painful than this one.

However, they were yet to come. He would not let his thoughts dwell on what might be until he lost his power to deal, with what was. He looked at Gwynna. She'd noticed his disappearing for a time into his own thoughts, but she'd also remained silent. She always did both.

She took his glance as a sign to speak again. "Other things also make the Hearth Mothers unhappy. The raiders are bringing back thrall-women and using them with either too much favor or too much of the stick. There are broken oaths in many longhouses already, and there will be broken heads in some before the summer is out."

Wandor laughed bitterly. "I doubt that broken heads among the warriors of the Sea Folk will be enough to keep them away from our coasts, unless they are broken by swords or axes in our hands."

Gwynna shook her head soberly. "No. But in such cases the Hearth Mothers are considered to have great wisdom, and therefore the right to speak and judge. It has been a long time since the full *Kym* of Hearth Mothers met, let alone stood equal to the *Kym* of Captains in great matters. But this is a matter of hearths and peace within them. The Hearth Mothers may choose to speak, even if no one listens."

"Are we supposed to wait until the Hearth Mothers find the courage to speak, then wait further until they may perhaps be heard and obeyed?" said Wandor. He knew before he'd spoken half the words that they were harsh. He did not know if he regretted them. There were times when Gwynna's constant dwelling on strange Powers and customs among stranger peoples itched like fleas under a coat of mail.

Gwynna's face did not change. Four times out of five she let his outbursts fly past without a word or an eye-blink. The fifth time her temper would explode about him like a mountain storm. At those times Wandor would gladly have taken refuge in the comparative peace and safety of a battle against odds of five to one.

"No, we cannot wait," she said. "I wish we could. It would give us the best chance of winning the Sea Folk to our side in the end. Sooner or later we must do that. Otherwise we are trapped here in the Viceroyalty as we were in the South Marches, waiting for Cragor to strike at a time and place of his own choosing."

Wandor was not sure that his question had been answered. He

was quite sure he could add nothing to Gwynna's words about the danger they faced.

Hooves thudded on the trail behind them and their escort rode up, a dozen armed horsemen with Sir Gilas Lanor at their head. The young knight's face was soot-darkened and grim, and his gestures were quick and nervous as he guided his men into a protective ring around Wandor and Gwynna.

"It were best that you did not ride so far ahead. The Sea Folk ships are long gone, but they have been known to leave behind scouts and spies, to be picked up later. Such men would have bows, and—"

Wandor nodded. "We shall take care, Sir Gilas." It was a half-empty promise. He knew it, Gwynna knew it, and Sir Gilas knew it. Wandor might rule the Viceroyalty, the Yhangi, and the Khindi. He did not yet rule the Warrior and Duelist in himself who would not set his own life above those of his followers, who would send no man where he would not go himself. Gwynna might be right when she said that in the end this could gain him nothing but a splendid funeral. He still would not set it aside.

Sir Gilas did not quite dare to sigh audibly. Instead he merely returned Wandor's nod and said, "Very good, my lord." Then he urged his horse up to the head of his men again, before Wandor could reply.

Gwynna sat in her saddle, her face twisted as if in pain, quivering slightly and giving small snorts and hisses of laughter. Wandor could sigh, and did. He should never have made it clear to Sir Gilas how he hated being treated with needless formality. He'd dangled an irresistible bait in front of the imp in Sir Gilas, and every so often the imp rose to that bait.

The trail climbed to the crest of the hill, then plunged down the far side, through close-grown pine trees into a valley that slanted northeast away from the sea. The trail followed the valley floor, winding from side to side and climbing up and down in a manner without logic or reason. Eventually it wound through an oak grove that filled the gap between two hills and turned into a road.

Beyond the oak grove the road turned again, and shortly met the high road leading south towards Fors. The riders turned toward the city, passing ox carts loaded with firewood, charcoal, and barrels of beer. The teamsters ignored the passing riders, too busy guiding their clumsy carts and clumsier beasts.

The riders clattered across a wooden bridge. From below came the smell of fresh tar and the sound of mauls and axes as new timbers were dressed and put into place. The carpenters took off their caps and bowed as they saw the Viceroy riding past and his lady taking off her famous green-leather hat to wave it at them.

The work Wandor had ordered on the bridges and roads had a double purpose. His strength in the Viceroyalty was greater than all but the largest army Cragor could bring across the Ocean. Yet that strength was scattered and would have to be assembled quickly if the Black Duke came. This meant building roads that did not turn into mud after every rainstorm and bridges that did not collapse under every pack mule. Such roads and bridges could carry armed men, horses, and wagons swiftly from one end of the Viceroyalty to the other.

The bridges and roads also meant work for men who might otherwise have been beggars or starved corpses, bread in their bellies, an occasional coin in their pockets, and, for the moment, fewer thoughts of trouble in their minds. There were many such men after two years of war in the Viceroyalty—peasants driven off their land and without the heart to start again, hunters who could no longer hunt Khind game and Khind women with impunity, mercenaries and Royal Army men with no place in the Viceroyalty's strength and small skill in anything but war. Few of these men were evil; but most were weak enough to become evil if no one helped them remain virtuous.

The road wound back and forth in broad loops, sliding steadily down out of the hills. The shadows of the trees on either side grew longer, while gold and crimson and orange slowly flooded the western sky. As the flaming disk of the sun touched the sea, they rode out of the forest on to the open land north of Fors. In the distance the city squatted on the end of its peninsula. The riders urged their horses from a walk up to a trot, and then up to a canter.

All colors but the purple of twilight were fading from the world by the time they reached the Shipwrights' Gate. They waited while a long, eight-wheeled cart rumbled through, drawn by twelve oxen and carrying an enormous rough timber—the future keel of some ship, perhaps. Then they rode in, the clatter of their horses' hooves echoing up the streets to rebound from the stone bulk of the castle and the temple towers. From the direction of the waterfront came the sound of men still at work fitting out the ships there.

Fear no longer blew through the streets of Fors on every breath of wind, as it had the night Wandor first rode into the city after his victory over Galkor's army. The new Viceroy's rule was firm but just; his men behaved themselves and his barbaric allies seldom entered the gates; there was work and food for all; and that which had the shape of King Nond no longer walked the halls by night and slew silently and horribly.

The fear was gone, but real happiness had not come. Nor could it, with all that might yet happen. The faces in the taverns, shops, and streets were still those of people certain that the gods had more unpleasant surprises in store for them.

Eventually the rider came to the castle and passed in through the main gate, tunneled through twenty feet of stone wall. Stablehands led off the horses, the guards scattered toward their quarters, and Sir Gilas Lanor himself went no farther than the old Great Hall on the third level of the keep. There were times when it was pleasant to sit for an hour over wine and a late supper, speaking of what the day had brought. This was not one of those times, and Sir Gilas could read it clearly on his master's face. He vanished as Wandor and Gwynna entered the Great Hall, and they were alone as they climbed the spiral stairs in the wall of the keep to their private chambers.

The steward had seen their arrival and done his duty. They barely had time to sit down on the bench under the window and pull off their boots when a knock on the door heralded the arrival of a party of servants with tubs, buckets of hot water, soap, towels, oil, and chamber robes. A quick look between Wandor and Gwynna, a quick jerk of Wandor's head, and the servants disappeared so quickly that it almost seemed they had never been there.

The water steamed temptingly in the tubs and the faint scent of the oil rose from the bottles on the floor. Wandor sat back down on the bench and began undoing his riding breeches.

"I suppose there'd be some purpose to having servants hovering about to do this for each of us," he said. "But I can't see what it would be."

"Keeping the nobles from saying that we live in no more state than shopkeepers or yeomen," said Gwynna, pulling off her tunic and throwing it into a corner.

"The nobles can bray as loudly as they please," said Wandor. "Try again."

"Making the steward feel needed," she said, pulling her shirt over her head and stretching as she stood bare to the waist.

Wandor shook his head. "I'll raise his pay, if he must feel needed."

Gwynna pulled off her breeches and massaged her thighs. "Better to spend the money on buying me a new saddle." She winced as her fingers probed sore muscles. "Also on paying the executioner to think of something really painful for whoever made the one I'm using now." She unknotted the silk loinguard that was her last garment and stepped naked into one of the tubs. With a blissful sigh she sank down until only her head and shoulders were visible.

"You'll get the saddle anyway," said Wandor, his voice muffled as he drew off tunic and shirt together.

"Keeping twenty people from begging or starving after the work is done on the roads and bridges," said Gwynna, reaching out for a jar of oil. Her tub tilted precariously, but didn't quite go over. "There are only so many roads one can drain and gravel and only so many streams that can't be crossed dry-shod even in flood."

"They can go to work in the shipyards," said Wandor, throwing aside his breechclout and stepping toward his own tub.

"Not the unskilled ones," said Gwynna. "Ships that won't sink the first time they leave harbor have to be built by men who know what they're doing." She began soaping herself.

"I suppose you could turn them over to Master Besz," she said after a moment. As she often did, she grimaced at the name. "The gods know he could make soldiers out of mules or apes, let alone men."

Wandor did not reply at once, because he was lowering himself into his tub. After a moment the first wave of delight passed and he could reply. "No doubt Master Besz could turn the men into soldiers, but could I pay them after he did? No, I was thinking of settling them on some of the abandoned farms, or having them clear new land."

Gwynna frowned. "That could mean trouble with the Khindi.

They've taken to hunting and even building camps on the vacant land. The Khindi will not easily turn against the wearer of the Helm of Jagnar. But they won't be happy about fighting for one who reaches out his hand against land they've claimed." Five minutes passed in silence as they soaped, oiled, and rinsed themselves. Then Wandor threw his hands wide, sending a chunk of soap flying across the room, and laughed.

"It seems that every solution raises a new problem in place of the old one. I somehow feel I've been through all this before."

"Oh?" said Gwynna, climbing out of her tub. She wrapped a towel around herself and came over to kneel beside Wandor's tub. "When was that?"

"When I was just sixteen or so, at the Duelists' House in Trorim. I was just beginning to realize that I had something out of the ordinary in the way of gifts as a Duelist. I began to get rather impatient and full of myself. Every time my instructor Sir Warin Marklor taught me a new system, I would make one or two changes in it."

"Just to show that you knew better than your elders, of course," said Gwynna.

"Of course," said Wandor. He reached out and patted one towel-clad thigh, feeling Gwynna's warmth through the rough cloth. "In any case, you can imagine what happened as soon as Sir Warin caught on. He took me down, four kills out of five in a single day. He hardly needed to say anything after that, but he wanted to make sure I understood, so he put it into words."

Wandor stepped out of the tub and began toweling himself dry as he searched his memory for his old arms instructor's words. "'Young Bertan, there is a reason for systems of fighting being as they are. Every part is intended to support every other part in achieving the purpose of the whole, whatever that may be.

"'Change one part, and you risk leaving some other part unsupported. Then the system may no longer work. Change one part when you are young and inexperienced, and you are certain to destroy the system and perhaps yourself.'" Wandor sighed. "I feel as though I'm back at school again. Well, I learned to fight and I suppose I can learn to rule. Self-denial, self-control, moderation, caution in everything. It worked before, and—"

Gwynna laughed. "Self-denial in everything?" In a single swift twisting movement she stripped off the towel, caught it by one end, and flicked the free end at Wandor's shin. As she almost always did, she scored a perfect hit.

Wandor looked at her—the sleek beauty and grace, the subtle gleams on skin and hair-and he shook his head. "No, not in everything." The warmth that was bubbling up inside him seemed to be clogging his throat, and his words came out hoarse and faint. Gwynna smiled, and reached out a hand to take him and lead him after her.

No, thought Wandor, there were things he would not need to deny himself. Not the fierce blazing joy in his joinings with Gwynna, nor the long sleepy moments of peace that came afterward.

The gods would ask only so much of a man and a woman before rewarding them.

CHAPTER 3

In the darkness, Jaira heard the wind whining through the holes in the wall of the hut. It almost drowned out the snores of the man sprawled on the pallet beside her. Hopefully it would drown out whatever sounds she made.

With exquisite care she rolled out from under the quilt and off the pallet. The dirty floor was icy against her bare skin. She rose on hands and knees and crawled to the corner of the hut where her gown hung on a peg beside Captain Tagor's war gear. She looked back toward the lump under the quilt that was the captain. The quilt rose and fell steadily, in time with Tagor's snores. She rose and pulled the gown from the peg. Without waiting to pull it on, she slipped through the narrow gap left by the sagging door. Rough wood scraped skin from her body both in front and behind, but that was better than risking a squeal from rusty hinges that could jerk even Tagor up out of sleep.

Outside the wind blew louder and much colder. Swiftly Jaira drew on the gown. In spite of the holes, it was good thick wool, better stuff than she'd ever worn before Tagor took her as his concubine. Some merchant's or master craftsman's wife had worn the gown once, perhaps in Avarmouth. Tagor's company had been among the first inside the walls when Cragor stormed the city and their chances for loot had been good.

The camp of Tagor's company lay in silence except for the wind and in darkness except for a single fire at the other end, beyond the soldiers' tents. Jaira's sharp Khind night-sight picked out the silhouettes of four sentries huddled around the fire. It had been over a month since the last alarm of Ponan raiders. The sentries were growing lax.

Jaira hitched the gown up around her knees so that it would not grow damp from the long grass and slow her down. Then swiftly she headed out into the darkness, toward the ruined farm where the rabbits now burrowed so thickly. She knew she had not the skills of a Khind of the Home Forests. She was town-born and town-bred, and Masutl the High Hunter turned his face away from such Khindi and withheld his blessings and his gifts of skill in the hunt. Yet she had all the skill she needed to pass silently through the darkness from the camp to the farm and fill her belly on the rabbits there.

She reached the farm, drew the snare from the sleeve of the gown, set it, then lay down behind a short stretch of wall. One hand held a fallen brick ready for striking. Now she could only wait and listen.

As it often did when she was alone, her mind turned to the idea of escape. As it always did a moment later, it turned away. Captain Tagor starved her, but mostly when there was barely enough food for himself and his men. He beat her, but mostly when he was drunk, and that was not often, since wine came only once a month to the soldiers who kept watch on the Ponans. He hardly ever turned her over to the other captains, and never to the Black Duke's chief captain on the border, whose slave girls often ended up mad or maimed. So her life with Tagor was not the worst that could happen to her.

Worse could have happened to her two years ago, in the massacre outside Benzos that slew her father and brothers. She would have died in her sixteenth year if it hadn't been for that swordsman, the Master Duelist who slew the men chasing her. She'd heard tales that the swordsman was the same Bertan Wandor who now ruled in the land that the Khindi called the Home Forests and that the Hond called the Viceroyalty of the East. She'd also heard that Bertan Wandor was nine feet tall and wielded in each hand a sword so heavy that no other man could lift it. Had it perhaps been someone else who'd saved her two years ago? She did not know.

She did know that there'd been no one to save her or any of the other Khindi in Benzos when the Black Duke turned against them.

Nothing at all had saved those who resisted or could not be made into useful slaves. She'd saved herself only by enduring too many men and half a dozen beatings, until Captain Tagor picked her out of a slave pen and took her north.

She could flee. She might even get clear of the patrols and not be brought back to be turned over to the company for as long as she might live. Then what? Some Khind slaves had reached the Hills, it was said. But the Sthi tracked them down and sacrificed them in the terrible caves far below the earth. No Khind's spirit could ever come back from those caves.

She might go north, to the Ponans. They would not sacrifice her, but they might well slay her. Even if they did not, slavery in their camps would certainly be a harsher life than the one she led now.

No, if there was wisdom in anything, it was in staying where she was. She—

A faint squeal reached her on the wind, the squeal of a rabbit caught in her snare. She darted out from behind the wall, the brick raised in her hand. She struck savagely at the writhing, furry shape on the ground in front of her, heard it squeal again, then saw it lie still. She dropped the brick and snatched up snare and rabbit, then darted for the shelter of the wall again.

Her teeth and nails were sharp enough to do the work of a knife, and hunger gave the raw meat as much flavor as a fire could have done. When at last her stomach was quiet, she took the ears and entrails, wrapped them around a fallen twig, then wrapped the whole bundle tightly in grass. She knelt, prayed briefly, then placed the bundle in a small bush, low down where no casually passing Hond would see it.

It was a small offering, and hardly a proper one without a fire to burn flesh and fur. Yet she had made it before and would make it again. Perhaps Masutl the High Hunter had turned his face away from her and from all the Khindi who lived under the rule of the Black Duke. It could still do no harm to make the best offering she could, to assure the High Hunter she had not turned her face away from him.

The Grand Master of the Order of Duelists sat in his carved

oak chair and stared at the wine cup on the table in front of him, a relic of the first Grand Master of the Order. Two and a half centuries of use had left the cup so scarred and scraped that it would have taken sorcery to give it a high polish.

The Grand Master made the gesture of aversion that all Duelists were taught to make at any mention or thought of sorcery. He made it slowly and more sloppily than he would have tolerated in any freshly-sworn apprentice. He was feeling his seventy years, but that was only a small part of the reason. When all was said and done, he wondered, did it matter anymore what the Order of Duelists thought of sorcery—or of anything else?

The Grand Master raised the cup to his lips and drained the last of the wine from it, then slammed it down on the table with more force than was really needed. He would not sink into doubt and despair. He could not. House Masters of the Order might despair and grow lax or sodden with wine. Two had done so, and he'd relieved them of all that they'd become unworthy to bear or hold.

If the Grand Master sank into despair and his hand grew weak, nothing except a Superior Conclave of all the House Masters could cast him aside and put a more worthy man in his place. Such a Conclave might not be allowed to meet at all. Certainly it could not hope to meet before the Order fell into a confusion from which only Duke Cragor could gain anything.

He would be true to his trust, like the twenty-two Grand Masters before him. The Duelists had survived many crises, beginning when King Stayor IV in a moment of extravagant generosity made them an Order. The jealousy of the other Orders at this outrageous and wholly unsought honor had nearly strangled the newborn Order of Duelists in its cradle. Could the Black Duke prove a more formidable enemy than those the Duelists had faced so long ago, when they had not the tenth part of their present strength and reputation?

The Grand Master pushed back his chair, went to the chamber window, pushed the shutters open, and peered out. The window was high in the tower of the Great House of the Order, and gave the Grand Master a view far and wide over Benzos.

The scrape of metal on stone sounded above him. Looking up, he saw two helmeted heads peering over the battlements on top of the tower. He made the "All's-well" gesture, saw the sentries return it, and saw the heads vanish.

That was one reason the Order might pass through this fire unburned. Every House of the Order had armed and alert sentries posted night and day. No House could be surprised, unless Cragor's fighting men had good fortune far beyond what could be reasonably expected.

Without surprise, any blow of Cragor's against the Duelists would most likely be a blow in the air. Every Duelist kept ready-to-hand weapons, clothing, food, and gold. In a single hour all the Duelists of any or all the Houses of the Order could vanish as thoroughly as chimney smoke whipped away in a winter gale. The swords of some of the deadliest fighting men in the world could be unleashed against Cragor, perhaps no more than a score, perhaps all three thousand. Would Cragor care to risk that?

The Grand Master doubted it. Cragor would know better than anyone else in Benzos that he could barely pay the fighting men needed to meet those enemies he already faced. In such a case, no man but a fool would lightly add to the ranks of his enemies, and Cragor was not a fool. Therefore the Duelists would be safe as long as they stood apart from both Cragor and Wandor, and they would do this as long as their safety depended on it. The Grand Master had not only dismissed a House Master for aiding Cragor's enemies, he had slain the man with his own hands.

The Grand Master had performed no harder task in all his life, for in his mind and soul he was firmly ranged on the side of Cragor's enemies. Cragor would sooner or later rule with a bloody hand and unbridled power, for all the moderation he might be showing now. Far too many of the great nobles already ruled thus in their home lands, believing the restraining hand of the kings gone forever. Kaldmor the Dark served Cragor, and Kaldmor the Dark had trod the grimmest path of any sorcerer in many generations of men to delve into the magic of long-dead Toshak. What he had already done made the Grand Master's blood run chill, and certainly neither Kaldmor nor Toshak had done his worst.

So be it. There was no choice, not when Cragor was willing to have the sorcery of Toshak called up to serve him. Yet Cragor's enemies had their own sorcery, and the Grand Master feared it only less than Kaldmor's.

There were tales that Bertan Wandor himself had mastered the Mind Speech. These were only tales, though, and in any case the Mind Speech was hardly true sorcery. It was a gift that could not be gained by those who altogether lacked it, and set aside only with the greatest difficulty by those who had it. Furthermore, it was small threat to the fairness of a duel. The Mind Speech seemed to take far more concentration than any sensible man matched against a strong opponent would dare to take away from his weapons. As far as the Grand Master knew, Bertan Wander himself had kept faith with the precepts of the Order he had once served.

But Wander was surrounded by true and formidable sorcery as completely as Eprim Blackblade had ever been surrounded by the twelve swordsmen of Baron Gostor. His wife, the Lady Gwynna, had Powers of her own and could command all the *Red Seers* of the Plainsmen in addition. Wander wore something called the Helm of Jagnar, which made all the Khindi follow him like sheep, and everyone knew how great were the Khindi's Tree Sisters. It was even said that Cheloth of the Woods had risen both from legend and from his long sleep to do battle once more with his ancient foe of Toshak. The Grand Master was prepared to believe even this tale. After all he had seen these past two years, he was unprepared to doubt any tale of sorcery, magic, or unleashed Powers.

Bertan Wander was a man greatly gifted and entirely honest. The temper of his soul had been as fine as the temper of his sword, and so it seemed to be still. He could be trusted in all that he could control.

Yet how much was that? The question tormented the Grand Master, and he did not expect the torment to end soon.

Count Ferjor straddled the branch of an oak tree and stared down the road. The orange glow of the lantern on the patrol leader's saddle grew slowly. Another minute and it would not matter whether the riders took alarm or not. Few would escape.

The Count shifted position, grasped the branch with one hand to steady himself, and locked the fingers of the other hand around the hilt of his sword. The sword was nearly all that remained of what now seemed like another life in another era of another world. In that life in that other world he had commanded the Tenth Regiment in the cavalry of the Royal Army of Benzos, met Bertan Wandor, fought the Ponans, and one day heard that King Nond had fled and Duke Cragor now ruled in Benzos.

In his present life he crouched on oak branches on dark nights, watching for two men who'd been his soldiers and ten farmers from nearby villages to spring an ambush on one of Cragor's patrols. The two lives were as different as eggs and diamonds, yet linked by a thread of loyalty to King Nond and to all those who held out for him and against the Black Duke. It was a thread that only Ferjor's own death would break.

The orange light was flickering more strongly now. The Count felt a prickling at the back of his neck as battle alertness flowed into him. He could see and hear nothing from below, but he knew the same was happening to the twelve men there. The orange light came on.

It came on the shapes of armored riders formed out of the darkness, then there were more shapes suddenly rising from ditches and from behind bushes. A crossbow went *spung*, then two more together. A horse screamed, then a man.

Count Ferjor hurled himself off the branch, dropping his own height into the wet grass. Another leap took him on to the road. He landed with a splat in ankle-deep mud. He drew his sword and tried to lift his feet, then nearly sprawled on his face as man with a raised billhook shouldered past him. From the darkness the count heard the *whusssh* of split air as the bill came down and the indescribable sound as it split the skull of the lead rider's horse. The horse toppled and its rider flung himself out of the saddle to land on his knees. Ferjor thrust at the man's exposed face with his dagger and felt the point grate on bone. The man jerked back, opening the distance enough for the Count to bring his sword around in a full swing. The slash missed its mark, the flat of the sword grating across the man's mailclad shoulder in a blaze of sparks and glancing off his helmet.

Half stunned, the man could not rise. Instead he lurched forward on his knees, wrapping his arms around Ferjor's thighs. The Count went over backward and pain shot up his arm as his wrist slammed down on a stone. His fingers went numb and his sword slipped to the ground. He doubled both legs violently, slamming his knees into the other man's chest. It felt as if his kneecaps had shattered against the man's breastplate, but the impact flung the man upward. The Count thrust again with his dagger at the man's face. This time he felt the steel sink deep and heard the man scream. The man twisted sideways, clapping one hand to his ripped cheek, as the Count heaved himself into a sitting position. He clamped one hand hard on the man's helmet and pushed him face down into the mud, then drove his dagger five times into the back of the exposed neck. The first three times the man jerked, the fourth time he gave a convulsive shudder, after the fifth time he went limp and lay still.

Count Ferjor forced himself to his feet, wondering what might have happened while he was wallowing around in the mud of the road like a rutting boar. As if called by his leader's uncertainty, one of the soldiers materialized out of the darkness, holding a mace thickly matted with blood and hair.

"Got seven, my lord. One got clean 'way. T'other was hurt but not enough to stop. Go after 'em?"

The Count shook his head. Seven out of nine would make enough of an impression on the dead men's comrades and on their captain. The last two enemies weren't worth the risk of widely scattering his own men in a chase.

"Ours?"

"One dead, two hurt. They can travel."

"Good. Get the litters, and—" He broke off suddenly as he saw one of the farmers bend to pick up a fallen sword. "Ho! Leave it there. Go through their saddlebags. Take food and money, but leave the weapons and armor." The farmer straightened up, the sword in his hand and the rebellious glare on his face visible even in the darkness.

"Why? Need good weapons, we do."

"You don't need these. I've heard that Kaldmor the Dark has cast a spell on every weapon wielded by one of Cragor's men. He can track a man who takes one as easily as you can track a hare across the snow. Do you want to challenge Toshakan sorcery for one sword?"

The farmer gasped and dropped the sword as if it had seared his fingers. His face turned the color of mushrooms seen by moonlight.

Then he backed away from the sword, keeping his eyes fixed on it as if expecting it to fly up and stab him in the throat.

The Count understood what drove the man, but the weapons and armor still had to be left where they fell. The yeomen laborers could not be allowed to arm themselves until the power lay in each one's hands to strike at Cragor when and where he pleased. That might win a few small victories at first. In the end it would bring a swarm of Cragor's soldiers tramping across the land, ending rebellion by ending the life of everyone they suspected. Then too many lives would end too soon and with too little to show for it.

There would be plenty of weapons when the right time came. In the days before the hammer of Cragor's treachery came down on King Nond's soldiers, Count Ferjor and certain trusted men of the Tenth Regiment had worked to make sure of that. Four hundred sets of armor and weapons for twice that many men lay hidden in caves, wrapped and greased against the attacks of the years that might pass before they could be brought out and put to use. All those who knew the secret had either died silently or fled to safety here in the borderland. Those who had died would watch from the House of Shadows with King Nond. They would watch until those who hid found the moment to strike.

It would not be easy to wait for that moment, and in the meantime keep the farmers disarmed with nothing more than lies and threats. The border farms were crowded with those who had fled south when Cragor's promises brought the Ponans swarming across the border. For five days' ride to the north, the land lay under Ponan rule, and along the roads the land was speckled with the whitened bones of those who had not fled fast enough. Those who had fled and those who sheltered them had a terrible hatred for Cragor and what he had brought upon them. It made them more than willing to hide Cragor's enemies and ambush his patrols often enough to keep them cautious. It also drove them past the bounds of good sense, so that swords flung carelessly into their hands would not remain un-blooded for long.

The stripping of the bodies was done now, and the men formed up for the march through the woods to safety. One of the wounded stood with his arm in a sling, the other lay in a litter carried by two of his comrades. Count Ferjor raised his hand, and suddenly there was only darkness and the fading sound of footfalls where the men had stood.

As he turned to follow them, a brief thought brought an even briefer smile to his lips. Might he be telling the truth about Kaldmor's casting a spell on all the weapons carried by Cragor's men? It was only a tale, as far as he knew, but his knowledge of high sorcery did not go far.

He could say that it was not likely. In the past few months all that was said of Kaldmor the Dark told of his having sought seclusion on some lonely hilltop to "improve his arts." Nothing had been said of his casting petty spells to aid his master.

The smile vanished from Count Ferjor's face. Kaldmor's "improving his arts" could mean only one thing—further delving into the secrets of Toshak, and the unleashing of things best not even imagined. Ferjor would almost rather have had Kaldmor casting trace-spells on Cragor's arsenal.

Duke Cragor strode through the door and two servants leaped to close it behind him. The guards on the far side crashed the butts of their halberds down on the stone floor. Cragor swept past them and turned toward the stairs leading up to his private chambers.

Anya would be waiting for him there. She had been waiting there for better than three hours. Hopefully she would have worked herself into a proper fever of impatience. The session in the prison had aroused him to an impatience of his own. The prisoner had been no more than a peasant girl turned prostitute, who'd tried to stab one of his mercenaries over a small matter of payment. The executioners had done extremely well with her, though, putting on an entirely pleasing and gratifying performance. The executioners were improving almost with each passing week, although this was hardly surprising, considering the amount of practice they were getting and the high standards of the master they served.

In any case, Cragor's own desire was now glowing, ready to burst into flame, and he was quite unfit for the business waiting for him in the state chambers. He would come to Anya in his roughest clothes, reeking of the smoke, sweat, and other less mentionable odors of the dungeon. That would discomfort her beyond what she could endure without protest. The Duke's pleasure in his wife's annoyance would be small, but his position did not yet permit him to take gross liberties with Anya. In law she was still Queen of Benzos, and as Nond's daughter she still stood for the memory of her father in the eyes of too many people.

Time would change that, however. In a few years memories would fade. Then he could cast off all the reins and go about reducing Anya to the most abject sort of obedience. He would still not be able to put her through the same treatment as the prostitute he'd just seen, still less through what he envisioned for Gwynna when her time came. That would go beyond what could be easily concealed. Besides, he could not afford to maim or kill Anya until the succession was more thoroughly ensured. A daughter five years old and a son still in his nurse's arms were not enough.

In any case, there were subtler ways of breaking a woman, and subtlety had its own delights. Suppose he'd put a powerful love potion in the wine sent up to Anya two hours ago? Suppose it had been working in her all this time, until her impatience now bordered on madness?

That was a possibility worth pursuing. It would require some skilled sorcery to remove the spells against poisons and love potions placed upon Anya before she was weaned. The gifted sorcerer who had placed those spells still lived, but he'd fled beyond the Duke's reach. Even if he could be found, there would be little hope of persuading him to undo his work.

Call upon Kaldmor the Dark? No. The sorcerer's own Powers were either too weak or too brutally clumsy for such a task. The terrible Powers he could wield through the *limar* of Nem of Toshak were too great to be used for merely Cragor's own gratification. Besides, Kaldmor was too busy exploring the lore of Toshak, and would be too busy for some time to come. He could not be taken from that task, for it was too important that he become able to meet any sorceries that might fight for Bertan Wandor.

There must be a few other competent sorcerers available in Benzos! To be sure, most sorcerers of any level of skill had fled into seclusion, fled from mobs half-crazed with terror of sorcery and releasing that terror on the handiest victims. But that same persecution should make at least one of the sorcerers willing to exchange a few weeks' hard work for a few years of Cragor's protection.

Perhaps the matter of Anya could wait. Sooner or later there would be Gwynna, and then the duke would speak to Kaldmor, though Nem of Toshak himself was rising from the House of Shadows to march across the world. He would bid Kaldmor use every Power he had or could call upon, to make sure that nothing Gwynna might do would keep her from feeling everything he would do to her. Cragor clamped his mind down firmly on the visions of Gwynna's agony. A wise man does not plan how to season the venison before he's shot the deer.

Cragor stopped before the door to the private chambers and took several deep breaths. He wished to greet an impatient Anya looking maddeningly at peace with the world and with himself.

A morning came when Bertan Wandor, Viceroy of the East, looked at the parchment on the desk before him. He looked at the documents stacked on either side of him. He looked at the young messenger, standing before him to receive the parchment he'd been about to seal and bear it off to its destination.

Then he looked at Gwynna, who sat on a cushion on the floor beside the desk, swinging a silver ring on a cord for the amusement of a leopard cub. Their eyes met for a moment; the messenger saw that meeting and disappeared. Wandor pushed his chair back so hard that it fell over, rose to his feet, and swore a long and tremendous oath that invoked many more than five gods.

Gwynna laughed. "If it isn't a joke, forgive me, but—"

"No, no, it deserves laughter more than anything else. It suddenly appeared clearly before me—"

"The way I did, the night in the forest when we first joined?"

Whatever Wandor had been about to say took flight in a choked gasp of laughter. He shook his head helplessly for a moment.

"No. But it was clear to me that if I tried to seal one more letter, I would tear it to shreds. Then I would pour the sealing wax on the messenger, and perhaps even throw the poor lad out the window."

"Perhaps we should leave Fors behind us for a few days. The Viceroyalty will stand without us that long."

"True. Where shall we go?"

"There's a manor farm to the north of the city. Its first master died at Delkum Pass, and the First Clerk to the Civic Council of Fors bought it. It's none too comfortable, but he's been in the habit of renting it for a few weeks at a time to people who want to get out of Fors: his fellow Councilors, Royal Army officers, the richer merchants, and so on.

"I'm sure he'd hardly balk at letting us use it. We'd not have much more comfort than we had that first night in the woods, but we'd be just as alone."

Wandor shook his head. "We could imagine we're alone, but we wouldn't be. If I gave no orders for a guard to be set around the manor, Sir Gilas would set one anyway. Better that we know where his men are and how to avoid them than always be stumbling over them on our way to bathe in the stream or find a patch of soft moss." Gwynna blushed faintly.

"We can also pass by Berek's ship on our way north," Wandor continued. "He must be within a few days of sailing for Yand. I owe him a proper farewell, at least." Particularly when he is going against the Beast Wizards, Wandor's mind added, and that farewell may be the last words you ever speak to him.

CHAPTER 4

Berek Strong-Ax stood beside the foremast of his ship *Fire of Elya* as the morning sun warmed the deck under his bare feet. His two axes, Thunderstone and Greenfoam, leaned against the mast. Berek himself stood as straight as the mast itself. He was of the HaroiLina, the Sea Folk, who did not show laziness or weariness aboard a ship. He was also filled with the joy of having a ship—*his* ship—once more under his feet. This was so great a joy that it seemed to Berek he would have been able to stand upright if all his bones had been shattered.

From aft came thuds and clatters and the grunts of men lifting heavy weights. One well-tarred barrel after another was coming up from the boat alongside and being lowered into the hold. More thuds told of the barrels being rolled forward until they formed a line along the ship's keel. There was cooking oil in those barrels, grain, salt meat and salt fish, water, beer and wine, extra weapons (well-oiled and wrapped in greased leather), and much else. There was a three-months' supply of everything needed for a voyage out into the Ocean and a long cruise off Yand Island.

For such a voyage a man not only stored his ship with food and weapons, he stored his mind with plans and schemes against all the dangers he might meet. They would be many. The Ocean itself, the ancient domain of Haro Sea Father. The ships and fighting men of the HaroiLina, thick off the coast of the Viceroyalty, perhaps thicker still off Yand.

Finally, the dangers to be found on Yand itself. These dangers arose not from the ordinary people, who were not great fighters and who seldom came to sea except to fish, but from the Beast Wizards. They had never been friends to honest men, from the day when the first High Wizard used his mastery of Beast Magic to create the Beasts. To be sure, Yevoda Slayer of Beasts had struck a mighty blow the night he killed forty of the monsters with his terrible Ax that held the Beast Wizards' own Powers. But Yevoda had slain neither all the Beasts nor all the Wizards, and in the end he had gone down into the depths of the sea and his Ax with him. Unclean Beast Magic was still strong on Yand. Now it called to the men of the HaroiLina.

Although the Beast Cult was a great and dreadful mystery, it was not the one Berek was sailing to Yand to explore. He was sailing to learn what men were doing there, with ships, swords, earthly gold, and their own wits. Men of Yand, men of the HaroiLina, men who served the Black Duke. Were the ships of the HaroiLina anchored or drawn up on shore when they came to Yand? Were their men allowed ashore, and if so, where did they camp? Had Cragor put men ashore on Yand, and if so, how many? And a hundred other questions, none of them touching more than slightly on the Beast Cult. That could wait, until the proper sort of Powers could be brought against it.

A last barrel thudded down into the hold, and after that came the clatter of oars. Berek saw the boats pulling away from the ship's side, toward the bank of the creek where she lay. Two more boatloads and *Fire of Elya* would be ready for sea. Then there would be nothing to do except get the rest of the crew aboard and wait for nightfall. They would have a struggle downstream against the incoming tide, but they would also have darkness to hide their departure.

Berek sprang lightly down into the hold and strode aft. A dozen men were already hard at work with ropes and mallets, lashing and wedging each barrel in place until it was nearly as immovable as a timber of the ship herself. He looked them over briefly and passed on.

They were doing well, as he had expected. The seventy men he was taking to Yand were an oddly-assorted lot—fishermen, HaroiLina, merchant sailors, officers and even rowers from what had once been King Nond's fleet. There was only one thing they all had in common. All were experienced sailors. They might not trust each other, but they would trust the Ocean even less. So they would leave nothing undone that might bring them safely home.

Berek scrambled up the ladder to the afterdeck to meet Kurash, the Second Captain. Kurash would lead the fighting men in any ship-to-ship duel.

"It goes well, Captain," said Kurash, raising the hat that shielded his bald head from the sun. He had Chongan blood and kept his head shaved in Chongan style, but substituted a broad-brimmed leather hat for the close-fitting silk wrappings of his father's people. "We shall not lack for anything."

Berek was about to reply, when on the path along the bank of the creek seven riders appeared. Beside the dark man in the lead rode a slim figure, gold feather bobbing above a green hat and the sunlight striking tints of fire from her hair.

Berek leaped on to the railing, then plunged over the side. As his head broke the surface, he saw Kurash dart a disapproving look at him, then hastily turn away. Berek smiled and began to swim with easy, powerful strokes that carried him swiftly toward the bank.

Kurash was a man of large gifts who had also enjoyed many blessings both from men and Haro Sea Father. Though a Chongan by birth and an exile from Dyroka, he had commanded a galley of Nond's fleet. When he could bear no more of Cragor's rule, he and three comrades made their way across the Ocean in a stolen fishing boat, when winter was already upon the world. Kurash and one comrade found favor in the eyes of Haro and reached the Viceroyalty alive.

Yet Haro had not given Kurash the gift of understanding a Captain of HaroiLina blood who would walk his decks clad only in a loincloth and would leap over the side and swim to shore rather than wait for the boat his dignity demanded. So be it, thought Berek. He did not require Kurash's understanding, only his wisdom and skill. Nor did he expect anyone not of the HaroiLina to understand why it seemed proper and even necessary for him to leap over the side and swim to the Master with whom he had sworn the Oath of the Drunk Blood.

The banks of the creek were steep. Berek's feet did not touch the gravel of the bottom until his hands could almost reach out and clutch the bushes on the bank. He scrambled out of the water, shook himself, and bowed to Wandor as his Master dismounted. He would rather have knelt, but Wandor had forbidden it.

"Greetings, Master. What is your wish?"

Wandor did not reply at once. Instead he scanned the hundred-foot length of *Fire of Elya* and the bustle on her decks. Then he laughed and turned back to Berek. "I won't pretend to be a good judge of anything about ships. I can tell at a glance whether the ship is afloat or not, but that's about all. Are you satisfied?"

Berek nodded. "I am, and so is Kurash. With Haro's favor, we shall succeed."

"Good. The gods know I would be happier to go with you, rather than send you to Yand. But—"

"Forgive me, Master, but I must remind you that all those aboard *Fire of Elya* together are of small worth beside you."

Wandor sighed. "Berek, I may forbid you to remind me of that, as I have forbidden you to kneel."

Berek bowed his head. "I will obey, Master, but I do not—"

"Well, I won't stop reminding you of your own value," said Gwynna briskly. "And since I haven't sworn the Oath of the Drunk Blood, you can't forbid me to do that."

Wandor laughed. "Or anything else, for that matter. Very well, Berek. Take my prayers and hopes, if you cannot take me. Learn what we need to know about Yand, and *come home safely*."

Berek bowed his head again. "With Haro's favor, Master." He turned to dive back into the water, then saw that the boat was loaded and just about to leave. He ran along the bank and sprang down into the boat as it pushed off from the shore.

In Benzos, on another morning, Duke Cragor's state barge came down the Avar. The current, the red sail, and the sweeps drove the barge steadily down the river through a gray world a mile from either bank. Gray, cloudy sky was overhead, and gray water on either hand. Even the green of trees and crops on the banks held tints of gray.

The Duke had made the river journey to Avarmouth three times in the last year, and each time he'd met different sights. The first time, he'd gone with his army to take Avarmouth. The banks had been deserted, the only movement smoke rising from burning manors and villages.

Then came the second journey, and he'd seen farmers once more at work in the fields and new houses rising in the place of blackened ruins. He looked upon this and drew hope from it. Most men could not forget that the crops must be brought in and the cows milked, the roof thatched against winter winds, shoes made for the children and new wheels made for the cart. In doing these things day after day, most men could forget or cease to care about the doings of kings and queens, dukes and distant viceroys, or sorcerers and witches. That was greatly to Cragor's satisfaction. The less people cared about who ruled high above them, the less willing they would be to resist him. Even those who might still care would think twice, for he was here in Benzos with his armies. He could put his enemies in a deadly peril from which the far-distant Bertan Wandor could not guard them.

Now as Cragor made the third journey he could see that he had not hoped in vain. One rebellious village remained a heap of ruins because he had ordered that it remain so. Little else showed that war had passed along this river. Even the fishing boats and ferries crept across the water as they had always done. From time to time Cragor heard cheers from the small craft, as they darted clear of the galleys escorting his barge. Cragor had not expected this, nor did he care much one way or the other. The people of Benzos could obey in silence, as long as they obeyed.

Yet because of those cheers he found that the grayness of the day would not enter his spirit, and he was pleased.

As they came down toward Avarmouth, the scenes on the banks at last began to change. Here was a grove of trees killed when fire spread from a cluster of Khind huts, the trunks standing black and gaunt. There was an empty place where another grove of trees had been cut down to make into the siege-engines that in the end had not been needed against Avarmouth. In a third place were two half-submerged hulks, royal greatships run ashore by their crews and now rotting slowly away into the mud. There were not so many ferries and fishing boats now, and no cheers from anyone aboard them.

Then at last there was Avarmouth itself, the great basin once more crowded with ships but with fire-blackened walls and empty spaces like missing teeth in the place of many sheds and warehouses along the quays. On the opposite side of the river stood the Naval

Arsenal, and its walls showed not only fire-blackening but fresh stonework where breaches had been repaired. Of all the greatships and galleys and river craft that had moored off the Arsenal until last year, only a handful remained. The men of Nond's fleet had gone down into the House of Shadows in the service of their king, but before they did they sent most of their ships on ahead of them.

The image made Cragor frown. Was there a spirit fleet waiting somewhere beyond the world, manned by spirit sailors ready to do the bidding of the spirit king they had served and strike at his enemies? It was a disquieting thought, but one that came easily in this land where the scars of war were not healing and people might still care very much that it was the Black Duke and not King Nond who ruled in Benzos.

Cragor went aft to his cabin and called for his squires to help him on with his armor. The black plate with the gilded engraving made him look rather more formidable, and it would make him a great deal safer as he passed through the streets of Avarmouth. His hand had come down very heavily upon the city when his soldiers entered its gates and gave themselves over to plunder, rape, and murder. Among those in Avarmouth who had neither died nor fled, some would certainly think their own lives a small price to pay for striking at the Black Duke.

A dusk grayer than the day was falling upon the city, the Arsenal, and the great river between them. Baron Galkor stood at a window high in the seaward tower of the Arsenal, watching the crews of his ships hang out the night lanterns. Beyond the mastheads of the ships, the Ocean rolled away toward the east into a horizon-less nothingness.

A mass of approaching feet sounded on the stairs and then on the stone floor just outside the chamber door. The door swung open with a squeal. Galkor stepped hastily from behind his desk, pinning his cloak into place as he went and going down on one knee as Cragor strode in. The Duke had changed from armor into a black doublet and hose. His sword swung from a red belt with a gold buckle and gold-washed mail was visible at his throat.

The Duke threw a quick glance around the chamber, a glance

which swept away messengers, servants, and guards. The door slammed shut with another pig-squeal of hinges and the Duke motioned Galkor to his feet.

Cragor dropped into a chair, took off his sword belt, and hung it over the back of the chair. Then he impaled Galkor with his stare. "Are you satisfied with your ships?"

Galkor shrugged. "I would say no, if I thought there was much hope of getting one more ship or another fifty good sailors. I gave up that hope some time ago."

"What about the soldiers?"

"I am happier with them. They seem to be six hundred good fighters, who will do all that any six hundred men can do. I have doubts about the captains, though. They are all proven in war, but can they maintain the order among the men that you have demanded?"

"They will find ways to do it, or pay the price," said the Duke. "I know I have asked much, but no more than what is necessary. The men must be kept from rape, theft, and drink both on Yand Island and among the Sea Folk. Otherwise we will hardly gain anything by sending them, and perhaps lose a great deal. Both the islanders and the Sea Folk are easily offended."

"In that case, are we wise in sending a fighting force at all? We must send living men, after all, not stone images."

The Duke frowned but did not flare up at Galkor's bluntness. He'd learned that such anger gained nothing and cost him Galkor's plain-spoken honesty, easily worth a thousand men. "We are wiser in sending them than not sending them. I have given the matter much thought. I will also give fifty gold crowns to any man of the force who returns without fault to his name, or to his family if he dies without fault. Tell your men this as soon as you are well out to sea. It should be enough to keep them all as chaste as priestesses of Yeza."

Nothing would do that for the war-toughened veterans who were sailing with him, Galkor thought. Not even fifty gold crowns, which would buy a yeoman's farm, a shop on a good street in Benzos, or all the drink and women a soldier could get through in half-a-year. He'd better make arrangements with certain trusted whoremongers in Avarmouth to provide a score or so of women to sail with the fleet. If necessary, he could add to them a few thrall-women purchased quietly among the Sea Folk. It was a minor detail, one Galkor could neither blame the Duke for neglecting nor afford to neglect himself.

"I have written nothing about what you are to do with the ships and the men," the Duke continued. "I dislike having this sort of matter put down for straying eyes to read and ill-disposed minds to remember. Our friends among the Sea Folk may need your help against the Hearth Mothers. But be careful. Entering into the quarrels of the Sea Folk could earn us two enemies for every friend we have now. Of course, if you can help our friends with a complete and final victory—then by all means do your best. I do not fear opposition from a heap of corpses."

Galkor nodded. Those were sensible words, and he was glad to hear them from his master. There was satisfaction in winning your enemies to your side, and perhaps there could be some in putting them slowly to death, if one's fancies ran as Cragor's did. But there was no satisfaction that Galkor knew quite equal to that of knowing that your enemies were completely and finally dead, beyond the power of even the gods.

Galkor stopped and swallowed, feeling a chill sweat breaking out on his forehead. He'd been about to think "beyond the power of even the gods to awaken." Then he'd remembered how something, god or not, had made King Nond walk golden-eyed along the walls of Fors last winter, slaying men horribly, until terror drove Galkor's army out of the protection of the city's walls into the open field and the hands of Bertan Wandor and Cheloth of the Woods. He remembered it all much too clearly.

The Duke noticed nothing. Galkor tried to silence his memories and turn his attention back to Cragor. After a time he succeeded.

"...help raid the coast of the Viceroyalty. Or defend Yand Island itself. Even our best friends among the Sea Folk don't always care to spend more time there than they have to. That leaves the island practically defenseless most of the time. The islanders are brave enough, but they're fishermen and shepherds, not warriors. Three hundred good men might sweep Yand from end to end. Our friends among the Sea Folk would fall into confusion then, and the Hearth Mothers would have a chance to rally our enemies. If they succeeded, we could lose the Sea Folk altogether, and I need not tell you what that would mean."

Galkor knew perfectly well. With the Sea Folk no longer aiding the Duke, the Ocean would lie open and free to both sides. Wandor could launch raids upon the shores of Benzos or reach south to trade and intrigue in the Twelve Cities of Chonga. Rebels in Benzos could take gold and weapons from Wandor's ships, or flee across the Ocean to swell his strength in a Viceroyalty that would be all but impregnable. And if the Sea Folk turned wholly to Wandor's side, as the Plainsmen and the Khindi had done...

Galkor told himself firmly to think no more on this. He had already faced one nightmare today, out of a past that could not be altered or denied. He would not face a second one, out of a future that might never be. One question still worried him, though.

"What of the Beasts? I thought they could be sent out at the command of the High Wizard, against any invaders of Yand."

"You have heard an old tale. Kaldmor the Dark has told me otherwise. The Beast Wizards no longer have all the Powers they once commanded. If the Beasts were to be loosed on an invader, there might be no controlling them again. Then they would have to be slain, and nothing could slay them except the Ax of Yevoda."

Which went down into the Ocean with Yevoda many centuries ago, thought Galkor, assuming that either Yevoda or his Ax ever existed. He neither knew nor cared. He did know and care that he or at least some of his men would have to spend a considerable time on Yand, too close to powerful sorcery for his peace of mind. But what duty demanded was as it must be.

CHAPTER 5

Fang of Giyo was the ship of Foyn Son of Thadul. She was fair-sailing and easy-rowing, sound, tight, and pleasing to the eye. Some among the HaroiLina said that Foyn did not deserve so good a ship.

Others saw that *Fang of Giyo* had only sixteen oars a side and bore only forty-five men along with her Captain. There was no other Captain among all the HaroiLina who had reached Foyn's age without having a ship that rowed at least forty oars and bore a fighting man for each oar and fifteen more besides. Those who saw the greater ships and compared them with *Fang of Giyo* said that Haro had given Foyn an open sign of his ill-luck for all to see.

Fewer spoke aloud against Foyn now that he had a name as one of the HaroiLina who faithfully served the Beast Wizards of Yand. Yet there were no more who would willingly sail and fight under a man of ill-luck, so his following grew no larger and *Fang of Giyo* remained his ship and his shame.

He had endured the shame until this night, for he had no other choice except to stay ashore, forsaking the pleasures of raiding and the rewards of the Black Duke's gold and the Beast Wizard's prayers, and enduring the sharp tongue of his sister. She was a Keeper of the Hearth of the Mother, and as high among the Hearth Mothers as he was low among the Captains. The Beast Cult disgusted her, and she had no fear of telling him what she thought about it or anything else.

Tonight, however, the smallness of *Fang of Giyo* seemed

Haro's own blessing—to give Foyn a chance to end forever his shame and his reputation for ill-luck. (A small but sharp-toned voice in his mind added: The smallness of your ship has helped, but so has all that Telek the Fatherless learned about this land and freely told you.)

The creek where *Fang* now lay hidden was barely deep enough to float her. A larger ship would never have crossed the bar at the mouth of the river into which the creek flowed. A larger ship would also have been hard to conceal behind the rippling curtain of willows. No one could peer through that curtain and see *Fang* without coming close and pulling the trailing leaves aside with his bare hands. Few men could be prowling along this creek tonight anyway, and none of them would be curious enough to examine every grove of willows on either bank.

The willow curtain fell to starboard of *Fang of Giyo*. To port, it was a short jump to a firm grassy bank. At the top of the bank lay the forest. Three miles to the north through that forest lay the manor house where Foyn sought to win tonight's victory. Telek had learned that in the manor house men high in the service of Bertan Wandor often spent a few days or weeks in search of quiet. Tonight they would have none. Tonight warriors of the HaroiLina would come down upon the manor. Those who slept would wake. Those who did not flee would soon sleep again forever, or become prisoners destined for sacrifice to the Beasts of Yand.

Foyn's breath came short at thoughts of the rewards which success tonight might bring him. The Beast Wizards of Yand were free with their blessings to those who brought high-ranking prisoners for the sacrifice. Those blessings now carried weight in the *Kym* of Captains. The Black Duke was just as free with his gold to those who slew Wandor's servants or carried them off to their deaths, and that gold also carried weight. A man so blessed by the Wizards and rewarded by the Duke might call himself equal even to one who had borne the Spear of Valkath as Speaker of the *Kym*. Ancient law and custom might say otherwise, but they did not speak as loudly as they once had.

If there was no one to slay or take?... That would be only lesser good fortune. There would be fires to set and perhaps a few of Wandor's soldiers for prey. After tonight Wandor's captains and councilors would have one less place to sleep easily. It was a small victory, but one that Cragor would hardly fail to recognize and reward. The Black Duke had great wisdom in war.

It was time to arm and march. Foyn took two steps aft and gently prodded the nearest of the shadowy forms on the deck with the toe of his boot. The man uncoiled himself, recognized his Captain, and elbowed the man beside him into sluggish life. One by one, like snakes coming awake after a long winter, Foyn's men rose to make themselves ready for battle.

Wandor let out a sigh of contentment heavy enough to make the flame of the candle on the chest beside the bed flicker and dance. The shadows on the smoke-grimed ceiling also seemed to dance, twisting into the shapes of strange beasts.

Strange, but friendly. The sort who might visit a Tree Sister of the Khindi, or Cheloth of the Woods in the distant hut by the sea where he sought knowledge of all that had passed during his long sleep and knowledge of what was yet to come. There could be nothing unfriendly in this old house, purged of its former master's body and spirit alike and now filled with the happiness he and Gwynna had known these past five days.

They had a night, a day, and another night remaining, and then it must come to an end. They must return to Fors and its life of stacks of parchment to read before breakfast and five-hour courts to hold after it. Duty would clamp down upon them again like a watchdog's jaws on a thief.

Wandor slipped out from under the furs and stood up. The air in the room held a chill that hadn't been there two hours ago, and he sensed a certain gnawing in his stomach. He crossed the room to the hamper standing by the door. A search inside produced the last flask of wine and two cheeses.

They would hunt tomorrow, Wandor decided. He and Gwynna would bring down a deer and some birds, while the guards went down to the river to fish. Then everything would be cooked over the great fires, sputtering and smoking and sending up rich smells to the very thrones of envious gods. A grand feast, with everyone gorging himself and no state or ceremony or dignity that Wandor did not choose to keep—and he would choose to keep none. It would be a proper ending to this time of peace and at least the beginning of a proper reward for all the men who'd kept watch so faithfully and so invisibly.

There would be other rewards for them, and for Sir Gilas Lanor above all. The young Knight had slept less, ridden farther, and kept longer watches than any of his men. He had endured saddle sores, insect bites, bird droppings in his hair, and much else. He would even have ridden through the virgin forest east of the manor if Wandor had not flatly forbidden it.

"We hardly need protection from the deer, the songbirds, and whatever Khindi may have wandered so far from their nearest hunting ground. Leave it be, friend. We know you will give us all your strength when it is needed. Save it until then."

Wandor picked up a cheese and the wine. As he did, a sudden gust of wind blew in through the sagging shutters. They rattled angrily. The candle flame danced wildly and Wandor heard a distant drumming of thunder.

The thunder brought Gwynna half awake. She turned over and reached out one bare arm toward where Wandor had been. She gave a little mutter of frustration as her reaching hand found nothing, and she started to sit up.

The rising wind blew chill on Wandor's skin, and he thought suddenly of Gwynna's body warm against his, of her gentle softness and the muscles like a finely-tempered sword blade under it. Warmth rose within him at the thought. He slid back under the furs, and this time when Gwynna reached for him he was there.

The thunder rolled louder and closer. It grew harder to distinguish the thunder from an angry wind that swelled just as fast.

A sudden tearing crash high above made Foyn start. The toe of one boot caught under a projecting root and he sprawled forward on his face, nearly catching his sword arm under him. He scrambled frantically to his feet again. Above all other things that might go wrong tonight, he feared losing the trail.

The rough blazes Telek had made the day before still showed

pale in the darkness. Would they be visible when the rain came down and the darkness grew still thicker? Perhaps to Telek—he had more wisdom in woodscraft than any of the HaroiLina. But to the men following Telek? Foyn shivered at the thought of losing the trail and blundering about this forest in a storm. It might be only another mile or so to the manor, but that might be as good as ten miles when it came to their reaching it. And if they lost the trail back to the ship!...

Foyn realized that in another minute he would start shaking, perhaps not with fear but certainly with the effort to fight it off. He would not do that. He would not. He would not.

By the time he'd repeated the words three times, body and mind were eased. By the time he'd repeated them three times more, the trail was turning sharply toward the left. Telek stopped so abruptly that Foyn bumped into him. The thin man pointed silently. Dimly visible at his feet was a path, snaking away through the trees. It wandered according to the whims of the trees and bushes on either side, but along it men could run and even horses might hope to move.

Minutes later Foyn stepped out from behind a great pine and looked past the crouching Telek out across open ground. His eyes could barely pierce the darkness to the manor house, a sprawling shape only a little darker than the night itself. As the storm rode in, it seemed to be sucking the last light out of the world.

Telek rose and turned to Foyn. "It is safe." He added no polite "Captain." Telek the Fatherless called no man by name or title, and those who wished the services of his bow and his other gifts ignored the habit.

"You're sure?" whispered Foyn. "This could be a trap."

"No," said Telek. "We may go forward."

Foyn shivered, and tried to tell himself that he shivered only from the wind. The cold-voiced remnant of warrior and honorable man within him refused to listen to that argument. You are afraid, Foyn, it said. You know you have come this far by luck and the knowledge and skills of others. Now you must step forward yourself if you would win the prize you seek. Do you still seek it?

I do.

Then pass on.

"We waste time," said Telek. "The men of Wandor may drink

wine and come where they should not." The wind blurred his words. It could not blur a note of open distaste for a Captain fumbling about in his own mind for the courage to complete what he'd begun.

"That is true," said Foyn, half to himself. It was even more true that if he failed to drive home this blow of his, so well launched, there would be more than Telek's scorn to face. There would be Daraun's, his sister's, Cragor's agents', and the Beast Wizards'——enough people to man a warship, which he would never be able to do again. There were always those reckless or desperate enough to ship with a man of ill-luck, but none who would pull an oar or wield a sword in the service of a coward.

Foyn realized that all of his men had come up behind him and now stood waiting for him to lead onward. He sensed an impatience in them also—a faint glow rather than the open flame that was in Telek, but still there.

Haro have mercy! he thought. If I do not lead them forward, I may not live long enough to face the scorn of others. A knife-thrust from behind...in this darkness who could see clearly enough to accuse, and who would ask blood-money or make blood-feud over the death of a man called coward?

No one, said the voice in his mind. You stand closer to death from your own hesitation than from all the steel and sorceries you may meet by going forward.

The voice of the wind rose suddenly, and Foyn heard a long ripping crash as a tree went down. Then the rain swept in, cold stinging sheets that turned the darkness liquid. Foyn sighed. Haro was indeed merciful, for in this rain no one in the manor would hear or see an approaching enemy until it was too late. He searched his mind for some sacrifice to promise or suitable prayer to utter.

No time for that.

He jabbed Telek in the shoulder, pointed toward the manor house, and nodded. He could have shouted at the top of his lungs. The manor house was three hundred paces upwind. Even the sound of many pairs of fast-moving boots did not carry far through the storm.

Wandor awoke from a misty half-sleep to see that the candle

had gone out. For a moment he thought he saw a faint pulse of light from Gwynna's hair, but that could not be. In the happy exhaustion that now washed over both of them, Gwynna had little more of her Powers left than he had of his swordsmanship.

The room was growing almost cold, and Wandor thought vaguely of building a fire when the warmth that now filled both of them finally died. The time for that was yet to come, though. The time for almost anything except sleep was yet to come. This was a rare moment for Wandor, in which he felt free of power, cares, gods, destinies, and all the other burdens that had come to him since he left the Duelists' House in Trorim.

A faint thud reached his ears through the wind and the rain. Bricks falling from the chimney at the north end of the house, no doubt. A mason would have to see to the manor before winter came, otherwise it would be uninhabitable by next spring.

Two more thuds, then a faint clatter. Wandor sat up, pushing away the happiness, the warmth, and some of the exhaustion. It sounded as if the house were beginning to fall apart already. He hated the thought of prowling the dark rooms with a candle, but he hated even more the thought of waking to find loose shingles, soot, and rain cascading down upon him. He remembered the apprentices' chambers in the Duelists' House in Trorim, the wind that always seemed to blow through the shutters even on the stillest winter days, how the sleeping pallets became little islands in a sea of scummy water after every heavy rain, how—

Then the sound of many booted feet trampled across Wandor's memories and routed them from his mind. He shouted to warn Gwynna, who was already stirring and sitting up, then leaped across the room toward his weapons. His hand closed on the hilt of his sword as an ax smashed against the shutters. One flew clear off its weakened hinges into the room, and after it came a tall human figure. Wandor could not make out garb or race, only the sword in the man's hand as it slashed toward his own head.

Wandor halted his rise in time for the enemy's blade to split the air instead of his skull. From a crouch he slashed at the man's legs. To kill would be best, to cripple would help, to do anything but keep moving and keep his distance would be death until he knew how many opponents he would be facing.

Wandor's sword was barely launched before he knew he'd swung too soon. The tip of the sword slashed across the man's leg, making him gasp but hardly slowing his next attack. Wandor's own guard was up just in time. A bell-clang, a shower of sparks blazing in the darkness, and the enemy's sword glanced from Wandor's to strike the floor. Wandor shifted from edge to point and thrust at the man's throat. If he'd never fought before against a Duelist's sword—

The man's luck held. In the darkness Wandor's thrust followed the wrong line, slashing along the man's jaw and cheek, spinning him halfway around. He lurched aside, just as another attacker leaped down from the window, round shield on one arm and ax in the other hand. He had no time to swing, only time to raise his shield before Wandor attacked.

Wandor struck three times at that shield, fiercely enough to make the man give ground. He backed away toward the window, effectively blocking the entry of the men now visible behind him.

Wandor took advantage of the moment's relief to shout to Gwynna. "Get to the door. Push the chest against it." A flash of white in the darkness and the sound of wood grating on stone told him she'd heard. When she finished their rear would be safe. Chest and bar would hold the inner door, their weapons and skill would hold the window, and both could be held as long as necessary. The rain that had allowed this surprise would hardly allow fire, they could endure smoke, and even sorcery they could meet if he could give Gwynna time to call upon the *Red Seers* and perhaps Cheloth. He would have called to Cheloth himself if he'd dared to turn his attention from his sword and the enemies before him. He couldn't risk it. For the moment there was nothing subtle to use against this attack, only strength and skill.

Now the axman and the wounded swordsman came on together. As they stepped away from the window, a third man at last jumped down into the room, out of Wandor's reach. A gap opened between the swordsman and the axman, and Wandor thrust his attack into it.

He closed, feinting at the axman's head. The shield flew up. Before the ax could come around it, Wandor pivoted on his right foot and drove his left into the axman's groin. The man doubled up with a scream. Wandor pivoted aside from the swordsman's furious downcut, ending up with his back against the wall. He had time to aim his own attack precisely and room to deliver it with all his strength. The swordsman's head flew from his shoulders and the headless body toppled forward. Blood sprayed from the neck, spreading swiftly across the floor. It spread to where Gwynna struggled to push the chest against the door, then spread all around her. As she gave one more tremendous shove her feet sailed out from under her. She dropped to her knees, her head slamming forward against the chest

Then Wandor had to meet the third attacker and his world shrank down to the man coming at him. The other's sword slid down along Wandor's with a grinding screech. Wandor twisted his blade clear and struck with his free hand clenched. The man's nose collapsed under Wandor's fist, then his boiled-leather coat and the shoulder beneath gaped under Wandor's sword.

Gwynna rose to her feet, a flickering pale shadow. Another man sprang up into the window, a dark shadow with a bow in his hands. An arrow hissed, then Gwynna gasped in pain. Wandor saw the arrow driven clean through the calf of her right leg and her lips twisting in the words of a light spell to banish the pain. Then two men came in through the window almost together, neither of them the archer. A swordsman came at Wandor and a man with a two-handed ax rushed Gwynna. Wounded and facing that ax, she could not live.

Wandor put that knowledge from him. He put all the years of learning what his body and his weapons could do into a single cut that sliced off his opponent's sword hand at the wrist. He split the man's shield with a second cut and his jaw with a third. Two more men leaped into the room as Wandor's ears waited for Gwynna's death-cry. He would join her soon, in a warrior's death—not all the gods together could keep him from winning that last prize for his skill.

Another arrow hissed and drove into human flesh, then a death-cry sounded that could not have been Gwynna's. Wandor saw the man who'd moved against her drop his ax to the floor. Both hands went up to grip the bloody point and shaft that stood out from his throat. He turned toward Wandor, a trickle of blood showing at the corner of his mouth and a sudden knowledge that the world was mad showing in his eyes. Then he fell on top of his ax, almost at Gwynna's feet.

Wandor suspected the dead man could be right, but knew for certain that two of the man's comrades were coming at him. If he could pass between them, he would have a clear path to join Gwynna. Side by side at last, they could stand more than twice as long as either could singly.

The two men came at Wandor as another attacker leaped down behind them, wearing a broad cloak that spread out on either side of him like a bat's wings. The two men drew apart from each other as they closed on Wandor and he passed easily through the gap. The cloaked man came down on him with sword and shield before he could break away toward Gwynna.

Wandor met the cloaked man, recognized the metal-studded belt of a Sea Folk Captain around his waist, and fought down a temptation to close and stay closed with the man until he was dead. He started to give, ground, then felt a hand clamp hard on his ankle. Before he could look down, an ax slammed hard into his stomach.

The flat of the ax struck Wandor, not the edge, spilling his wind instead of his guts. He saw the axman he'd kicked in the groin lying on the floor, still doubled up but swinging his weapon back for another blow. Wandor fought his body straight, fought breath back into his throat, fought vision into his eyes and strength into his sword arm to meet the attack. His sword sank into the ax handle instead of the man's arm, while the edge of the ax drew sparks from the floor instead of blood from Wandor.

In the next moment Staz the Warrior himself would have been helpless to keep the Sea Folk Captain from pushing home his attack. The flat of his sword came down on Wandor's right hand, breaking its grip and all but breaking its bones. Wandor lunged for the fallen sword with his other hand. No Duelist rose high in the Order without a fair measure of skill in both hands.

Wandor hadn't won back the breath to move fast enough. As his left hand closed on his sword, the Captain dropped shield and sword, tore the ax from its owner's grip, and swung it at Wandor's head. It struck, and the power to move left Wandor. It struck again, and Wandor felt as if he had been pushed over the edge of a great hole filled with icy darkness, to fall and fall and fall until the iciness numbed him so thoroughly that he could no longer feel it or anything else.

CHAPTER 6

Gwynna's will to fight did not leave her even when she saw Wandor sprawled on the floor, but will alone could not keep her fighting after Telek sank an arrow into her other leg. She fell to her knees, unable to drive away either the pain or life itself before Foyn struck her as senseless as Wandor.

Foyn stood over his captives until both were thoroughly bound, his white-knuckled hands gripping the ax as if releasing it would release the life from his body. He stood in silence, but his mind churned with so many thoughts that he could not have spoken all of them if he'd had three heads and three mouths in each head, like Bayu the Golden Serpent.

How it had come about for him to do this he did not know. He only knew that Wandor and Gwynna were helpless in his hands, and with a further blessing or two he might bring them away safely. Then none of Wandor's enemies could withhold any reward he might ask. All among the HaroiLina and the Beast Wizards of Yand would forget the past ill-luck of Foyn Son of Thadul and remember only that he had put an end to Wandor and Gwynna. His fame might even be so great that no one would believe Telek the Fatherless if he spoke the truth about whose plan had brought this night's victory. If that fame was not enough, there would doubtless also be enough gold to buy Telek's silence, one way or another.

Yet he would not rejoice now, not when the victory was still as incomplete as a sword without an edge. He saw the men rise from around Gwynna. The darkness could not hide her beauty or the lust on their faces, but their hands fell only on her wrists and ankles. Foyn would ship strange or desperate men, but not fools who would lose themselves in lust this close to the enemy. Nor would they be indulging it with Gwynna, even afterward. There were blemishes enough already on her if she was to be any sort of acceptable sacrifice to the Beasts. There would be far too many, and perhaps not even a living spirit in her, if his men had their way.

Telek would help—indeed he had already done so. Foyn's eyes met the archer's as he sat cross-legged on the floor, cleaning the arrows and arrowheads he'd drawn from Gwynna. Then he looked at the body of the axman Telek had shot down to save the woman, and finally at the rest of his men. No one understood why Telek had done this thing. No one cared for it in the least. No one doubted that Telek would do it again if he saw fit. Above all, no one wanted to be Telek's next victim.

The other men of the party now crowded into the room. Foyn looked down at his two cripples. Both deserved better luck than to die here because they could not travel, but neither could escape their fate. He bent over the two men, dagger in hand.

"You will lack nothing in the rites," he said softly. "I shall make it my first charge." He uttered their names even more softly, casting each one into the Earth Tongue as custom demanded. Then two quick thrusts and the spirits of two more of his children departed toward Haro Sea Father. Foyn stood up, sheathed his dagger, and motioned for the newcomers to pick up Wandor. Four of them lifted him. Foyn motioned two more into place. They would have not only to bear Wandor's considerable weight, but bear it fast and far, in darkness, over wet rough ground, perhaps fighting a battle on the way.

Foyn would have prayed to avoid that battle altogether, but knew it would be unwise. He had not quite forgotten that the strong Sea Father refused the prayers of weak children. So he prayed only for victory if battle should come upon them, and led his men back out into the night.

Sir Gilas Lanor rode where he had promised not to be, but was ready to face any danger that might come from this breaking of his word.

The danger was not in what might slip out of the dark, rain-sodden forest around him. Bertan Wandor was doubtless right that nothing and no one would reach the manor from the east—certainly not tonight in the face of the storm. The danger Sir Gilas faced was Wandor's anger for disobeying an order. There might also be Gwynna's wrath, which could sting even more painfully because of the dreams the young Knight had put aside where she was concerned. That was a small danger, compared to what might come about if by some chance they were all of them wrong about the forest. Sir Gilas doubted that they were, but he would no longer let himself be certain until he had seen with his own eyes and heard with his own ears that the forest to the east held no enemies. Sir Gilas was not a Duelist, but he saw a great deal of wisdom for all fighting men and their leaders in the words of the Duelists' Oath.

Besides, his not riding east these past five nights might have given some of the guards the idea that he was growing lax and they could drift about as they chose. Sir Gilas was proud of his men, but not proud enough to trust them altogether unheard and unseen. Some were wild spirits, some might even be spies. None should have an easy time of it.

Sir Gilas and the six men with him rode between two birches and reined in at the edge of the clearing around the manor house. The rain was beginning to slacken, and Sir Gilas could see the manor house clearly. It showed no lights, no sign of human life, and no great changes since he'd last seen it. A shutter on one window hung broken and askew from a single hinge, but that spoke of nothing except the force of the storm winds.

A sudden *Ho!* of surprise echoed around Sir Gilas' mind. The other shutter of the pair had vanished entirely. The ground below the window showed traces of a churning-up that could hardly have been done by the storm alone. A faint line of disturbed earth led toward the window from the forest and another line away from it, back toward the forest. Doubt and the first hints of fear began to echo around Sir Gilas' mind along with the surprise.

His hands danced, picking out men for duties. "Three mount

guard, two hold the horses. Dirok, you come with me." He slipped from the saddle, tossed the reins to a horse-holder, and drew his sword.

The two men closed in on the manor house. Sir Gilas would have forsworn his Knight's Oath in return for a spell to let him move without making a sound. They approached the window, and saw on the dangling shutter splinters and tool marks that no wind had left behind. Sir Gilas did not run, as much as he wanted to. With Dirok guarding his back, he walked to the window, pulled himself up until he could see into the room beyond, and looked.

He could feel relief that Wandor and Gwynna were not among the sprawled bodies in the bloody room, but nothing else. Now he and Dirok did run, back to the others. Sir Gilas' voice was remote as he spoke.

"The Viceroy and his lady have been taken. Sea Folk. Korm and Herdo—ride to Captain Gimor and give him the word. Have him divide the men into parties of—oh, ten—and start searching the country between here and the seashore, as far south as the river."

The Sea Folk had somehow come out of the forest. Yet they were not badgers or deer or Khindi. They were men who came and went in ships across the Ocean. Somehow, and sooner rather than later, they would strike for the shore and the open sea.

"Dirok, you're the best woodsman. Take the lead. The rest of us will follow you." He sheathed his sword and leaped into the saddle. Korm and Herdo touched their caps, mounted, and spurred their horses away to the north. Dirok crouched low and began casting from side to side, trying to pick out a definite trail from the blurred footprints.

Sea Folk on land can leave a trail that endures as if cast in bronze. In minutes Dirok had reached trees and was pointing frantically. Sir Gilas motioned him into his saddle, then all five men formed a single line with Dirok at the head and rode into the forest.

Sir Gilas knew that his five men would be attacking a band of Sea Folk at least twice their strength. But a quick attack by a handful now might do more than a stronger one in an hour or two, when any blow at all might land in the air. His men now had their horses and their knowledge of land fighting. They might also have surprise. They would certainly have the desire to do all that could be done for either Wandor and Gwynna, or their spirits. Such a desire could make any man fight like a silver bear. These things and the favor of the gods might be enough.

Telek the Fatherless made a hissing sound. It was so like the warning of a serpent coiled and ready to strike that Foyn started and jumped back from where he'd been about to step.

"We have men on our trail," said Telek.

Foyn kept a warrior's face drawn tightly across the sudden withering of his spirit. "We'll have to turn deeper into the forest, then."

"No," said Telek. "We take this path to the end."

"They'll catch us for certain."

"Of course," said Telek. "We will then kill them faster. It will take time for others to come. Time for us to reach the ship."

"They will be coming on horseback," said Foyn. The withering of his spirit came from the ancient fear of mounted warriors, an enemy the HaroiLina had never really been able to meet on equal terms.

"Of course," said Telek again. "A horse is faster than a man. It is also bigger, and without armor. On the path my bow can do its work better."

Foyn fell silent. It would be foolish to risk Telek's scorn now, when they had come so far and done so well. The words of Telek the Fatherless could still spread among the HaroiLina, gnawing away at Foyn's hoped-for reputation and honor like a school of sharks at a whale calf.

"We hold to the path, then," he said. "Change the bearers, and let two men keep watch in each direction." He saw a clumsy dance of shadow-shapes, heard an oath or two, then saw his men reforming behind him. The raiders moved on, Telek now in the rear and looping a fresh string to his bow as he moved.

A natural path and a blazed trail that guide raiders to their goal can just as easily guide their pursuers in the opposite direction. Sir Gilas saw the first few blazes on tree trunks, clearly visible even in the light-swallowing darkness of the forest. He rejoiced and also cursed himself for not disobeying Wandor's orders long before this night. The

Sea Folk raiders must have found their hiding place in the forest and their path to the manor long before this night. The most casual of searches would have revealed their presence, but the search had not been made and the fault was his. He had sworn no Oath of the Drunk Blood to make him obey without question. His body was not chained in a dungeon, nor his wits chained by the ignorance of youth or the failings of great age. He had wrought much evil this night, or at least allowed it to be wrought by others. Which it was did not make much difference to a man who would stand dishonored and shamed before all the world, even if he and Wandor and Gwynna all survived this night.

For some time he rode lost in this misery that was nearly as dark as the forest, certain that Dirok would lead them to the right place if there was one. He rode until suddenly Dirok raised a hand and pointed. The beaten trail unmistakably led off that way, into a stretch of open ground. The trail was fresh; their quarry was not far ahead.

Sir Gilas' misery began to lift. Perhaps they would come up with the raiders in time to undo all their work. That was the only thought in his mind as he urged his horse forward into the lead. There was no room for any other thought, and no need for one that he could see. He drew his sword and dug in his spurs. His horse bounded forward. He was only dimly aware of the other four riders doing the same, or of their frantic efforts to stay in their saddles as they tried to keep pace with him. He'd always been a superb rider, more than willing to spend a few extra crowns for a little more speed in his horses.

The open ground was narrow and winding, but Sir Gilas' vision ahead was as clear as it was dim in every other direction. He could have counted every branch on every tree as they swept past him, every twist and tum in the raiders' footprints.

He counted the men ahead as he swept around a bend and saw them barely a hundred paces away. He counted about fifteen in a rough square, with two more lying on the ground in the middle. He counted five leaping in panic for the shelter of the trees. He counted one tall figure taking a stand in the rear, raising a sword, and he gave a mighty shout of triumph.

Then an arrow flew from the darkness and drove so hard into his chest that stunned and shocked flesh was slow to wake in pain. The next thing he knew was another arrow taking his horse in the chest and a terrible scream as the animal went down. He felt himself hurled out and plunging down, felt and heard the cracking and crashing as the branches of two saplings plucked him out of the air. Then he neither felt nor heard anything more.

He did not feel the blood oozing out around the arrow shaft, through linen, mail, and leather. He did not hear the two arrows that struck Dirok out of the saddle, or the man's wild scream. He did not hear his last three men frantically reining in, or how they died as the five enemies who'd fled into the trees suddenly sprang out with axes and swords. He did not feel the probing hands of Telek the Fatherless or hear the man's words, "Dead or dying, all of them." He did not hear Captain Foyn's sigh of relief or the fading steps of the Sea Folk as they continued their interrupted journey.

He did not hear or feel anything until morning brought the searchers along the trail. It was too late by many hours for Wandor and Gwynna, but the gods and Sir Gilas' own stubborn life-force contrived that it was not too late for him. They lifted him gently, washed his cuts and bruises, splinted his broken bones, then laid him on an improvised litter to bear him to the manor. They left the arrow in his chest, for they had no skills they dared match against such a wound. All they dared was prayer, and that only after they had finished their prayers for Wandor and Gwynna.

Through a haze of pain Sir Gilas was aware of this, but did not hold it against them. Had he been able to form prayers into sensible words and then direct those words to a destination, he also would have prayed for Wandor and Gwynna. He would have prayed for himself hardly at all, unless it were for a quick death.

CHAPTER 7

With the night having begun as it had, nothing could have easily brought it to an end without further disorder. So strange and confused happenings continued until some hours after the most wretched of dawns crept over the forest.

Korm and Herdo rode as fast as their horses could find a way through the forest. It took them some time to find Captain Gimor. In the meantime, they cried their news to all the guards they met. Few of these waited for their captain to divide them up into search parties and give them orders. With admirable zeal they dashed off helter-skelter, in practically every direction except the right one.

In any case, it would have made no difference if some of them had found the raiders' trail. Before Korm and Herdo met the first of their comrades to give the alarm, the raiders and their captives were approaching their ship. Before the first search parties plunged into the forest, *Fang of Giyo* was casting off, pushing her way through the curtain of willow leaves and out into the creek. She moved swiftly downstream toward the river and the safety of the sea beyond.

Gimor might still have gathered his men and hurled them south, to command the ford of the river. He might then have caught *Fang of Giyo* and done something more than let her slip unseen and unharmed out to sea. That would have needed good luck and quick wits, though, and he was denied both.

By the time Korm and Herdo brought Gimor himself word of the disaster, half the men were already scattering on their private searches and were no longer where the messengers from their captain sought them. The messengers chased their comrades about the forest as energetically as their comrades chased the phantom raiders, but to little more purpose.

Meanwhile word came from the south. Guards moving down the road to the ford had encountered twelve men left there by Foyn to block the road until *Fang of Giyo* was safely past the ford. Captain Gimor, assuming that he had all the raiders within his grasp, promptly led all the men on hand south along the road. If he'd had more of his men on hand he could perhaps have fought his way through to the river in time to accomplish something.

As it was, half of Gimor's men were nowhere to be found, and many of the rest were seeking the missing. Against the men Gimor had with him, twelve desperate Sea Folk could stand for a good while, even on land. It was a vicious and vile battle there in the dark, wet woods. The Sea Folk neither gave nor asked quarter, and would all have been slain if Gimor hadn't remembered that prisoners might explain what was going on.

Only two of the Sea Folk were taken alive. All the others died with a stubborn courage worthy of a far better Captain than the man the dying cursed so roundly. None knew that they'd accomplished their task. Before the first of Gimor's men stood on the bank of the river, *Fang of Giyo* was miles past the ford. Her sails were filled and all her oars at work, carrying her down to the sea more than fast enough to outpace men pushing through the forest along the banks of the river.

Some hours passed before anyone under Captain Gimor realized that the bird had flown. By then *Fang of Giyo* was nearly out of sight of land. Foyn sat below in his tiny cabin, pouring the contents of a wine jug into himself and singing songs that grew steadily more triumphant or obscene or both as his spirits rose and the wine in the jug sank.

No one can say what this knowledge might have done for Captain Gimor. It is only certain what he did. With zeal and energy and the most profound loyalty to his captive Viceroy, he proceeded to make matters still worse.

He sent off a messenger at once, with orders to ride like the wind to Fors and bear word to Count Arlor. The messenger departed before the prisoners had been questioned or Sir Gilas Lanor found. He therefore bore no message except that Wandor and Gwynna had been carried off by mysterious Sea Folk, striking mysteriously out of the forest under cover of darkness and the storm.

The man thundered off into the night at a horse-killing, buttock-bruising pace. Two hours later a second messenger followed, and just after dawn a third. These two bore a more coherent tale of what had happened, obtained from the captured Sea Folk and from the mumblings of Sir Gilas Lanor.

The first messenger's horse dropped dead at a full gallop and he fell so heavily that he was lucky to escape with only bruises and a twisted ankle. He found himself some hours' painful hobbling from any place where he could get another horse. The other two messengers rode nearly as fast but had better luck with their horses. So they both arrived in Fors many hours before their comrade, having covered in a day and a half what was normally a three-days' ride. They brought their news straight to Count Arlor, just as he was sitting down to his dinner.

His digestion was not improved when he discovered what else the messengers had done on their frantic dash south. Gimor had neglected to warn them to give their news to Arlor and no one else. So they shouted it out as they passed, to all who would listen, as loudly as every fishmongers cried fresh-caught turbot or salt brownfish in the marketplace. They also found a better market for their wares than any fishmonger ever enjoyed. Behind them as they rode they left fear—sputtering, smoking, and here and there blazing up into an open flame of panic.

Count Arlor promptly sent off his own messengers: to Yost, to members of the High Council of the Viceroyalty not in Fors (which was nearly all of them), and to Cheloth of the Woods. He ordered every one of the messengers to say nothing of the news he bore, under the threat of the direst penalties.

Before Arlor could do anything more, a fourth messenger arrived from the north, bearing what almost deserved to be called good news. Captain Gimor had come sufficiently to his senses to realize that guarding the manor house now was like locking the stable door after the horse was stolen. Indeed, it was like locking a stable after the doors themselves had been removed from their hinges and carried away. So Gimor sent word that he was on his way south, with all his men, the one surviving prisoner, Sir Gilas Lanor (who badly needed a doctor), and all his knowledge of what had happened that night. Count Arlor sent off a curt acknowledgement and also a doctor with two assistants: a surgeon, and a Tree Sister of the Khindi. Sir Gilas would need all the help he could get, and the doctor was warned that a refusal to work with the Tree Sister would cost him the price of his head.

Burdened as they were by wounded men, Gimor's party took more than the usual three days to reach Fors.

Count Arlor ate little and slept less during those days. He spent some of the time contemplating the undignified but agreeable vision of strangling Gimor with his bare hands. He spent a great deal more time in the saddle, leading soldiers of the garrison of Fors to a dozen different places on a dozen different errands.

The panic still rose, and an announcement of what had really happened (as far as this was known) did little to fight it. On the third day after word reached Fors, Zakonta the *Red Seer* rode into the city and said that she sensed a *luor*—an aura—of fear over the land so thick that she could almost reach out and gather it in handfuls from the air.

Count Arlor did not disagree. He had seen that fear at work, as he rode about putting out fires, dispersing riots, and snatching victims from the clutching hands and hurtling stones of mobs. Fear was riding about the Viceroyalty, faster than he could follow it. Fear had thrust home a mortal blow to King Nond's rule in Benzos. Would it do the same to Wandor's cause here, even before the people knew whether Wandor and Gwynna were alive or dead? Would they know that, and if so, when? Cheloth of the Woods might know it, but he was silent. The only voice heard was that of fear.

Eventually Captain Gimor reached Fors. Count Arlor found that the vision of strangling Gimor was far more satisfactory than the prospect of actually doing it. He merely cursed all of the Captain's ancestors and descendants, took his company from him, and sent him off to serve as a common soldier in a tumbledown fort in the far south of the Viceroyalty.

"There is nothing down there but tree adders and bears," said the Count. "I think their wits are even slower than yours."

Count Arlor could send Captain Gimor off to the South Marches, but he could send no one to deal with the High Council of the Viceroyalty. Now that Wandor and Gwynna were...*elsewhere*, that task fell squarely on him, like the contents of a chamber pot cast down from a high window.

Elsewhere was a carefully chosen word he used in his own mind, to drive back the fear lurking there like wolves in a winter forest. He had to choose the many more words needed for his speech to the High Council just as carefully.

Of all the Council, he knew only three who could face everything which was known or suspected about this affair without flinching. They were Zakonta, Sir Gilas Lanor, and Cheloth of the Woods. Only Zakonta was present. Sir Gilas lay in a bed in the castle, using his own strength and the skills of doctors and Tree Sisters to fight for his life. Cheloth of the Woods was still silent, and it hardly would have been wise to let the sorcerer appear before the full Council in any case. The less the Councilors thought of how powerless mere humans might be in this affair, the more able they might be to do all that they could do.

Good fortune was on Arlor's side in one way. He was able to delay the meeting of the Council until every one of its members could reach Fors. "After all," he told those who objected, "to ignore anyone would be to cast doubts on his wisdom or even his honor. Do you wish that? I thought not. So let me hear no more of hastening the meeting of the Council."

He had no need of the Council for the work of the daytime; sending ships to sea, mounting patrols along the roads, ordering rioters and rumor-mongers clapped into prison, and much else. He had even less need of it for the work of too many long nights: listening to spies' and prisoners' accounts of what had happened, and choosing the words he would use to tell the story to the Council.

When the day at last came, Arlor spoke plainly. He admitted everything that was already known far and wide. Wandor and Gwynna had indeed been captured by the Sea Folk, but there was good reason to believe that they still lived. The Sea Folk often saved valuable prisoners for sacrifice to the Beasts of Yand Island. Who could be more valuable than Wandor and Gwynna, or more likely to be saved for such a sacrifice?

True, their being saved for that purpose would gain nothing but time. Yet time could do much for those who could put it to use. Wandor and Gwynna certainly could. Furthermore, Berek Strong-Ax should already be nearing Yand Island, and he was a man from whom few secrets could be hidden if he wished to know them.

The wise folk of the Viceroyalty would not be backward in using this gift of time, either. They should spare no effort to meet the raids of the Sea Folk and take as many prisoners as possible. Who could know who might be taken? A Captain of the Sea Folk who knew that his son would die by torture if Wandor and Gwynna went to the Beasts might find that he no longer loved the Black Duke's gold quite so much as before.

They should also muster a fleet in the Viceroyalty—a fleet of all the ships that could keep the Ocean—on a voyage to the lands of the Sea Folk. The ships should be equipped, provisioned, manned, and sent forth. Then Cragor's victory might well be snatched from him before he could even gloat over it.

Not one word of this was a lie, nor was one word of the answers Arlor gave to the Councilors' questions. There were not many of those questions, and Arlor was glad of that. He was also glad to see the Councilors leave the chamber without asking any of the many questions he could not have answered easily.

He'd said nothing of the work spies had certainly done in telling Captain Foyn what he'd needed to know for the raid. If he had, tales of a horde of spies in the Viceroyalty would certainly have gotten about. Then there would have been a mad rush to turn the Viceroyalty upside down and inside out, searching for spies who would certainly be in any place but where they were sought.

He'd said nothing of Telek the Fatherless, who'd lent his Chongan-trained mind and bow to bring Foyn a victory he did not deserve and could never in all the ages of the world have gained without Telek's help. Arlor knew as much as any outsider could know about Telek, guessed more, and was uneasy about all of it.

Telek had spent a full ten years learning all the murderous skills of mind and body taught by the *mungans* of Chonga. There were few men or women not of Chonga who'd done this, and few men or women of any people who'd ever left the service of the *mungans*. Or had Telek left them? Could he be serving someone high in Chonga? Perhaps. A *mungan* had also tried to strike down King Nond, in the very hour of the flight from Manga Castle. Might someone high in Chonga be taking subtle steps toward an alliance with the Black Duke? Arlor wondered.

If Arlor could wonder about that, others, who knew less and imagined more, would be certain that ten thousand *mungans* were about to descend on the Viceroyalty and reduce its people to bleeding corpses strewn about the streets of their burning towns. There were not so many *mungans* in all of Chonga, but neither were there so many people in the Viceroyalty who thought clearly enough to realize this. Once more, there would be panic and confusion. Sooner or later, the hunt would turn against the colony of Chongan traders in Fors. By the time the mob was through with them, Pirnaush of Dyroka would have hundreds of dead countrymen to avenge. Then he would take steps toward an alliance with Cragor—and these would not be subtle steps.

Arlor had said nothing about what the Viceroyalty could actually send to sea by way of a fleet. They did not have the time to gather a fleet that could rout the Sea Folk in their home waters, even if such a fleet were possible. They had the rest of the spring and part of the summer, a few months at most. In that time they could gather at most thirty ships manned by two thousand sailors and carrying as many more soldiers. It would be enough for a raid, but no more.

Finally, he'd left unsaid anything that might make the Councilors think too deeply about how little time they might have. No one knew when the next sacrifice to the Beasts would take place. Wandor and Gwynna might be rushed off to Yand the moment they landed in the Sea Folk lands, or even be carried straight there by Captain Foyn. On the other hand, they might still be sitting in some dank hut on the shores of Stohra Bay when the snow began to fall.

It was not even certain that Wandor and Gwynna would live until the time of sacrifice. Death could come to them from a shipwreck, the hands of a drunken mob, during one of their certain attempts to escape, or from the instigation of Duke Cragor, who would doubtless be happy to send every Sea Folk Captain a sack of gold if they were to send him Wandor's head—and Gwynna, alive and in a condition to feel all the tortures he would inflict on her. The Black Duke surely would speak and act, the moment he learned of Captain Foyn's and Telek's unexpected victory.

Arlor rose from his chair and walked toward the door, his mind on getting enough wine to blunt his thirst without blunting his wits. He had so little thought for anything else that he nearly collided with Zakonta in the doorway.

"My apologies, my lady," he said formally. "You will be staying among us, I trust?"

She shook her head. "I was coming to tell you that I must leave Fors at once and seek out Tree Sisters of the Khindi."

"For Sir Gilas? He is already in the care of—" She held up one golden-brown hand to interrupt him. "No, not for Sir Gilas. I must assemble the strength both of the Tree Sisters and of the *Red Seers*. We must be prepared to reach out to the Hearth Mothers of the HaroiLina if they need our help to stand against those who worship the Beasts of Yand."

"*If* they stand against them."

"They will, in time. But they may also have to stand against the sorcery of Toshak."

"It is said that Kaldmor is in seclusion. Can he do his work from where he is?"

"I would not care to say what he could not do. Also, the more gifted Beast Wizards may now have learned enough about Toshakan Powers to make some use of them. There are certain spells which came down from Toshak in the Beast Cult. They will not have to learn that much." She started to turn away.

Arlor dropped a hand on her shoulder, not gently. He did not wish to anger her, but he had a strong sense of much left unsaid that he needed to hear.

"There is something more?"

She turned, twisting out of his grip and looking at him. She was a head shorter than the Count, but he had the sensation that she was looking down at him from a great height, though with pity rather than contempt. The gray eyes were very wide.

"You did not tell the Council all that you knew or thought, did you?"

"I did not."

"You did not want them to be uneasy to the depths of their souls about things they could not understand?"

"I did not."

"Cannot I do the same when I speak to you?"

"You are afraid of making me afraid?" Ten years ago Arlor would have asked that question in the hope of provoking the speaker into an insult worth a challenge. Many Knights would do so at any time in their lives. But then, they hadn't served King Nond for ten years, learning to slow their tongues and quicken their wits.

Zakonta nodded. "You are not a man at ease with the knowledge of how suddenly the world beyond may leap down on us, like a leopard on a deer?"

"I am not," said Arlor. "But I am also a man who sits in the Viceroy's seat, wields all the Viceroy's power, and must know everything the Viceroy would know. You would not hide anything from Wandor, would you?"

"No. At least not altogether. I would tell Gwynna, and she would tell him in better words than I could choose. Then he would see clearly and not be afraid."

"Doubtless. But I have inherited the Viceroy's power without inheriting the Viceroy's lady. Put aside your fears and I shall put aside mine. Speak." Arlor did not doubt Zakonta's wisdom or good faith, but he doubted his own ability to endure her good intentions much longer.

"Very well. It is known that Kaldmor secludes himself to increase his knowledge of the sorcery of Toshak. One skill he may have sought is that of giving the *limar* of Nem of Toshak the power to act and wield Powers as though it were a living sorcerer."

"What kind of Powers?"

"Any that Kaldmor can wield himself."

As clearly as before, Arlor sensed something left unsaid, but this time he did not feel like pressing Zakonta to reveal it. The *Red Seer* was partly right. He would grimly pursue every bit of knowledge he needed to do his duty. He was afraid to pursue certain kinds of knowledge beyond that point.

"So we have the chance of facing two Kaldmors instead of one?"

"Yes."

Arlor had nothing to say in reply, and Zakonta took that as dismissal. She was gone so swiftly that the sound of her feet on the stairs was fading before Arlor realized that she no longer stood before him.

A party of servants came tramping up the stairs to clean the Council Chamber. They stopped and bowed as they caught sight of the Count. He dismissed them with a silent wave of his hand and hurried down the stairs. The thought of wine was with him again, more wine than he'd wanted the first time.

That would be an easy matter. He could call a servant for the wine. He wished he could call Cheloth of the Woods as easily.

CHAPTER 8

The wind blew from the northwest and the Sea of the Frozen Gods. Daraun's raiders had sailed out when the spring was new and the northwest winds still held the chill of the ice packs as they swept the ships south toward the Viceroyalty.

Now *Mistwing* and the four seal ships that still followed in her wake were on their way home. The wind no longer blew so chill, but it still blew, and now the raiders were beating north against it. They'd already been a long weary time coming north, and there would be a time almost as long and even wearier, before they reached the mouth of Stohra Bay and could approach the land under oars.

Daraun stood on *Mistwing*'s foredeck, beside the anchor and its coiled rope, bracing himself against the ship's heel with one hand clamped on the railing. Above him loomed sails taut as drumheads. His eyes ran up and down the rigging, noting where leather pads might soon be needed to prevent chafing. Then Daraun's eyes looked beyond his own ship to the others thrashing along astern of her.

Like *Mistwing*, they were heeled over until it took feet wide apart or a firm hand on the railing to keep one's footing. Like her, they showed patched sails, spliced rigging, and shield hooks with no shields on them. One sailed with a hastily trimmed pine trunk jutting up where her foremast had been.

Like her, they also sailed under a burden of prisoners, loot, and memories of the past weeks of raiding. Some of those memories were less pleasant than others, for there were missing faces aboard all five ships. The men of the Viceroyalty were not a herd of spotted whales, to be driven into a bay and slaughtered easily as they thrashed and gasped in mortal panic. Those of the HaroiLina who thought otherwise did not live to receive the Black Duke's gold.

Captain Foyn had always been one to despise his foes. That explained the half-witted bravery that won him his War Name so many years ago, and much of the ill-luck that followed him thereafter. Doubtless, it also explained why *Fang of Giyo* was not following in Daraun's wake as the raiders beat their way north.

Telek the Fatherless could have warned Foyn on this matter and much else. But could anything make Foyn listen to another's advice, even such excellent advice as Telek the Fatherless was known to give? Probably not. Probably Telek the Fatherless had found Foyn Son of Thadul as deaf as ever, and had gone with him to meet whatever fate came upon *Fang of Giyo* and her men. Why, in the name of Halo Sea Father, had Telek chosen to sail with Foyn on this voyage? That was a question that would never have an answer, now that Telek had gone to Haro or perhaps to Khoshi Swift in Battle, war god of the Chonga where he'd learned his strange arts.

A cry came from the foretop.

"Ho! Sail ahead! Looks to be a seal ship."

A momentous announcement, thought Daraun. In these waters there'd been few other ships for more than twenty years. He thought of telling the lookout as much.

The raiders held their course. As the minutes passed, the ship ahead came in sight from the foredeck. She was on the same course as Daraun's five. A raider bound home from the Viceroyalty, or a merchant returning from Chonga?

The lookout shouted again.

"Ho, Captain! I think it's *Fang of Giyo*!"

Daraun leaped into the rigging and scrambled up to join the lookout. The man was right. There was no mistaking the badge on the approaching ship's badly set foresail or the red-painted stern. For a moment Daraun was tempted to make a gesture of aversion, then restrained himself. *Fang* and her captain had not returned from the dead, although it would be most interesting to find out just where they had been.

Minutes later Daraun saw that *Fang*'s crew was taking in sail. Then she came about and lay waiting for *Mistwing* to come up, the men manning the oars to keep her head into the sea. Daraun wondered if Foyn needed help, or if, perhaps, he had some tale to tell that made him willing to be overhauled so he could tell it.

Within half an hour Daraun had drawn within hailing distance of *Fang of Giyo*. Both ships lay to on their oars, *Mistwing*'s bow cutting the waves only a few spear's lengths from *Fang*'s stern. The other four raiders held their course under shortened sail. Daraun would have ample time to rejoin them before nightfall.

Daraun held his place on *Mistwing*'s foredeck, with his Second Captain standing behind him and his Right and Left Hands on either side. All four men were armed and armored. Daraun expected no violence, but he did expect to find a warlike air useful in shortening Foyn's tales and explanations.

Foyn sprang up from below, and Daraun's first thought was that the man was drunk. Either drunk, or with something just as potent as wine or mead at work in his mind and body. He swayed as he stood, his long arms waved like the branches of a tree in a storm, and his face was one immense grin. He wore neither armor nor weapons.

Beside Foyn stood Telek the Fatherless, wearing mail coat and Chongan helmet with its tail of overlapping plates. He carried sword, bow, quiver, and two knives, and his face was less than friendly. Foyn and Telek might have been the carvings of *Mirth* and *Sobriety* in the *Kym* House of the Captains.

Daraun cupped his hands and shouted across the water. "Ho, Foyn! What tales do you have of deeds done since we parted?"

Impossibly, Foyn's grin became even wider and Telek's face grew even darker. "No tales," shouted Foyn. "No tales, but a victory for the Children of Haro such as they have never won before. A mighty victory, and the trophies to prove it!"

The wind blurred his words, but wine had not. There seemed to be a sober joy filling Foyn. Daraun found himself growing uneasy about what sort of victory might have done this to Foyn, and what the trophies might be. *Fang* did not appear to be riding lower in the water, so at least the trophies could be nothing of any great weight.

Foyn turned and waved to someone standing farther aft. The

wind carried to Daraun a sharp wordless command, the clatter of weapons, and the unmistakable clank of chains. Then Daraun sucked in his breath as two lean figures scrambled clumsily up into view.

They stood just behind Foyn, swaying with the motion of the ship. Both wore ragged leggings and still more ragged shirts. Their feet were bare and through the rents in their clothes showed skin darkened with filth. Through this skin showed bones and sinews not commonly meant to see the light of day. They were chained at the wrists and ankles.

Rags and filth, starvation and chains might alter or confine what these people could do, but not what they were. They stood so that Daraun found himself trying to guess how far they could reach, and their faces were such that he found it impossible to meet their eyes—particularly the woman's.

They were Wandor and Gwynna. At the sight of them Daraun's stomach twisted until he wondered if the fish he'd had for breakfast were going to return to their home. Then the feeling passed, the more swiftly because he would not show his unease before Foyn and still less before Foyn's captives. He found his voice again.

"You have...done that which will certainly make your name live long." This was true enough, Foyn would take it as praise, and it would spare him the need to say "...won a great victory." Daraun could barely form those words in his mind, let alone his throat.

Foyn could not grin more widely, for there was not enough room on his face. But he tossed his arms about and did a little dance on the deck, until Daraun wondered if he would float away in the breeze like a tuft of feathers tossed into air rising from a fire. Telek remained as stiff as before. Without at least Mind Speech, no one was going to discover what he thought of all this.

Daraun thought a great many things, but the next words to come to his lips were, "Are they safely secured? To have them escape while among us could be worse than to have them in Fors leading their men against us."

"I have done all that is needed," said Foyn. "They have not been allowed to speak one word to each other since I took them. They have been chained as you see them. I have kept their food so scant that neither Wandor's sword nor Gwynna's Powers need be feared. The eyes of armed men are upon them every moment they are on deck."

"Has anything else happened to them?"

"The woman had to be wounded in both legs before we could take her." Telek stirred briefly at those words, and a look passed between him and Foyn. "She is healing well enough. Otherwise they are quite whole. I know well that the Wizards of Yand accept only the most perfect of sacrifices to the Beasts."

"Indeed, that is well known," said Daraun. "You have been wise." And indeed Foyn—or more probably Telek, who doubtless knew far more about keeping dangerous prisoners safely—had been wise. Wandor and Gwynna had not been permitted to make a slaughterhouse of *Fang of Giyo* and get themselves killed while doing it. Wandor had not been crippled, nor Gwynna raped.

Yet might it not have been better if she had been? Against Gwynna's rape a howl of protest would have gone up from countless throats: from the Hearth Mothers, for the blasphemy of having so treated a woman of Powers, initiated by the *Red Seers* of the Yhangi; from the Beast Wizards, for having irreparably blemished a prime sacrifice; perhaps even from Duke Cragor, for having taken from him some of the pleasure that his twisted soul had so long anticipated. Wrath would have crashed down upon the head of Foyn Son of Thadul. His death or disgrace would not have healed Gwynna, but it would have meant at least one less fool dashing about to leave chaos in his wake.

Daraun wanted to laugh and go on laughing. There was madness abroad, when it might be better for a free woman of high rank and Powers to be pounded under the bodies of a whole ship's crew. There was madness in the world, there might be madness in the gods above it, and there would certainly be madness in him, if he had to endure looking upon Foyn and his captives much longer while hiding all that he felt.

So he said, "Your name will live when the trees grow tall upon your grave barrow." Then he headed aft, calling out orders. The oarsmen backed water and *Mistwing* began to draw away.

Foyn's face clouded. Perhaps he'd been expecting Daraun to remain with him and escort him home in triumph, like the guards of a Battle Captain or a *Kym* Speaker? Daraun almost groaned aloud at the thought of Foyn running free, with more followers and fame than ever before but no more wisdom. Telek's face was as unreadable as ever, and Daraun could still not meet the eyes of Wandor and Gwynna.

By the time *Mistwing* had steadied on her course to rejoin the other four ships, *Fang*'s deck was bare of both Foyn and the captives. Daraun was able to resume his place on the foredeck while he tried to put his thoughts in some sort of order.

Should he have struck boldly, leading his men over *Fang*'s railing to snatch Wandor and Gwynna from Foyn's hands? It might have been possible, though certainly bloody now, and still bloodier later. There might not be blood-feud over Foyn for Telek, but others aboard *Fang* had families who would demand vengeance.

No, he had been wise in standing aside. But this was perhaps the last time such would be the case. Foyn had brought an end to the time of easy raiding with no thought but of pleasing the Black Duke or the Beast Wizards. He had opened a new time for the Children of Haro, one that would bring little that was easy and much that might cost blood.

Daraun was happiest with easy ways, in war and peace, (A voice had sometimes pricked at him with the question: Is that why you have no War Name?) Now those easy ways could bring more blood and misery than other courses a man might see opening ahead of him.

For the moment Daraun would not push his thoughts farther than that.

Wandor and Gwynna were hustled back to their space in the hold and the leather curtains tied back in place. They lay down side by side on their sleeping pallets and Gwynna stretched her legs cautiously. Under the bandages the arrow wounds were healing swiftly and with no traces of festering—luck, her own health, the Sea Folk's crude medicine, or perhaps something about Telek's arrows? The wounds still called themselves brutally to her attention if she had to stand for more than a few minutes.

Wandor lay back at full length. The pallet under him was as damp and lumpy as ever and the deck under it as hard. He noticed none of this, as he took several deep breaths and opened his mind.

Instantly he sensed Gwynna, ready and receptive. With an ease built from their natural gifts by long practice, the Mind Speech link formed.

("I think perhaps we have met a friend today.")

("Who?")

("Captain Daraun. Berek has often spoken of an uncle, Daraun Son of Hymok.")

("Daraun is not so rare a name among the Sea Folk.")

("No, and we do not know his father. But he has that family look of Berek, that is certain. He may well be the same man.")

("Why should he prove a friend, even so?")

("Very well. Perhaps we should call him someone who may be the enemy of our enemies.")

("Why?")

Wandor sensed in that question a weary disbelief that there could be anything but deadly enemies within many days' sailing, except for those Hearth Mothers who might find both the courage and the opportunity to act.

Wandor found he wanted to mask his thoughts as he tried to form his answer. It was not an easy task, for how could he explain his faith in Berek to someone who had not seen or heard everything that gave Wandor his trust in the man's judgement?

He found he could not mask them well enough, not from Gwynna. A few moments, then:

("I see. Berek spoke of his uncle as a good man, who often avoided hard decisions when he could. But Daraun also sees clearly and thinks before he speaks, so he will not shy away from a decision when he must make one. From what you know of Berek, a man he spoke of in that way might in time turn against the alliance of the Sea Folk with Cragor and the Beast Wizards of Yand.")

("That is so. Berek is a man who does not easily forgive folly or those who endure too much of it in others. So I think one thing his uncle may see clearly is how much harm may come to the Sea Folk from our capture.")

("Yes, perhaps. But how can we find out what he truly thinks, let alone guide it? We have to lay many of our plans before we make landfall off Stohra Bay.")

By Wandor's reckoning that could be no more than five or six days away. Any reckoning he made about the progress of ships was rough in the extreme, but he was reasonably confident about this one. He'd talked at length with Captain Thargor, who had sailed with the last raid into Sea Folk Waters more than twenty years ago and probably knew as much about them as anyone in the Viceroyalty.

("So soon?")

("Yes. We have to reckon on not being able to use the Mind Speech once we enter the homeland of the Sea Folk.")

("I thought they did not have it.")

("They seldom do. But they know there is such a thing. Some can recognize it or at least guess wisely when it is being used. There are no such aboard this ship, Mother Yeza be praised!") She hesitated. ("Except perhaps Telek the Fatherless, and I doubt if we shall ever learn what he knows or does not know until it is too late.")

Wandor did not even need to put his agreement into words.

Gwynna continued. ("The Keepers of the Hearth and some of the Hearth Mothers do have the Mind Speech. One may have secretly turned against her sisters and so be able to betray us. Even if the Hearth Mothers are all true, we still have to face the Beast Wizards. It is said that most of the full Wizards among them have the Mind Speech and even skill in preventing others from using it. Some of them will almost certainly be among the Sea Folk. Or Kaldmor the Dark may have sent Nem's *limar*. Or—oh, any number of things that could keep our minds bound as tightly as our hands were the night we were taken.")

Only Cheloth of the Woods could truly number all their enemies, and they'd heard nothing from him since weeks before their capture.

The Mind Speech link slowly faded, as both realized there was nothing more to say. Wandor had further thoughts of his own on possible enemies, but they would be worth putting into words only for Cheloth.

During the last few days of the voyage, he'd sensed a third presence when he was forming or breaking a Mind Speech link. This presence always vanished as the bond formed itself or broke, as insubstantial and fleeting as the foam on the crests of the waves. It was not Cheloth of the Woods. It was nothing and nobody Wandor had ever sensed or imagined.

It was also something that seemed to be passing Gwynna by. Certainly she gave no sign of the slightest awareness of this third presence. Perhaps then it was only his imagination, fed by fatigue and hunger and the ordeal of captivity?

Perhaps. Certainly it seemed that, with her greater sensitivity and trained Powers, Gwynna would have been aware of anything he could sense. Not only aware, but actively listening, even probing into it.

Just as certainly, Wandor could not bring himself to mention these quirks of his inner senses to Gwynna. He could not even put description of this presence into plain Hond words, and vague murmurings of vaguely sensed things would only add to Gwynna's burdens. He would keep his silence, and perhaps in time this third presence would do the same.

CHAPTER 9

Darkness lay upon the land and the sea, and in that darkness men and women did whatever their gods and their circumstances allowed or compelled.

In Trorim, a master goldsmith named Desoud Wandor lay dying in the bed he had not left for three years. In the cellar of his house, an apprentice of Sthi blood named Kayrin did carpenter's work. He was putting up four new posts, and he would tell his master's widow that it was to make the house stronger and ensure a better price when she sold it, as she doubtless would. She would not ask more, not being one to let idle curiosity stand between her and money.

In one of those four posts was a hollow space, and in that space lay a pyramidal pendant of gold and crystal. The pendant had come from the body of the woman said to be the true mother of Desoud Wandor's foster son. That was the Bertan Wandor who now ruled in the Viceroyalty of the East and of whom much else was said.

Desoud Wandor had taken as his second wife the sister of a man strong for Duke Cragor. This and his sickness kept the duke's men from the house. Desoud Wandor's death might open the doors and would certainly open his widow's path to selling the house.

Kayrin did not know more about the pendant than rumor told him. But he was of the Sthi, so those rumors told him more than they told most men. They told him clearly enough that the pendant should not fall into the hands of anyone friendly to Cragor. If possible it should not even leave the house of Desoud Wandor, hence this night's work.

The work would be finished soon, about the time Desoud Wandor's spirit departed. Then Kayrin would also depart, for the Hills and his people there. They would not be kind to him, for he had become of the towns and not of the Hills. In their eyes that was a betrayal. It was enough for him that none of them would be serving the Black Duke.

In the Hills the *limar* of Nem of Toshak lay on a pallet, doing those things which *limars* do in place of the sleep of flesh-and-blood creatures. On another pallet lay an exhausted Kaldmor the Dark, drifting off to sleep with the knowledge that he had done well this day.

A few more such days, and the *limar* would have all it needed to move about the world like a living man. A few more days or perhaps weeks after that, and he could give it all his own Powers. Wherever the *limar* was, there he would be also. He could hold Mind Speech with it, see and hear what it saw, speak with its mouth...

Kaldmor fell asleep at that point, and for once his dreams were entirely pleasant ones.

In a hut in a soldiers' camp on the Ponan border, the Khind girl Jaira huddled in a corner. Captain Tagor lurched toward her, grease-smeared hands reaching out.

It would be bad tonight, she knew. Tagor was drunk, because bandits had burned three farms that his company should have kept safe. The chief captain beat him with words, and now he would beat her with his fists.

So be it. If the High Hunter had abandoned her as he seemed to have done, she could expect no better. Perhaps she ought to thank whatever gods ruled this land and Tagor's heart that she could expect no worse.

* * *

In a forest camp not far from Jaira's hut, Count Ferjor peered down into a skillet where a last sausage lay sputtering quietly to itself. He looked at the other men seated around the fire. None of them seemed hungry any more. He stabbed the sausage with his dagger and disposed of it in two quick bites. The last mouthful was washed down with a wooden mugful of ale.

There was plenty of food for his band now. This happy situation might even last until winter, now that they had a loose alliance with the bands prowling close to the rich and untouched farms in the south.

The Count wondered on what terms the food was obtained. The leaders said they only stole from those who favored Cragor and paid all others. The Count had his doubts. Some of those who fought Cragor (or at least Cragor's men) were bandits in all but name.

These doubts did not make Ferjor willing to cast aside the alliance. A year in the woods had toughened both his body and his conscience.

In a cellar room in the Duelists' House in Avarmouth, the Grand Master watched two apprentices fight a test match. They were both fighting well, although they fought in a dank, low-ceilinged chamber fitfully lit by rush dips.

In times past such a match would have been fought in a sunlit courtyard or even a market square, with other apprentices collecting copper and silver from appreciative onlookers. No more. The Order of Duelists had no wish to remind anyone of its purpose or its prowess. None of the Order unsheathed his steel except in the greatest privacy. Inevitably, this pruned away the wealth of the order, so that rush dips replaced candles, ale replaced wine, and porridge replaced meat. Only weapons and armor were as they had been.

One of the dips went out, and the darkness thickened. The apprentices halted and stepped apart. "Go on, go on," the Grand Master called. After a moment the grind of steel and the thud of booted feet began again. Why not go on fighting in the dark? thought the Grand Master. It was good training for the battles that might yet come to the Order of Duelists.

* * *

Duke Cragor slept, alone and motionless in his great bed of state. He slept after a day that had brought neither good nor harm to either him or his enemies. With this he was content. Such days worked for him more than they worked for Bertan Wandor.

On Yand Island the High Beast Wizard strode up a flight of weathered stone steps cut in the hillside, staff in hand and a lampbearer scurrying before him. At the top of the steps he turned on to the stone-paved walk around the rim of the pit of the Beasts. His stride did not slow, nor did the steady beat of his iron-shod staff on the stone.

He came to the point on the rim opposite the iron gate that held the Beasts within their Caves except on the days of sacrifice. He looked down. Just below the rim was a small stone ledge, and on it stood the two Initiates who had charge of maintaining the proper spells on the gate. At least they should have been standing. One of the brown-robed figures was sitting down, his legs dangling over the edge of the platform.

The High Wizard thrust the staff sharply downward, sending the tip inches over the sitting man's shaven head. Then he brought it back against the stone with a crash that echoed around the pit.

The Initiate jumped up so violently that he nearly lost his balance and fell into the pit. The High Wizard almost regretted he hadn't. The fall would certainly have broken enough bones to give the young lout a lesson not soon forgotten.

"*Stand* while you watch the pit," the High Wizard snapped. His voice raised more echoes and a low grumbling mutter from some wakeful Beast in the foul darkness beyond the gate. The two Initiates stiffened and bowed deeply.

The High Wizard nodded and moved on, muttered curses now marking his progress along with the pounding staff. Was there no regard for the laws of Yand any more, or respect for The Way of Sacrifice?

There was, but no longer enough. It was the new richness of the sacrifices that had brought about this decline. In the days when a single flaw in the annual sacrifice could bring a year of evil to Yand, there was thought, there was care, there was obedience. Now there was a sacrifice every month and sometimes every week. Only a few Wizards held to the old standards, and too many of those were feeble with age. The most skilled and reliable of the younger Wizards was Mykto, and he'd been sent to the mainland to keep a proper watch on the HaroiLina. He was too badly needed there to permit keeping him on Yand, as much as that would have eased the High Wizard's mind.

The High Wizard stopped cursing and sighed wearily. He had prayed before and he would pray again. Perhaps those prayers would be answered, and the laws and customs he'd learned as a boy would last out his life. This was not too great a prayer, not for a man nearing his eightieth year.

In Yost, the southern city of the Viceroyalty of the East, lights burned in the chambers above a sailors' tavern. Count Arlor sat at a scarred and wine-stained table with Captain Bendo Thargo, whose ship *Red Pearl* had brought first Wandor and Berek, then Arlor and Nond, across the Ocean.

They sat, they drank wine, and they talked of how many ships the Viceroyalty might send north against the Sea Folk and how many fighting men might be crowded aboard those ships. The numbers were ominously small. The Viceroyalty had seaward defenses and seaborne trade to maintain, and both demanded their share of ships.

In the forest between Yost and Fors, Jos-Pran, War Chief of the Gray Mares and the man who spoke for Wandor among the Yhangi of the Plains, kept a solemn vigil. He would rather have been with Zakonta, but she had sent him away on this vigil that she might better keep hers. Jos-Pran had obeyed. There was great strength in Zakonta, strength beyond what was common even in *Red Seers*, strength to stand against a man and warrior and bend him to her will.

There should be shame in that, but Jos-Pran felt none. He was not as proud as he had been the day he challenged Bertan Wandor to ride the King Horse of the Yhangi. He had seen too much. Now he saw that the wise thing to do with Zakonta was to grip the lance and drink the wedding-ale with her. If she would be his wife, her strength (as well as his) might be bred into the warriors and *Red Seers* she would bear him.

Such would surely be needed among the Yhangi, for even if Bertan Wandor should win a great victory, it would not make the elk herds strong through the winter, the foals numerous in the spring, the women fertile, or the war-singers gifted.

Sir Gilas Lanor tossed in a feverish half-sleep. An immense weight seemed to lie on his wounded chest while pale faces and paler things without form or name came and went.

Wandor's face did not come, but Gwynna's did. The part of the Knight's mind not gripped by the fever felt vaguely guilty about this. Wandor was the chosen one, not Gwynna. His grief should not be for Gwynna, even though she might be already dead or doomed to face the Beasts of Yand along with Wandor.

Yet it was. Waking, he could keep what he still felt for Gwynna from his lips and even from his mind. Asleep or in fever, this was not so.

In another part of the forest, Zakonta stood in the Seer trance. Tree Sisters of the Khindi guarded all paths toward her, while with her mind she reached out in one direction toward the Keepers of the Hearth of the Mother among the HaroiLina, in the other toward the *Red Seers* of the Yhangi.

She was cautious in her reaching out toward the Keepers. She was still not altogether sure of their willingness to act, although she'd feigned confidence with Arlor. She was still less sure of their ability, for their Powers had lain long disused and might now be weakened almost into uselessness. She was least of all sure that she could reach the Keepers without finding some Beast Wizard reaching out to attack the link and perhaps her as well.

Yet she had to seek to form that link between the Keepers and the *Red Seers*. Nothing else could do as much to move the Keepers and the Hearth Mothers to act. No one among the HaroiLina could do as much as the Keepers and Hearth Mothers to aid Wandor and Gwynna.

Cheloth of the Woods sat on a log of driftwood, his feet half-buried in the sand and a breeze from the Ocean making his cloak ripple about his lean frame.

His body sat on this narrow beach with the surf booming only paces away, while his mind reached out across the Ocean, listening. He did not probe or try to push aside any of the barriers he sensed there. He had never done so and never would. Neither had Nem of Toshak. It was nearly the only limitation the Master of Toshak had ever accepted, and he'd accepted and lived with it even during his great duel with Cheloth. In the end that duel sank a continent, but neither sorcerer ever made the slightest move against what lay in the waters of the Ocean.

Cheloth would have been happier to leave the shore and return to the forest for Mind Speech with Zakonta, since he could reach neither Wandor nor Gwynna. He would even have considered going directly to Fors, to speak directly to as many of the Council as might be able to hear him without fear.

He could not have done either of these things without revealing that, for the moment, he could not reach the captives. Indeed, he was too concerned with other matters to make any real effort to do so. He did not wish it known that anything could hamper or distract him in this way. This was not vanity but simple wisdom. Humans were not made to accept without terror how little they knew about the universe around them.

In the land where the HaroiLina built their ships and raised their crops and buried their fathers, the fire burned higher and later than usual in the Hearth House. The nine Keepers who ruled the Hearth Mothers were all gathered around it, tending it with their own hands.

Foyn Son of Thadul lay in a noisy, drunken slumber beside a thrall-woman who was even drunker.

Daraun Son of Hymok walked along the shore, seeking answers amid the rumble of the waves on the rocks and the gravel—

answers that he would not find.

Telek the Fatherless sat in the branches of a tree outside a village. No one knew what he sought and no one cared to ask him.

Wandor and Gwynna lay in an exhausted, hunger-haunted sleep on straw pallets spread on the floor of a log-walled chamber in a longhouse on the shore of Stohra Bay.

Out in the middle of Stohra Bay, all was darkness and the slow surge of water that tells of great depths below. The three greatships and the pinnace came in from the Ocean with all their sails spread. They still moved slowly, for they were heavy and heavily laden. From the mainmast of the lead ship flew Duke Cragor's banner, and from the foremast, Baron Galkor's.

CHAPTER 10

Baron Galkor and the sun rose at about the same time. Galkor seldom rose so early, but today he expected to be meeting Sea Folk of high rank in their own longhouses or at least on the decks of their own ships. He had already met the Beast Wizards of Yand and left little undone to please them, so he could do no less with the Sea Folk.

He washed in a basin of tepid water and allowed the barber to mutilate his hair and beard into a less ragged shape than they had achieved in two weeks at sea. He breakfasted on flat ale, dry bread, and drier cheese, sitting before the door of his cabin in drawers and hose.

Then he began to dress. Shoes of dark gray leather with tarnished silver spurs. A linen shirt from which nearly all the lice had been shaken. A tunic with the breast quartered in red and white and the long sleeves green where the moths hadn't nibbled. A heavy cloak, blue with a black lining. This was intact although damp; as was its gold clasp of the best Chongan work, Galkor's last gift from his father. His servants knew it. He would have flogged anyone who let the clasp tarnish.

At last, a belt with sword and dagger of the plainest steel, bone, and leather, that shouted "I am only for killing" so clearly that no one could mistake it. The Sea Folk had this among their other good customs: they required no free man to disarm or wear weapons that were for show rather than for use.

In the end Galkor knew that he'd done as well as the contents of his chests and their condition after a long voyage permitted. Now that he had spent so much time dressing, doubtless the day would bring no meeting with any Sea Folker of higher rank than captain over half-a-dozen fishing boats. He tightened his belt and went out on deck.

Some of his sourness vanished upon seeing the sunlight, and more upon seeing the crew's work so well done. The decks were scrubbed white, the rigging taut, the paintwork freshened, even clean sand laid down in the cookbox forward. A dozen sailors sat on the fo'c'sle deck, pulling on fresh breeches and tying fresh rags around their hair. The men on watch had already finished dressing in whatever clean clothes they possessed.

Galkor walked to the railing and looked out. The other three ships presented much the same sight. On the rearmost one, the sun already winked on the armor and helmets of soldiers coming up from below. All four bows pushed ahead of them broad beards of foam and all four sterns trailed even broader white cloaks. The four ships were heading up the bay at a good six knots, praise be to whoever had care of the winds this far north!

So his work and that of his men was done for the moment. Now there was nothing to do but wait for whatever meetings the day might bring. For once, Galkor felt the rare peace that comes with good weather, few cares, and the sense that over the past few weeks one has worked to some purpose.

Five of his ships with all their crews and five hundred of his soldiers now held Yand Island securely—for whom, he was not entirely sure, but certainly against Wandor. Cragor had been quite right. Before the fleet landed, three hundred good men could have swept Yand Island from end to end. Now Wandor could no longer reach out across the Ocean and pluck Yand like a ripe fig.

The other ships now carried him and the last hundred soldiers up Stohra Bay toward *Kym-Thass*. The Field of the *Kym* was the best place to start when there was business to be done with the Sea Folk, whether that business involved walrus tusks, furs, slaves, bribery, or assassinations.

All the ships were sound, or so the captains told him. Of the sailors and soldiers, twenty or so were dead of accidents or shipboard fevers—no great toll out of nearly a thousand men. Perhaps a hundred more were sickly, but putting land under their feet would swiftly restore them.

The ships sailed for another hour as the day turned to blazing brightness. At the end of that hour, a Sea Folk ship appeared dead ahead, bearing down on Galkor with all her oars at work.

The approaching ship was one of the light open rowing vessels the Sea Folk used in their home waters, and she came down fast toward Galkor. She flew no banner that anyone could recognize; but a cluster of armored men standing amidships suggested she bore an important messenger or at least an important message. The Sea Folk ship made a complete circle around Galkor's squadron, her oars throwing up flashing arcs of foam in a flaunting display of her independence of the wind. Then she pulled to within hailing distance of Galkor.

"*Horoooooo*! Lord Galkor! Come you?" The speaker's accent was so thick Galkor could barely make out his words, but at least he wouldn't have to call for his interpreter.

Galkor cupped his hands and shouted back. "I am here. It is I, Galkor. I come from Cragor, my master. Honor to the *Kym* of Captains."

"Great word have we for you. Great word. We have Wander and Gwynna. I, Foyn Son of Thadul, took them in the night. Come to see them. Come!"

For a long moment Galkor could not have spoken a word, polite or otherwise, to save his own life or indeed to keep all four of his ships and every man aboard them from sinking to the bottom of the sea. He would have more readily expected a thunderbolt from the cloudless sky above than what he'd just heard.

Galkor's moment of silence stretched on into a minute before he was able to bring it to an end. "Honor to you, Foyn Son of Thadul. Honor to you and rich reward, for you have done well. Indeed we shall come to see what you have taken." And to see if you are telling the truth, he added to himself.

It was indeed great news—so great that Galkor found it hard to grasp, let alone believe. Yet the fact that something sounded incredible did not make it false. Also, there was no reason for a Captain of the Sea Folk to tell any sort of lie or jest in such a matter, especially to one who spoke for Duke Cragor.

"Will you follow us?" shouted Foyn.

"Yes, we shall," replied Galkor. Now he recognized the slurring in Foyn's words. The man was simply drunk. Galkor threw back his head and let out a roar of triumphant laughter. Perhaps he also would find himself of a mind to get drunk tonight.

He waved to Captain Foyn and strode forward. As he went, cheers rose around him—from the sailors at first, then from the soldiers as they scrambled up from below, and at last echoed from the Sea Folk ship alongside. The cheering ran on for a while, then died away as Foyn's ship took station ahead of Galkor's.

The men cheered several more times before sunset that day. The last time they cheered, Galkor's four ships lay anchored off the *Kym-Thass* and the baron was rowing ashore to meet the Speaker of the *Kym* of Captains. He'd already seen the dim chamber in the prison longhouse, and he'd seen Wandor and Gwynna asleep in that chamber. Now he was going ashore again while the men cheered him, cheered the news, cheered loudest of all the barrels of beer and the joints of roasted meat they could see being rowed out to them.

They cheered loudly enough to be heard in the longhouse that held Wandor and Gwynna. The chamber had a small window that let in some air and a good many buzzing insects, and gave a view toward the shore and the bay. At the sound of the cheers Wandor stepped to the window and knelt. Gwynna scrambled up onto his shoulders and peered out. He heard her hiss of indrawn breath, then she dropped down again. Her legs gave under her and she dropped to her knees, her face bleached by pain, exhaustion, and a despair that Wandor had seen in her only once before. That had been in a chill tent on the snow-covered northern Plains where he lay wounded. She had crept into his arms, shaking with cold, fever, hunger, and doubt that she'd been able to reach out to the *Red Seers* of the Yhangi. It was not good to see.

He drew her against him and heard her murmur, "Four ships of Benzos, and Galkor's banner on the first. Another wolf joins the pack around us."

It was a true image, although wolves did not lock up their prey before closing in for the kill. Only men did that.

Then Wandor's thoughts began to turn, slowly, like a millwheel long unused, but to some purpose. Though there was no Mind Speech between them, Gwynna seemed to sense this mental awakening and respond to it. The despair slowly left her face, although the exhaustion and the hunger remained.

"Yes, we're surrounded by a pack of wolves," he said quietly. "But it's a pack without a leader. They need one, but they'll be hard put to find him."

"Yes," said Gwynna slowly. "Galkor comes, no doubt from Cragor. He will want you killed out of hand and me in chains to take back across the Ocean for..." She broke off and her face showed bleakness again. The death awaiting her if she fell into Cragor's hands would break into anyone's thoughts or words.

After a moment she continued. "But the Beast Wizards of Yand also have people on hand to speak for them. They will certainly demand we be turned over for sacrifice to the Beasts. Perhaps Galkor will let them have you, but will he risk what Cragor might say if he can't have me? Then what will the Beast Wizards say? What will those among the Sea Folk who follow the Beast Wizards say?"

"I'd give a thousand crowns to hear it," said Wandor with a thin smile. "That's not all, either. There's Daraun, who may well be hatching schemes of his own. I doubt if they'll be friendly to Galkor or the Wizards. There's Telek the Fatherless, who will certainly have some plan of his own, although, I'll wager, even the gods don't know what it is. Something about you draws his attention."

"I drew his arrows first," said Gwynna. "I could have done better with more attention and fewer arrows. But you're right. I don't know what the mating of Sea Folk blood and *mungan* training has done, but certainly he's been willing to stand between me and death. Then there are the Keepers of the Hearth—I think."

"You do more than hope, now?"

"Yes. I can listen just well enough to have some idea of what they are doing. Zakonta has reached out to them, and the *Red Seers* with her. The Keepers of the Hearth accept the link, but there are only nine of them and they haven't yet reached their decision. They seem to doubt they can do anything for us that justifies the risk to them, since we do not know what Cheloth may be doing."

Wandor refused to waste strength cursing Cheloth or pounding his fist against the wall. He sighed. "So they may love us enough to steal a kiss in the dark, but not to walk with us in the daylight?"

Gwynna laughed. "You should turn bard. Yes, that is the position of the Keepers of the Hearth of the Mother—for now."

Wandor sighed again. "Well, we can live with that. The pack around us is already of four different minds. Without a leader, will they keep their attention on our throats alone? I wonder."

"So will Baron Galkor, the moment he learns what he faces here."

They slept the deep sleep of exhaustion that night, and Galkor slept the deep sleep of drunkenness. The gods were kind enough to send him, as reward for his labors, one night of peace of spirit and of joy in victory.

CHAPTER 11

Gray waves marched like ranks of pikemen behind *Fire of Elya* as she drove toward the land. Berek stood amidships, as secure on his legs as only a man could be who'd learned to balance himself on a rolling deck the same year he'd learned to walk. Three strong men gripped the bar of the steering oar, and Kurash's unsleeping eye watched every other part of the ship. Berek watched the waves, waiting to see them steepen into the ugly breaking sea that told of shoal water, hoping he would see them roll onward as they had done for so many hours.

Fire of Elya was coming home after only six weeks, although she still had stores for as many more. She was coming home, although there was not a missing sail or spar and only five missing faces from her crew-two had drowned, one was lost to the sharks, and two had died in battle. She was coming home, because neither Berek nor Kurash could see that there was anything more to learn off Yand Island.

They knew now that a man (who could only be Baron Galkor) had come to Yand with a fleet, then sailed on to Stohra Bay, leaving behind five tall ships and five hundred soldiers. They knew the soldiers had made a camp and were building fortifications. They knew that the island's fishermen were watching for strange ships and reporting them to the new garrison. So they took seven fishermen as prisoners and set sail for home. There was nothing to be gained by letting Galkor's captains know that Yand was being watched, and perhaps much to be learned from the fishermen by more thorough and skilled questioning than was possible aboard *Fire of Elya*.

Both his heart and his mind told Berek that he'd done good work for his Master. He sang no songs, though. Haro had a short way with men who boasted of their victories before they were on dry land and safely out of his reach. Nor could Berek forget that for all his success in gathering news to bring to Wandor, most of that news was bad. To snatch Yand Island would once have been easy, but this was no longer so. To face the HaroiLina knowing that Baron Galkor was among them promised even less pleasure. Berek knew that Galkor had more skill than his ill luck had so far let show. If Galkor's luck were to turn while he was in the north?...

Within the hour the coast of the Viceroyalty appeared ahead, a dark and featureless mass to eyes less experienced than Berek's. He saw that they were a good two hours' sailing north of Fors Bay. With this wind, it would be tempting Haro to head straight north, with a rocky shore so close under their lee. A long beat to seaward would avoid that, but would also end with their running in toward Fors Bay in the darkness. That also would be tempting the Sea Father.

Better to tempt no one. A half-hour to the south lay a bay with deep enough water for *Fire of Elya*. Doubtless it would be crowded with fishing boats also waiting out the storm, and those boats would be filled with curious eyes. Yet *Fire* might have been anywhere, and if her men kept silent no one would learn her business or the news she bore.

The half hour was closer to an hour, but at last Berek could order the sails down and Kurash and the drummer could send the men to the oars. *Fire* crept into sheltered water, and her anchor went down with a scraping of fast-running rope. A score of fishing boats were drawn up on the shore. As *Fire* swung to her anchor, two men climbed into the smallest of the boats and started rowing out toward her.

Berek waited amidships as the boat sped toward the ship, and gradually the crew gathered behind him. They all saw clearly the way the boat was coming. The two men in it bent low and rowed as furiously as if the water was drying up inches behind them. They caught crabs, yawed wildly, and nearly capsized twice, but came on nonetheless.

A ship's-length away one of the men turned around and saw

Berek. He quivered like a man with a palsy and stopped rowing. The other man did the same. The boat began to drift away from *Fire*.

Those men must have what they think I will call bad news, Berek thought. They do not want to be bad-news bringers, and I do not blame them. But in another minute they will be out of hailing distance, and we will have to send a boat ashore to learn what they fear to tell us. We have no time to waste with their foolish fears.

He cupped his hands and hailed. "Ahoy, the boat! Now, by the gods, will you tell us what you came out here for, or must we come after you?" He shook his ax, Greenfoam, in the air to give point to his words.

The bow rower shouted back, "Will you promise that no harm will come to us, if we tell true?"

"Harm will surely come to you if you don't, and swiftly!" roared Kurash.

The silence lasted a few heartbeats longer, then: "Wandor the Viceroy and his lady Gwynna are taken by the Sea Folk, under one they call Telek the Fatherless. No one knows if they yet be living or gone now into the Shadow House."

Then both rowers were furiously digging their oars into the water, bringing the boat around so sharply that once again it nearly capsized. They thrashed away toward the shore still more frantically than they'd come out.

"We go north," said Berek, turning to Kurash. But Kurash was no longer there, and neither were the men who'd been standing behind Berek. The Second Captain was halfway to the bow already, leading the anchor party. Others were unshipping the oars they'd shipped only a few minutes ago.

There'd been no need for Berek to say a word. As if all the men aboard *Fire of Elya* were part of a single Mind Speech link, they knew what to do. Hoist anchor and go north. Risk wind, risk waves, risk sharp rocks, risk the anger of Haro, risk the anger of all the gods or of none. Risk anything, but do not delay one minute in bringing the ship to Fors.

Fire of Elya beat her way north during the remaining hours of daylight, then ran into Fors Bay in the darkness. She ran in so fast and with so little warning that the garrison of the castle turned out, thinking the Sea Folk were daring a raid into the bay itself. Fortunately, someone identified the ship before the alarm spread to the city, but not before Count Arlor was dragged from a bed in which he'd lain down only an hour before.

So the Count was less than half-awake and more than half out of temper when he met a Berek who was in a mood to punish someone—anyone—for whatever follies and failings had led to the capture of his Master and Gwynna.

To Arlor, Berek seemed at least a foot taller than normal, and his dark bronze hair stood out in all directions. He bore no weapons, but the twitching of his enormous hands took away much of Arlor's comfort in that fact.

"Is it certain that they are gone?" Berek's voice bit like a carpenter's adze and grated like a rusty file on rough stone.

"It is, and you never doubted it yourself. Otherwise you would not have come north as you did, setting us by the ears."

"If other men had been as watchful as those in the castle, Wandor and Gwynna might yet be among us."

"We cannot say. We do not know enough of the skills of Telek the Fatherless. What do you know of him?"

"I know that he was a man before the *mungans* taught him, and is still a man now. No man should have been able to come against Wandor and Gwynna and take them if others had been watching as they should. I must know—"

"Berek, you have returned from a long voyage. You have your ship and men to see to, and after that you must read of what has happened while you were gone."

"I cannot read, Count. You—"

"You can read well enough when you are not—"

"I do not need to read scribblings on dirty parchment to know that my Master and Gwynna are gone. What else can have happened, that I must know?"

"Much." Arlor flogged sleep-dulled wits in an effort to find other events worthy of note since Berek's departure. He hesitated a little too long.

"You do not speak the truth," said Berek. His hands were twitching more than before, and he raised them to the level of his waist. Arlor stepped back two paces and barely refrained from resting one hand on the hilt of his sword. He abandoned his search for noteworthy events and turned his attention to finding words that would keep Berek from erupting like a geyser of boiling mud.

"Berek, I have done nothing to make you call me a liar to my face, and I will not submit to it. I cannot give you the names of those who failed when I do not know who they are. Still less can I let you—" (He nearly said "...go rampaging about like a wild bull in rut.") "—go searching the Viceroyalty for those who failed your Master. If we have not found them in a month of searching, do you think you will be able to succeed now? It is far more likely that you will sow anger and confusion and make men lose work and time when every day counts. We are gathering a fleet to sail north in search of Wandor and Gwynna, and all our efforts must go into that."

"You prepare a fleet?" said Berek.

"We do. You would have seen signs of it at the docks if..." Instead of "...if you hadn't been too angry to see your hand in front of your face," Arlor said, "...if you had come into port by daylight. If Wandor and Gwynna live, you do them harm by anything that will delay the fleet a single hour."

Berek shook his head. "Perhaps that is so." His eyes speared Arlor again. "You swear that those who failed Wandor and Gwynna are unknown to you?"

"I swear it, by Alfod the Judge, Staz the Warrior, and your own Haro Sea Father."

"You are not a man who will call three gods to witness a lie," said Berek grudgingly. "Very well. The gods must judge the man if my Master or I cannot. Now, I have learned much off Yand Island. There are men of Cragor—"

Arlor held up a hand. "Berek. I said before, and I will say again, you have business with your ship. Certainly your news is not fresh fish, that a few more hours will spoil it."

Berek managed a faint smile. "No, it is not." His hands dropped to his side again and he turned away without another word. Arlor stood without moving or even taking a deep breath until he saw the door close behind Berek, then turned toward his bedchamber.

He hoped he'd said enough to keep Berek from searching for those who did not truly exist. He doubted it, though. He knew he'd been closer to death in those moments face to face with Berek than in some of the battles and duels he'd fought. Berek's rage was not one to be more than briefly turned aside by any words that a tired man dragged from his bed could muster up. And there was still the Council meeting tomorrow—although it was only the War Council, all the gods be praised.

Enough. For tonight he would do neither himself nor anyone else any good anywhere but in his bed.

CHAPTER 12

The War Council met soon after dawn. The waves still boomed in through the channel before the northwest wind and threw clouds of spray halfway up the seaward face of Fors Castle. The wind itself swept around the castle with howls and moans like giants being tortured, from time to time rising until no one in the Council chamber could make himself heard without shouting. At last Arlor ordered the servants in to wedge the shutters closed and light the candles. After that the thick stone of the tower kept out the sound of the wind, although it held within the chamber a dank chill more fit for late autumn than for late spring.

In the chamber facing Arlor were Jos-Pran, Zakonta, Berek, Master Besz, and Captain Thargor. In time many others would have the right or the need to learn what was said and what was decided by these six, but for the moment the six were enough. Arlor was Viceroy in all but name. Zakonta wielded her Powers and those of the *Red Seers* for their cause. Jos-Pran spoke for the Yhangi. Berek bore the news that had them gathered here. Master Besz would lead the fighting men sent north against the Sea Folk, and Captain Thargor would lead the ships which carried those men.

Berek told his tale briefly, in well-chosen words that showed no anger. Jos-Pran was the first to speak after Berek was finished.

"Clearly, we now need more men aboard the fleet. There will be a place for the two hundred Yhangi I have offered."

"There will be no place for them if they will not follow my

orders," said Besz. "I have accepted the Khindi because their chiefs have sworn before a priest of Staz and two of their own Tree Sisters to obey me in all things. Where is such a promise from the Yhangi?"

"Why should the Yhangi obey your orders, Besz? You served Cragor and slew many of our people in his service. It is even said that you were once captain for the slave raiders of the Seven Towns. Who knows, perhaps you led them when they slew my wife and children?"

Besz's eyebrows rose. "Much is said that is not heeded by men not too proud to be wise. There cannot be more than one captain in a battle. Who is Jos-Pran, that he has forgotten this?"

"One who thinks of the honor of his people," said Jos-Pran.

"You do?" said Zakonta sharply. "Then why do you think there is honor for the Yhangi in being cast out of this venture because of your pride? It is your pride that makes you unwilling to follow Master Besz. Firehair herself was once taken by this man, but she has trusted him with her life."

The Count sighed. They were all snappish as half-starved dogs from too little sleep, too much work, and now Berek's news. He did not hope for great wisdom from today's meeting, merely for common sense, but so far he'd seen little of that.

Normally Zakonta's sharp tongue could lance Jos-Pran and let the pride drain out of him. Today it merely made him still more obstinate.

"We have offered enough by abandoning our horses," he said. "To fight on foot in a battle so important is not the way of the Yhangi. We will offer no more, certainly not to Master Besz."

"You need think no more of Master Besz," said Arlor. "I will be captain over all the men and ships that sail north. Will the Yhangi refuse to obey me?"

"*Hauuuuuu!*" exclaimed Besz, startled out of his usual impassivity. "My lord Count, you have just this moment chosen to lead us, have you not?"

Arlor would have liked to call Besz a liar. It wasn't the first time the man had spoken aloud words better whispered or not said at all. But Arlor could not meet the blank, all-seeing eyes in the face that was now returning to its usual frozen calm and still deny what Besz had said.

"I have. It seems to me that with Wandor and Gwynna both absent, I am the one who will be most readily obeyed by all."

"This is certain," said Besz. "But I see reasons why you should not sail north, even so. We shall—"

"What reasons?" said Jos-Pran. "Are you afraid of having anyone over you, so that you will not be able to do as you wish, for whomever you wish?"

Master Besz's eyes opened a little wider, which was his normal equivalent of jumping up and down and shouting. Captain Thargor was less self-restrained. His fist came down on the table with a crash.

"Now by the gods, you dirty—! Shut your mouth, or I won't let a single one of the Yhangi aboard any ship in the fleet. If I have to—"

"Silence!" shouted Arlor, springing to his feet. The fury in his voice and on his face hammered everyone into attentive silence. "Enough of this. There will be no more questioning of Master Besz's loyalty. There will be no more threatening of Jos-Pran and the Yhangi. There will be no more squabbling like spitboys from the castle kitchen. Do you all hear?" Jerky nods. "Good. The Yhangi will obey whatever captain leads us north. Any of them who refuse will not sail, whether it is Jos-Pran himself or, the youngest girl among the *umnera*. That is my decision, and there will be no more words spent on it."

His eyes met Jos-Pran's, and he was relieved to see the War Chief bow his head in reluctant submission. It was always risky to press Jos-Pran hard. When his mighty pride rose to the surface he made a team of mules look docile. Yet the question of command had to be settled, and if the price of settling it was Jos-Pran's sullen rage, then that price would be paid. Jos-Pran would not turn aside from his duty to Wandor and Gwynna. Sooner or later his sense of that duty would rein in his pride and make him once more the strong and wise leader in war that he could be when his pride did not run away with him.

As for Master Besz—

"Master Besz, you appear to have something to say to us from your great knowledge of war. Please say it and nothing else, as you value your place among us."

The threat drew no reaction from Besz. He would have sat

unmoved at a threat of impalement or burning alive. The threat was intended mainly for the ears of Jos-Pran, to assure him of Arlor's willingness to deal harshly with the mercenary Captain.

"We do not know if Wandor and Gwynna still live," said Besz. "If they are gone, we face a new and desperate battle. For that battle we must have at least a few strong leaders, and Count Arlor is the strongest."

Under other circumstances Arlor would have laughed. Here was Besz, throwing at him the same argument he had so often thrown at Wandor when the Viceroy chose to risk his life for no apparently good reason.

"I will think of this, I promise you," said Arlor. "I will promise no more, and we will leave the matter for today." He wanted to pass on to other subjects before some other painfully honest soul pointed out that, with Wandor and Gwynna dead, any new battle would probably be lost from the beginning and only worth fighting in the hope of dying with dignity. "Now—Captain Thargor. How many ships have we mustered, and how many can we hope for?"

"We've twelve fit for the voyage north to the Sea Folk now, three more in another month, and five more a month after that. We'd not do well to wait longer. Then we'll be facing the autumn gales, and I'd not be happy chancing ships with soldiers aboard against them."

Twenty ships, plus *Fire of Elya*. Twenty-one in all, to bear the whole weight of their cause. "How many men?"

"We'll not have trouble finding the stores for any number. But I'd not be happy sailing without a good four months' food and water in each ship. Then the fighters'll be taking armor and all the rest... Say a thousand. Maybe two, three hundred more if they'll stand being packed like salt fish. No, more. Maybe two hundred more sailors you could arm and take ashore without risking the ships."

Fifteen hundred fighting men. And that was if they waited another two months, by which time Wandor and Gwynna might well be dead. In that time prison fever or a congestion of the lungs could take them off, let alone what the human enemies all around them might do. But if he sailed north now, with only twelve ships and half as many men, would he be gaining anything? Would he not simply be throwing away the ships and the men, as well as making it certain that Wandor and Gwynna would die?

Master Besz cleared his throat. "My lord. I see another course for us. Captain Thargor, can the twelve ships we have now carry seven hundred fighting men to Yand?" Slowly Thargor nodded. "Seven hundred men under me and my chosen captains can make an end of any five hundred Baron Galkor can have left on Yand Island and any strength the islanders can add to them. If the fleet goes to Yand, we can take it in days. If Wandor and Gwynna are there and alive, we will then have them safe. If they live and are not there, we will already be in the place to which they may well come.

"If we go north, on the other hand, we must wait to have enough men and ships. By the time we sail we are likely to come only to the place where Wandor and Gwynna have been. It is always wiser to go ahead of the enemy and wait for him than to pursue him after he has gone onward."

Zakonta frowned. "But it is not certain that Wandor and Gwynna will be taken to Yand. The Keepers have been thinking more and more of calling the Hearth Mothers to speak out against such a monstrous sacrifice."

"Have they done more than think of it?" said Besz.

Zakonta's dark skin turned darker as she flushed. "I fear not."

"Then nothing may come from the thoughts of the Keepers. If something does, Wandor and Gwynna may still be snatched away to Yand. If the Hearth Mothers not only speak out but are heard and obeyed—"

"Small chance of that," said Berek. He and Zakonta exchanged glares, leaving Besz to go on.

"If Wandor and Gwynna come under the protection of the Hearth Mothers, they will no longer be in great danger. Baron Galkor is among the Sea Folk, of course. But he will hardly risk war against them by striking openly at Wandor and Gwynna. Against hired assassins they have great power themselves.

"Finally, if we do go to Yand and strike down the Beast Wizards and Galkor's men, the Hearth Mothers may find the courage they have not had before." Zakonta transferred her glare to Besz, who ignored her. "If they do not, we can still sail north to the lands of the Sea Folk. While we are taking Yand, other ships and men can be assembling at Fors. The two fleets can meet in the north, then sail together against the Sea Folk. If we sail north first, we cannot so easily hope to sail against Yand afterward. They will be ready. The Sea Folk and even Duke Cragor may send more men to the island to meet us."

There was a good deal more to Master Besz's plan, and he went on explaining it without anyone interrupting him or anyone taking his eyes off the immobile brown face. Arlor stared with the rest, but his thoughts were elsewhere. The remorseless logic of Besz's mind had taken him and his men into the service of Duke Cragor. It had then taken him out of the Duke's service into Wandor's. Now it had conjured up a plan that seemed to offer more hope of victory than anything else Arlor could imagine.

Soberly, he realized that those left behind had done Wandor and Gwynna poor service by the very passion of their devotion. All of them, himself not the least, had believed too much in the god-sent king and his warrior queen. All of them, except Master Besz. The mercenary Captain believed in nothing but his own skill in war and the invincibility in battle of good men led by him.

So Wandor and Gwynna could vanish and perhaps be horribly dead, and Master Besz would still be thinking as swiftly and as clearly as ever. Nothing could thaw his chill soul, nor could anything short of death weaken him. This was a frightful gift, and Arlor thanked the gods that he himself had been spared it. He also thanked the gods that Master Besz had it, and was devoting it to Wandor's service.

Arlor realized that Besz must have finished his explanation, because now Zakonta was speaking. Besz was giving her the same attention she'd given him. "...we do, must be done soon. When I let myself be aware of it, the *luor* of fear in Fors almost overpowers me. If we do not act quickly, I think we shall see the people beginning to think we fear something. Then there will be no way to keep them at work. We can lose our battle other ways than by the death of Wandor and Gwynna. Let us follow the course Master Besz has given us."

Captain Thargor nodded. "Aye. We've got few choices, and none of them good. We'd do well to take the least bad, and that's yours," he said with a jerk of one leather-skinned thumb at Besz.

Arlor thrust himself into the silence that followed. "Does anyone wish to speak against Master Besz?" The silence continued. "Then we shall take his plan as ours."

Arlor rose. "Captain Thargor. Tomorrow we shall visit the docks with Master Besz and—"

That was as far as he got before several pairs of fists began pounding desperately on the door of the chamber. Above the pounding, Arlor could hear what sounded like men gasping and sobbing in exhaustion or desperate fear. Before Arlor could take a single step, everyone in the chamber had drawn a weapon. The Count motioned Master Besz to stand on one side of the door and Jos-Pran to stand on the other. Then he went to the door and lifted the latch. If the castle's men had flown into another panic like last night's and over something equally absurd—

The door flew open under the pressure of three frantic soldiers so violently that it knocked Count Arlor sprawling on his back on the floor. The rug kept him from cracking his skull, but not from jarring himself badly. It was fortunate for the soldiers that he was not able to get to his feet at once. Master Besz stepped in front of them, halting their progress as if an iron portcullis had slammed down in their path.

"What is happening?" he asked, in his levelest voice.

"Cheloth—thin air—flying—out of nowhere—not speaking—" was all anyone could make out of the jumble of words that poured from the men's lips. Besz finally held up a hand to silence them, then turned to Arlor.

"It seems that Cheloth of the Woods has returned," he said. "Something about that return has frightened the guards."

Arlor shook his buzzing head and stood up. As he did, brisk footsteps sounded on the stairs. The guards shuddered and tried to plaster themselves as flat on the floor as the rug itself.

A moment later Cheloth of the Woods strode into the chamber.

CHAPTER 13

Cheloth swept in with an air so regal that beside him Wandor—or perhaps even Nond—would have seemed like a swineherd and Gwynna like a dairymaid. The only people affected by the sorcerer's manner were the three soldiers. They flattened themselves on the rug and their hands and feet twitched as if they would have liked to burrow out of sight.

"Up!" snapped Arlor. In this moment he had no patience with Cheloth's grand manner, nor would he willingly see anyone giving the sorcerer the slightest encouragement. The three soldiers lifted their heads enough to see the expression on Arlor's face and also on that of Master Besz. Those faces frightened them more than Cheloth of the Woods. They sprang up and were gone.

Cheloth adjusted the pointed silver helmet that concealed his whole head, brushed dust from the sleeves of his green tunic and the knees of his green breeches, then sat down in the nearest chair.

"Where have you been?" said Arlor. "I think we have some right to know."

"I have been about matters important for both my purposes and yours," said Cheloth. "You would not have understood these matters, so I said nothing about them until I felt that a proper time had come."

"The time has come now, I trust?" said Zakonta. No one could miss the edge in her voice, and no one except Cheloth could have ignored it.

"Yes. So I came as rapidly as I could from where I have been.

It is unfortunate that I had to come in such a way as to frighten the soldiers, but it seems that such men are easily frightened. I could not risk appearing in a place that I could not see exactly in my mind. There would have been great danger to others, as well as to myself."

"You used your Power of Passage?" said Zakonta. "You seem to know a good deal about my Powers."

"The *Red Seers* may have forgotten what you know, but not that you know it. So do not waste time we cannot spare by seeking to make of yourself a greater mystery than you are."

"Harsh words, Zakonta."

"Soft words, beside what the Lady Gwynna would have said to you."

"So be it," said Cheloth. The three words came down like an executioner's ax. Arlor realized that they would get no more explanation or apology from the sorcerer, even if they waited in this chamber for five years. They would be more likely to find Master Besz dancing drunk in a brothel.

"So be it," Arlor echoed. "Now—you have some matter which brought you here, I think. Speak, and we will listen."

Cheloth inclined his gleaming, silvery head in what was for him a gracious nod, and began to speak.

In all the created world short of infinity, there were four great forces, each one emerging through one of the four elements: air, fire, earth, and water. Each sorcerer since the creation of the world drew on Powers rising from one of these four elemental forces.

From the air came the complex sorcery of Toshak, brought to its supreme height by Nem and now being revived as best as could be by Kaldmor the Dark.

From fire came many Powers, great and small. The ones those in the chamber knew best were certain healing spells and the gifts of the Guardian of the Mountain who had sent Wandor forth on his quest.

From earth came the hundred clean and unclean forms of Beast Magic, the Powers of the Red Seers of the Yhangi, the Tree Sisters of the Khindi, and the Keepers of the Hearth among the HaroiLina, as well as the greater part of Cheloth's own Powers. His arts encompassed all of the other Earth Powers and many more that were his alone.

From the water came...nothing. At least, nothing that the Being who held the force of water and was held by it in turn did not send forth of its own free will.

Water is the center of creation. It excludes air, drowns fire, swallows or wears away earth. So no sorcerer whose Powers are of air, fire, or earth can hope to work successfully against it or draw from it, and what lies in water has never chosen to send forth any Powers of its own.

In fact, what lay within the water seldom did anything at all except lie there. It was like a sleeping lion, for it knew that none would willingly come near it. Yet even a sleeping lion will wake, if there is a loud enough sound close at hand, penetrating its sleep. It will not wake out of fear, but it will wake in order to see what is happening and whether anything should be done.

That which lay within the water—apparently the Being had no other name—was now like that waking lion. The air Power of Toshak, the fire Power of the Guardian, the earth Power of Cheloth and a hundred lesser sorcerers—these were making a mighty sound, such as had not been heard in the created world for two thousand years.

Two thousand years ago, Nem of Toshak and the Guardian of the Mountain and Cheloth of the Woods had fought their first great battle and had each gone to their destinies. They had fought that battle, from the first moment to the last, in the knowledge that one greater than they watched and listened and waited to see if there was any need to act.

Now the second battle was at hand, and that which had watched the first battle was slowly waking to do as it had done before.

These were not Cheloth's words. They were the words into which Arlor formed what Cheloth said. Then he tossed them back at Cheloth, asking for the sorcerer's judgement. He was not sure what he would do or say if Cheloth refused to give that judgement.

To Arlor's surprise Cheloth spoke without even the moment's hesitation that would have lent mystery to his words. Perhaps what

Zakonta had said or thoughts of what Gwynna might say had made Cheloth grasp the wisdom of being understood by those human beings whose purposes were part of his.

"For a human without Powers you understand clearly," said Cheloth. "You have also chosen the right words to show that understanding."

Thank all the gods for sharp-tongued women, thought Arlor. They are a Power mightier even than Cheloth of the Woods. Aloud, he said, "So now we know that something new has been added to the battles we have to fight. Cheloth, exactly what difference will this waking of the waters make for the tasks at hand?"

"You need not spend time looking over your shoulders, watching for that which lies in the water to leap upon you," said Cheloth. "That task will be mine. Continue gathering the ships and the men to save Wandor and Gwynna. Spare nothing in arming and equipping them. It is certain that it will not be easy for me to aid the fleet when it goes forth upon the Ocean. The Powers of earth, air, and fire do not altogether cease there, but the price for using them can be heavier than it is wise to pay.

"Zakonta, it is time to gather the *Red Seers* again and with them reach out for what we must know. Do you feel yourself ready?"

"Yes. We have already reached out to the Keepers of the Hearth, though not for long. There is at least one Beast Wizard close at hand with enough skill to learn what our link carries. So we have been cautious."

"You have been wise in that," said Cheloth. "But with my help you may set that caution aside, and learn what must be known."

Under those last four words everyone in the chamber sensed the brutal question: Are Wandor and Gwynna still alive? Now the time and the Power were at hand to answer it.

Arlor rose. "I think it is time we went about our separate affairs." No one wasted words agreeing with him. They also rose as Arlor crossed to open the chamber door. Cheloth was the first to leave, slightly disappointing the Court by walking out on his feet instead of vanishing in a puff of smoke. Zakonta was about to follow him when Arlor stopped her.

"What is the Passage Power?"

"Oh, that? It is Cheloth's ability to transport himself from one place to another by willing himself to do so. He can only do this safely if he has a clear picture in his mind of the place where he will arrive. So he had to appear in the open courtyard, which he knew well and which he knew would not be crowded at this hour of the day."

Arlor shrugged. He appreciated Cheloth's desire to arrive quickly, but not his frightening already skittish soldiers into fits by doing so. There was little to be said or done either way.

"Thank you."

Zakonta smiled and went out, followed in succession by Jos-Pran, Master Besz, and Captain Thargor. Berek was about to follow when a page boy came trotting up the stairs, panting as though he'd had not only the long climb but a long run before that. The page bowed jerkily to Arlor, then spoke to Berek.

"Lord Berek. I bear word from Sir Gilas Lanor. He would see you in his chambers, as quickly as you can come."

Arlor opened his mouth to forbid Berek to go, then shut it abruptly. Both the Tree Sister and the doctor caring for Sir Gilas had urged him to see no one who might excite him and destroy the precariously restored balance of humors in his healing body. A talk with Berek would do just that.

Yet forbidding Berek to go would not keep him away. It would only ensure that when he went, he would go by stealth, suspicious and perhaps angry. His stealth would cause rumors to fly about. His anger and suspicion would do Sir Gilas no good at all.

"By all means go," said Arlor. "I will tell Master Besz and Captain Thargor to ride on down to the docks without waiting for us."

"Thank you, my lord Count," said Berek. He followed the boy down the stairs.

CHAPTER 14

The page danced ahead of Berek as though he were passing barefoot over hot stones. Either he knew the reason for Sir Gilas' call and knew that it was urgent, or he didn't know and was in a fever to find out. He still could not stay far ahead of Berek, who was a foot and a half taller and wasting no time either. They reached the door of Sir Gilas' chamber almost together.

Berek shut the door quietly but firmly in the page's face and turned toward the bed. Sir Gilas slowly raised himself on the cushions to greet his visitor. The young Knight was twenty pounds lighter and looked twenty years older than when Berek had last seen him. The combined effect was ghastly. Sir Gilas Lanor did not look like a man slowly but steadily healing of his wounds. He looked like a man whose wounds were still festering, draining strength from body and spirit alike. His face was gaunt, the sharp chin and nose so prominent that they seemed to overpower all the rest of his features except the inhumanly large eyes. The hand he raised in greeting was a claw, gleaming faintly with sweat.

"Thank you for coming." The voice was no louder than one would expect from a man in Sir Gilas' condition. It was, however, clear and steady and there was nothing to be read in it one way or another.

"The page seemed eager. I think Count Arlor did not wish me to come, but—"

"The page spoke in Arlor's hearing?"

"Yes, I—"

"Oh, gods! Now he'll know that someone told me you had returned. He'll be asking all the maids and the serving boys and—" He broke off, with the air of a man realizing he's said rather too much.

"Count Arlor did not wish you to know that I had returned?"

Under Berek's gaze Sir Gilas nodded slowly. "It is not really his fault. The doctor and the Tree Sister—"

"Would not go against Count Arlor," Berek finished for him. "It seems that Count Arlor thinks he may act as our father. This is not his right. Only—"

He broke off, listening. Then in a single leap he was at the door. One massive fist crashed down against the lock. Metal boomed and clanged loudly enough to raise echoes. From the other side of the door came a yelp of pained surprise, then feet scurrying away down the hall. Berek laughed, walked over to the window, and tore off a long string of curtain. He stuffed the cloth into the keyhole, still laughing.

"No harm done, and none will be." He stopped laughing as the overpowering miasma of the room pierced his lungs. Drugs and herbs, sweat and stale bedding and dressings, soup bowls and chamber pots taken out a little too late, the dampness and mold of any castle, and the scent of fear, as unmistakable to Berek as to any hunting animal.

He stepped up to the window again, and this time he ripped the curtains completely away with one hand and tore open the shutters with the other. Chill sea air blew in, driving the miasma out of his lungs and nostrils and starting to drive it out of the room. It would be a long time before the Sea Father's salt wind cleansed this room of all its stenches, but be made a beginning. Now he and Sir Gilas could speak without feeling that they were shut away in the diseased bowels of the earth.

The scent of fear was gone, but the traces of it were still there on the Knight's face. What did he fear? thought Berek. Aloud, he said, "Sir Gilas. What did you want to tell me?"

"You seek those whose fault it was, that Wandor and Gwynna were taken?"

"That is no secret."

"The fault was mine, Berek. If you wish to punish anyone for what happened to your Master and Gwynna, let it be me."

Berek's fists were clenched and he'd taken two steps toward the bed in the time it took the words to pass from his ears into his mind. Then he stopped, his thoughts churning like a riptide.

He lies.

He would not lie about this.

He would if Count Arlor asked him. Count Arlor would not ask him.

You have so much faith in the Count?

No.

Then Arlor may well be seeking to surround you with lies.

Why?

He rules in all but name here, with Wandor and Gwynna gone. If you were not surrounded by lies, you might ques- tion what he does.

He would not be questioned. Why not?

He may have many reasons. Or Cragor may have—

"No!" roared Berek. "Haro—give me strength!" He was still holding a shutter from the window. His hands clamped down, and with a crack the shutter split in two pieces. One clattered to the floor.

Shouts and pounding feet filled the hall outside. Swiftly Berek seized one end of the chest that stood under the window and pushed it across the chamber. It thudded into place against the inside of the door just as fists started thudding against the outside.

"May all their fathers have no manhood," said Berek, to no one in particular. He sat down on the chest, adding his own two hundred and sixty pounds to the weight already holding the door in place. "Now, Sir Gilas—how did you come to have done this thing?"

The Knight told his story, and as he told it Berek slowly began to believe him. Sir Gilas told his story not like a man giving a well-rehearsed performance, but like a man pouring out something that had been a painful burden for weeks, something he had lost all hope of being able to tell anyone. He was shivering as he talked, shivering with a chill from Haro's wind but also with fear.

Berek had no Mind Speech nor even the small Truth Seeing Power known among the Hearth Mothers. But he knew fear when he saw it and he knew the Knights of Benzos well enough to know how rare it was for one to show so much fear. Count Arlor could have told Sir Gilas to do much, but not to show anyone this face of fear, ash-gray and slick with sweat. Sir Gilas was telling the truth—or if he was not telling the truth, then he still expected to pay with his life for the lie he was telling. He expected no help from Count Arlor or anyone else, and no mercy from Berek Strong-Ax.

Even if the Knight were telling a lie—Berek suddenly realized how badly he himself would be serving Wandor and Gwynna if he raged about like a bull seal in the mating season, hurling himself at every man he might suspect of the smallest failing toward his Master. Count Arlor had said as much, yet he'd been on the point of believing that Arlor said it out of folly or even treason. Arlor said it out of wisdom, and nothing else.

And Sir Gilas? For a second time, the Knight had thrown himself into battle for Wandor and Gwynna, not expecting to come out alive, or perhaps not even caring whether he did or not. The first time he'd gone into battle against the raiders. This time he'd had to go into battle against the folly of the very man who'd sworn the Oath of the Drunk Blood to Bertan Wandor.

Berek was not sure whether to laugh or weep.

While he was trying to decide, the swelling uproar in the hall outside reached his ears. Swords and spear butts had joined the pounding fists. The heavy oak planks of the door were shivering. Someone shouted, "Go to the kitchen and get a log. We'll have to batter it down. Somebody go and call the archers, and somebody else call Count Arlor!"

Sir Gilas threw off the quilts, and with the help of a firm grip on a bedpost pulled himself to his feet. "Open the door, Berek," he said, with a faint smile that was actually a recognizable cousin of his usual grin. "If you're not going to murder me, we'd better prove it before those fools set the whole castle by the ears again."

Berek pushed the chest aside, then took a firm grip on the door with one hand and drew the bolt with the other. Half-a-dozen armed men instantly tried to crowd through a gap that would have been tight for a small boy in a breechclout. Berek kept the firm grip on the door until he could be sure that everyone trying to get through it had seen Sir Gilas standing by his bed, chalk-pale and tottering but, beyond any dispute, alive.

Silence fell, and Sir Gilas' words cracked through that silence.

"All of you—get out and stay out."

Sir Gilas might have spoken more elegantly, but no words could have emptied the doorway in a shorter time. Berek slammed the door in the face of the last man, threw the bolt, and sat down on the chest. Then he began to laugh, and stopped only when he was out of breath and in danger of falling off the chest.

By this time Sir Gilas had wrapped a chamber robe around himself and was sitting on the edge of the bed. "This is the first time I've put my feet on the floor since they dug the arrow out of me," he said. "I think I'll just sit here and enjoy the feeling until the doctor and the Tree Sister come howling around to get me back under the covers."

"Sir Gilas," said Berek slowly. "There is an oath among the HaroiLina, an oath to be sworn between those who have sworn the Drunk Blood to the same Master."

Sir Gilas shook his head. "I have not sworn the Drunk Blood to Wandor, Berek. Nor could I. A Knight's Oath—"

"I know," said Berek. "Yet—there is what a man swears, and there is what a man does. You have twice, these past two months, been ready to throw down your life for Bertan Wandor. You could not have done more if you had sworn the Drunk Blood. You have done more for Wandor in that time than I."

"Berek, I—"

"We each know how strong the other can be in the service of...*our* Master." Sir Gilas did not seem ready to question the phrase. "We also have seen how weak we can be. I have seen your fear, you have heard my foolish words." Again Sir Gilas was silent. "Sir Gilas— brother—let us swear the Oath of the Brothers to Serve."

Sir Gilas pulled himself to his feet again and stretched out one hand toward Berek while gripping the bedpost with the other. "Give me your hand on that, brother."

Berek crossed the room and took the outstretched hand. It felt as small and fine as a woman's, and in his great happiness he had to force himself to hold it gently.

Count Arlor was on the seaward ramparts of the castle when Berek came to him and in five quick sentences told of what had passed in Sir Gilas Lanor's room.

"You have sworn the oath?" was all the Count said.

"No. It means the mingling of blood. Sir Gilas said that if I shed any of his blood in the oath, the doctor would probably shed rather more of mine."

"The doctor will take his orders from me," said Arlor.

He smiled. "That's the first jest I've heard from Sir Gilas since he was wounded. He must be mending faster than I thought."

"When I entered his chamber, he looked like a man who was dying, not healing. When I left the chamber—"

"I understand," said Arlor. He gripped Berek by both shoulders, trying to put into the gesture what he could not put into words. "Thank the gods he found someone to ease him of his burden."

Although the day was wearing on, the clouds were breaking up and it was brighter than it had been at noon. Shafts of sunlight thrust down here and there, and all the seaward horizon lay clear.

The noise of hooves in the courtyard made Arlor turn and look. Cheloth was riding toward the gate on the gray mule that some said was his familiar, with Zakonta following on her Plains mare. They rode without an escort, and that would have left the Count uneasy if they hadn't flatly forbidden him to send anyone with them.

The two riders vanished around the spreading base of the north tower. In the lengthening shadow of the keep, a score of mounted men waited, Master Besz at their head. It was time to ride down to the docks.

Together the Count and Berek went down the stairs.

CHAPTER 15

The great Hearth itself was dark, and the other fires in the niches of the walls of the Hearth House were dying down into red patches of coals. The nine Keepers of the Hearth sat on furs spread over two rock-slab benches arranged to face one of the niches.

The faint light from the glowing coals left the nine women for the most part wrapped in shadow. Here was a booted foot, with a snakeskin band around the ankle; there a long-fingered hand, holding a battered silver cup; elsewhere a long face, brown and wrinkled, aged with a burden of judgements made and years endured.

There was little left for them to say to each other, and the time had not come to speak to others. That time was close, though, and with it the time of deciding the fate of the Hearth of the Mother.

It could no longer be otherwise, and three of the women had been saying it could not have been otherwise since the ship of Foyn Son of Thadul returned with the captives. The others had held back, but they did so no longer. All spoke with their lips, for there could be others reaching out toward them to listen if they spoke mind to mind. Some of those listeners would not be friendly.

A noise in the darkness drew Wandor up from sleep. He saw Gwynna seated cross-legged on her blankets. In the darkness only her face and shoulders were clearly visible, tinted pink by the glow from her hair. The rest of her was only graceful shadows, hinted rather than told.

Wandor lay still and tried to keep his mind as quiet as possible. This was not ordinary Mind Speech she was using to listen to the Keepers of the Hearth, but something much closer to the heart of her Powers, where he could not have followed her even if he'd wanted to. There was no sense of the passing of time in the dark chamber, nothing but Gwynna's faint breathing and the coming and going of the glow from her hair. At last the glow died. She reached out in the darkness and gripped Wandor's hand. She sighed deeply, but for once the sigh held relief and not just terrible weariness.

"The Keepers again?"

"Yes. They've reached their decision."

"For us?"

"Yes. They will have the matter raised openly in the *Kym* of Hearth Mothers. They will seek to have it raised in the *Kym* of Captains. I heard them mention the name of Daraun in such a way that I think they reckon him as an ally."

"That was not wise of them, if the Beast Wizard was listening."

"I heard no one, and I doubt that the Beast Wizard could conceal himself so completely from me. Perhaps he cannot enter the minds of the Keepers where they speak only with their lips."

All this left too much uncertain, but for now there was no hope of things being any other way. He and Gwynna both would have more freedom if the Beast Wizard could be silenced, but there was little hope of that.

"What do they expect from Daraun?"

"I don't know. He seems to have plans of his own already. They doubted whether he would willingly become part of theirs."

That did not surprise Wandor. Daraun might move the earth to see justice done or a monstrous crime prevented. He would move the earth and the sea as well to avoid being caught in the middle of the ancient rivalry of the Captains and the Hearth Mothers.

Were he and Gwynna any better off, even with the Hearth Mothers on their side?

How many swords could the Hearth Mothers send into battle?

Did anything else but swords matter, here and now?

The three questions ran quickly through Wandor's mind without finding answers. He started to bring them back for more thought, then suddenly sat up on his pallet, throwing off his own blankets. His hand clamped down on Gwynna's so hard that she gasped with the pain, then gasped again with something quite different.

A Mind Speech pattern was forming, one they could both detect, one that was reaching out to link with them. It was reaching out behind wave after wave of the strangest and most jumbled pulses Wandor had ever sensed, but he could recognize the minds lurking behind those waves.

"Cheloth!" he gasped.

And from Gwynna, "Zakonta!"

Awareness of the response flared in both Cheloth and Zakonta. It formed words:

("You live?")

("We live. We live. We live.")

If Wandor and Gwynna had been shouting out loud, they could have been heard through the walls of their prison and halfway to the beach at the foot of the hill.

Then came the sudden sense of an intruder's presence, so strong that even Wandor could detect it. The glow from her hair showed Gwynna's body arching in sudden pain. In the next moment pulses from Zakonta and Cheloth swept roaring over everything.

Wandor let his mind go blank and held Gwynna against him until the easing of the pain lines in her face showed that she had done the same. Then somehow they found the strength to join, and in that joining they found an exaltation and a release they had not felt since their capture. After that came sleep.

In a sullen dawn Count Arlor awoke, to find two cloaked figures standing beside his bed. They had so much of the dawn's paleness on them that at first sight he did not know who or even what they were.

Then he saw that they were Cheloth of the Woods and Zakonta, and he was instantly awake.

"Our night's work is done," said Cheloth. "We know that

Wandor and Gwynna live. They are held close prisoners, but—"

Arlor made a choking sound and rolled out of bed. For a moment he thought he would sink to his knees on the cold stone floor, from the weakness of relief and joy that was seizing all his limbs. He did not, and in a moment he could stand and give attention to what Cheloth was saying. Cheloth did not speak at length, and Zakonta did not speak at all. The *Red Seer*'s body sagged under a terrible weight of exhaustion, and Arlor would have said that Cheloth was also tired, if there'd been any sense in applying human concepts to the sorcerer.

In his mind Arlor shaped Cheloth's words into three certainties.

Wandor and Gwynna were alive, confined, but fit to help their rescuers or themselves, once freed.

The Keepers of the Hearth had decided to do as much as they could to aid Wandor and Gwynna, but did not know how much that would be.

Among the HaroiLina there was now one of the Beast Wizards, a man of large Powers and gifts named Mykto, strong-willed, cool-headed, and dangerous.

In his own mind Arlor added a fourth certainty, then spoke it out loud.

"Then we have even more reason to strike first at Yand. What holds back the Hearth Mothers seems to be fear of an open breach with the Captains, particularly those who follow the Beast Cult." He looked inquiringly at Zakonta.

She was too exhausted even to glare at him for calling the Hearth Mothers afraid. She merely nodded.

"Then when there are no Beast Wizards, there will be much less to hold back the Hearth Mothers. They will be able to do what is needed to keep Wandor and Gwynna safe until we send our ships for them."

Zakonta nodded again. Arlor was content with his logic. It was fair enough for logic conjured up at the fourth hour of the morning by a man who'd not slept well.

Then the sorcerer and the *Red Seer* were gone on silent feet, and Arlor was ringing the bell for his servants. Beyond the narrow window, he could see the light growing stronger. The new day had come to Fors, and with it, by the favor of the gods and the Powers of Cheloth and Zakonta, new hope.

He would have the news cried from the towers and in the streets this day. Perhaps then the *luor* of fear would no longer stifle Zakonta, or make hardened veterans in the castle garrison ready to jump at their own shadows.

Baron Galkor was starting his day on raisins and ship's bread, salt fish and watered wine, when the servant entered.

"Yes?"

"My lord—a man to speak with you."

"Who?"

The servant swallowed. "Telek the Fatherless."

Galkor put down his cup and reached for his sword. The appearance of Wandor and Gwynna themselves, steel in hand, would have been hardly more surprising, hardly less welcome, and a great deal less mysterious.

In peace and in daylight, there was no aura of terror, skill, or mystery about Telek the Fatherless to the unknowing eye. He was a trifle smaller than the average warrior of the Sea Folk, and his beard was dark and close-trimmed. Otherwise he looked much like any other fighting man whose skill had earned him enough to live but not to live well.

Galkor's eye was not unknowing, and he made quite sure that his back was to the wall before he spoke. "What do you wish of me?" he said.

"For you—there is news I have." Telek's Hond held a Chongan accent, rather than that of the Sea Folk.

"I am always ready to receive news, and even to reward its bearers if they have done me a service."

"I think this does you a service. The Keepers of the Hearth— they want Wandor and Gwynna not sacrificed."

Where the Keepers of the Hearth led, the Hearth Mothers of the Sea Folk would follow, as far as they were called or at least as far as they dared. How far would that be?

"How did you learn this?"

Galkor did not really expect an answer to that question. He did expect to learn from Telek's manner of refusing to answer it something more about the man. Any knowledge of Telek would be greater than what he had now.

"The Beast Wizard, Mykto, used his Powers at night, when from the south they talked to the Keepers."

"They? Cheloth, or who?"

Telek ignored that question. "The Beast Wizard talked of what he heard, where his servant had ears. That servant has a mouth, and I listen."

That was an answer longer than Galkor had expected, although still too short to tell him all he would have liked to know—such as what had happened to the Beast Wizard's servant. Still, it deserved its reward. Galkor counted out three small bags, each holding twenty gold crowns. Telek stuffed them into his belt pouch and was gone without a single word or a single moment's delay to count even one bag.

The Baron found he'd lost his appetite. He stared out a window that happened to give him a view of the shore. The three ships from Yand were anchored in clear sight. From a tripod of poles on the beach floated the banner of the Beast Wizards—silver-gray, with the weird arrangement of green triangles that was said to be a greatly stylized portrayal of one of the Beasts.

He wondered how many men the Beast Wizard had with him, apart from that indiscreet servant. As he wondered, a thought struck him. Could the Beast Wizard perhaps need help—the kind of help best provided by a force of armed men?

It began to seem possible. If it were possible, then so was an alliance between him and the Beast Wizard. Cragor had said nothing against such an alliance—perhaps he'd thought there would be no possible occasion for it. Once again, the Duke hadn't thought of everything.

He would not go at once to Mykto. That would show too much eagerness. If the man wasn't a fool he'd be suspicious, and he'd be quite right. Galkor's men could raise a solid wall of swords and pikes between the Hearth Mothers and the captives. If they could do that, then it would be time to think of raising another such wall—between the captives and the Beast Wizards of Yand.

Much good might come of that, if it could be managed without an open challenge to the Beast Wizards. Gwynna might be delivered into Cragor's hands, earning Galkor a rich reward. Wandor might be sent down into the House of Shadows without delay, and that would be final victory.

Yes, it was definitely something that deserved further thought.

CHAPTER 16

An evening came, one week from the day Cheloth woke Count Arlor and Telek the Fatherless took gold from Baron Galkor.

Captain Daraun and a Keeper of the Hearth walked along the beach, a ship's length from the nearest cover where unwanted ears might lie hidden. The damp sand was firm underfoot, so they walked briskly.

"It is certain you cannot bring the matter before the *Kym* of Captains?"

"It is certain," said Daraun. "Seven who have borne the Spear of Valkath as Speaker must agree if the *Kym* is to be called together out of its proper time. I have promises from only three. There may be a fourth in a week or two, but I see little hope of getting more. Even then, the Captains would have to come together. That takes time. Then they must agree to speak out, which will take more time."

"Surely they cannot remain silent before the foulness of this sacrifice to the Beasts?"

Daraun thought of answering, "Good Keeper, you know far too little of the way men think." It would have been the truth, but a Keeper of the Hearth deserved more respect even when her words did not. He could also have said, "The Captains may indeed remain silent, since to speak out would shame too many of them," but did not want to show what his comrades had done, like the Ax of Yevoda Slayer of Beasts

131

lighting up the Beast Caves. He himself had taken Cragor's gold, and his hands were far less clean than he would have wished.

"Perhaps they will not speak out," the Keeper went on. "But surely if the Captains gather, that will give pause to the Beast Wizards and Cragor's men?"

"It will not," said Daraun. He spoke sharply, from bitter memories. He himself had long considered each course the Keeper was offering, and rejected them all because of certain harsh truths. He had no desire to plod with this woman over the same ground again, no matter how much respect she deserved.

"It will not," he repeated. "Neither Baron Galkor nor the Beast Wizard, Mykto, respect anything but men with swords in their hands. The Hearth Mothers have no such thoughts and the *Kym* of Captains will have none until it is too late."

He saw the Keeper's shoulders sag and the wrinkles in her brown face deepen. He did not wait for her to reply. "I have fifty men who will follow me where I lead them, with their swords ready and their mouths closed. I can bring these men to fight against the sacrifice of Wandor and Gwynna. If I do, will I have the blessing of the Keepers and the Hearth Mothers for them and for myself?"

The Keeper straightened. "When will they strike?"

Daraun shook his head. "That must be my secret."

"You do not trust the Hearth Mothers?"

"I do not trust anyone but myself."

"How can we promise to stand with you when we do not know with whom we will be standing?"

"By your blessing, you will stand with men who may otherwise face blood-feud, outlawry, perhaps daggers in the night or *fon*-fish venom in their ale. They are all brave, but not brave enough to face these things without the Hearth Mothers to guard their backs."

The Keeper turned to him. Like warriors on the deck of a ship, distrust fought with hope back and forth across her face. "Think, Mother," said Daraun. "Have you anything to lose by giving us your blessing, when otherwise Wandor and Gwynna may go to the Beasts without a hand being raised to prevent it?"

He had found the right words. Hope drove the distrust from the Keeper's face. "It can be done, Daraun. It shall be done. I swear it for myself, and each Keeper shall come to you and swear it for herself as well."

"No. They shall not come to me, nor I to them. You will ask each one to swear. If I hear nothing, I will know that all have sworn and the blessing of the Keepers is ours."

"But—"

"It must be so. Too many eyes watch. Mykto has his Powers, Telek the Fatherless has a sea hawk's sight, and there are certain to be others."

He turned and walked rapidly away along the beach, before the Keeper could have time to argue further. When he rounded the headland to the west of the cove, he looked back to see her still standing where he'd left her.

It was the kind of evening when a man could still illuminate a fine scroll outdoors, while behind walls lamps were already needed to drive back the dark. In the longhouse given over to the Beast Wizards, the lamps gave enough light for Baron Galkor to see clearly the man he faced.

Mykto was no more than forty, with steady dark eyes that seemed to overpower his thin face and a way of moving that suggested a trained and hardened warrior's body under the russet robes. Galkor suspected there was an equally trained and tough mind under the shaven skull.

"So you offer me fifty armed men," Mykto said. "These will help guard our sacrifices from the prison to the ships."

"Yes. And even after they are aboard the ships, if necessary."

"It may not be necessary."

Galkor was silent. He had no wish to disagree with this man so soon. Then Mykto frowned. "On the other hand, I have heard of the skills of Wandor and Gwynna. Perhaps we will indeed have some use for your men on the voyage to Yand."

Galkor decided to press on. The more that could be arranged beforehand, the less would have to be left to the chances of battle, darkness, and steel applied at well-chosen moments. "Indeed, I see no reason why we cannot take Wandor and Gwynna to Yand aboard my own ship."

"Why?" The unmistakable hint of suspicion in the word made Galkor draw back and set him to thinking furiously. When he replied, he used a more servile tone of voice than he needed with Duke Cragor.

"My greatship can better stand against the attacks of Sea Folk craft than your vessels. The danger is even greater if by chance we encounter ships of the Viceroyalty. I would not speak ill of the vessels of Yand at other times. But I now beg you to consider that they are made neither to fight nor to flee."

"That may be so. But why do you fear an attack on the sea?"

"For the same reason I fear one on land. The Keepers who rule the Hearth Mothers have spoken against this sacrifice. You yourself have told me this." That was exceedingly fortunate. The less said of Telek the Fatherless, the better. "Some may be encouraged by the Keepers to strike against us. In fact, I believe they may be more willing to strike against us at sea than on land. At sea there is no one we can call to our aid, and no rack or hot irons can make the sea give up its secrets."

"That is true enough," said Mykto. "As for the rest—we will speak of it another time. For now—the fifty men you offer?"

Galkor nodded. "I would send more if I could, but I would not care to leave my ships weakly guarded. Fifty will be enough, I think. No one among the Sea Folk will be gathering enough men to sweep aside both my men and yours without our getting some word of it." At least no one would do so, as long as Telek the Fatherless kept watch and did not lose his appetite for gold.

"You speak as one who has thought deeply on this matter," said the Wizard. Galkor controlled his irritation at the man's patronizing tone. One of these days he might encounter a sorcerer with the common manners of civilized men, but he would not hold his breath.

"Thank you," he said. "Now—I think it would be best if my men came in from the ships just before we march to the prison. I would also suggest that they wear robes like those worn by your own men.

"No one knows for certain how many men you have aboard your ships or in your camp. So no one will be quick to suspect anything if they see fifty or so rowing ashore that night.

"They will not be needed before then. As long as Wandor and Gwynna are in the prison, no one will dare to lift a sword for them. The prison is guarded by men sworn to the *Kym* of Captains. Anyone attacking it will be outlawed, and all the Keepers and Hearth Mothers together could not save him.

"So your enemies and mine will be hoping to strike between the prison and the boats. By that time my men will have joined yours, with no one the wiser. Any attack after that—" He shrugged.

"Indeed, we may certainly hope so," said Mykto, with a curl of the lips that might have been a smile. "I think little more needs to be said. I accept your offer. I shall send word to you the day before we wish to take our sacrifices aboard ship. Will you need cloth for the disguising of your men?"

"No. We can find cloth and dye it aboard our own ships. It will not pass by daylight, but my men are not going to be assisting at the High Sacrifice."

The Beast Wizard let Galkor's little joke pass without a blink or the most fleeting of smiles. Galkor stood, realizing that nothing could really ease him except getting out of there. He clasped hands and shoulders with Mykto, then turned and left the longhouse.

Outside, the light was beginning to go. Galkor tramped back down the hill, his guards on either side and his thoughts dancing.

There would be a price to pay for what he planned, one that he hadn't expected. He'd heard tales that Mykto aspired to the highest place among the Beast Wizards of Yand. Now he'd seen for himself a man who certainly seemed to have the necessary gifts and might well have the ambition. To carry out his plan could mean throwing away all chance of having this man in his debt—in his own personal debt, not just that of Duke Cragor. Galkor regretted the loss, for he was too wise a servant to be content with only the crumbs from his master's table.

But neither did a wise servant ever leave anything within reason undone to carry out his master's dearest wishes. Cragor wanted his hands on Gwynna, and there was an end to it. So matters would go forward as planned, at least until the Beast Wizard grew too suspicious or openly hostile.

Who could know? Perhaps the gods would smile after all. It was not impossible that Wandor and Gwynna would actually try to escape. Indeed it seemed likely enough, considering their skills and their pride. If matters came to that, there might quite honestly be no way to prevent them from escaping without killing them both. However great the wrath of the Beast Wizards or Cragor then, neither could bring Wandor and Gwynna back to life—for sacrifice, for torture, or for any other reason.

Galkor shivered slightly, not from the evening chill or the thought of anyone's wrath. He shivered at the memory of the scene in the chamber of Fors Castle, where Arlor and Gwynna and King Nond had slaughtered his men like sharks among herring. Wandor and Gwynna would do as well—perhaps better—for they would doubtless have learned how to fight together as a team, using all the arts of the Duelists. The deck of his ship would look like the streets of Avarmouth after Cragor's army sacked it, and Galkor himself might be among the bodies.

Well, he would leave it in the hands of Staz and Alfod whether he would live to reap any reward from his victory. Perhaps he should pray to Haro Sea Father too? Yes, and then put the matter out of his mind. If he died, he died. If he lived, sooner or later Cragor and even Mykto would recognize that he'd helped them to a victory.

Overhead the stars were beginning to come out.

"More chicken?"

Gwynna had her mouth full, so she merely nodded and reached out. Wandor tore another of the birds on the wooden platter in two and handed Gwynna half. Then he returned to his own meal. The sound of busy jaws and the crackling of bones and nutshells filled the chamber.

As he ate, Wandor couldn't help contrasting this feast of roast chicken and pork, bread, nuts, fruit, cider, and beer with what they'd been living on until a few days before. Then it had been hard biscuit and harder salt meat aboard the ship, mushy porridge laced with salty pork fat in the prison. Now they were being fattened—for the slaughter? Eventually Wandor dropped the last of the apple cores on top of the last of the chicken bones, poured out the last of the cider, and raised his cup.

"To our captors' cooks," he said.

Gwynna laughed and raised her own cup in hands smeared with grease and juice. "To the cooks."

They drank and set the cups aside along with everything else. There were no knives—that would have been too much to hope for. But perhaps something could be done with a pork or even a chicken bone, concealed and sharpened?

Wandor found himself examining the idea with an interest possible only these past few days. Before that the scanty food had fogged mind and dragged down body—Gwynna's even more than his, since she had had to use her Powers and thereby increase her burden. Now Wandor felt himself growing stronger and more clearheaded almost by the hour, more and more ready to take advantage of any mistake their captors might make. He could see Gwynna doing the same.

There was still Mykto the Beast Wizard, whose skill and strength made any use of Power a risky business here. Yet Mykto was also one more powerful, snarling wolf in the pack around them, eyes fixed on his prey and ear given to no leader. He was a menace, but perhaps also an opportunity (very much in spite of himself).

Wandor wiped his hands as best he could in the straw, which was now changed every other day instead of lying stinking for a week at a time. He leaned back against a pile of the straw-stuffed leather cushions that now covered the stones, and Gwynna crept close to him, her head on his chest.

"I've eaten and slept worse than this at inns where they took good silver," he said. "I wonder if Galkor knows that we grow stronger each day?"

"Perhaps, but I doubt if he has any voice in the matter. I think this is Mykto's doing. The sacrifices to the Beasts must be strong spirits in strong bodies. This is the oldest law of the Beast Cult. So those who are to be sacrificed are given everything they need to make them strong and as happy as possible, for at least a month before they go to the Beasts."

"Then our time may be coming," said Wandor.

"Yes."

"We shall have to start training again, then," he said. "Tomorrow, if the guards will allow it."

"Why not?" said Gwynna, with an impish grin. "If we say it is needed to keep us happy, Mykto will not dare say a word."

A faint glow over the sea was all that was left of the day, but torches blazed in sockets all along the quay to drive back the night. The smell of oil and paint and pitch, the splutter of burning resin, and the thud of hammers and mauls and adzes surrounded Sir Gilas Lanor and Berek as they watched the carpenters at work on the ship.

Sir Gilas stood with his legs spread wide apart, leaning on a stick. In the flickering torchlight his still-gaunt form looked like some three-legged creature, perhaps bred from human stock but certainly not at all human. At last the young Knight had seen enough. Slowly he turned to Berek. "Call our horses, brother. I think the ladders will serve."

"A horse, not a litter?"

"A horse," said Sir Gilas, smiling. "And when we return to the castle, a meal. Bread and a good leg of—"

"The doctor said—"

Sir Gilas suggested various improbable and degrading acts the doctor could perform on himself. "I can't waste any time following that old maid's instructions. The Tree Sister is far wiser. She will have me strong enough when the fleet sails. I cannot be left behind, Berek. As my brother, you cannot stand in my path, either."

"No, I shall not stand in your path," said Berek, resting a hand on the smaller man's shoulder. "Do not fear that. But do not test your strength every day, or you will have none when you need it." He led Sir Gilas to a stone bollard, drew off his own cloak, and draped it over the Knight's shoulders. "Sit here, while I go for the horses."

Utter darkness, in the sky overhead, on the sea to the west, on Fors Bay to the east. Light only in the city and the castle, and there only where armorers or carpenters worked late or torches burned to give light for sentries. No moon, no stars, no wind, an easing of even the endless roll of the sea below the castle wall. A sudden rumble and squeal, then the clop-clop of hooves at a trot.

From his perch on the wall, Count Arlor saw Berek and Sir Gilas Lanor ride in through the main gate. The Knight was trying unsuccessfully to keep from swaying in his saddle like a drunkard. *Sir Gilas does not need to drive himself this way,* thought Arlor. *He will be aboard the fleet when it sails. I will not stand in his way even if he has to be carried aboard on a litter. And the bond that grows between him and Berek—I will not stand in the way of that either. We have too many captains whose only bond is that they follow the god-sent Wandor. We need some captains who are joined by more than that, who will guard each other's backs as readily in a tavern brawl as in a battle against Cragor's assembled hosts, who will—*

("You are still not a man to be content, Arlor. You still would have matters go a trifle better than they do, and give up your life for that trifle.")

The voice was in his mind, but there was no mistaking its quality or its choice of words. Arlor remembered the frozen darkness beyond a camp in the forest south of Fors and the voice that called him out into that darkness. Once again King Nond walked and spoke to him.

("Sire?") Arlor looked around him, eyes searching the darkness for the familiar shape with the deep-set eyes that now blazed gold.

("I speak now without appearing on the walls. If I did, your men would leap their own heights in fear and then run screaming through the streets. You've had enough of that, I think?")

("Very true, sire.")

("Arlor, you go into more danger than you know in sailing to Yand.")

("Cragor has landed more men?")

("No. Have you given any thought to the Ax of Yevoda?")

("Little enough. The Guardian of the Mountain named it part of Wandor's quest, but all that we have heard of it says that it went down into the sea with Yevoda. Wandor and I have pondered why the Guardian would send him in quest of something which no longer exists.")

("You would set up a tale so old that the coral has covered it over, against the very words of the Guardian of the Mountain?") Scorn was in Nond's voice, stabbing like a dagger.

("It is no tale?")

("It is not. The Ax still exists.")

("Then Wandor can seek it out, since it is part of his destiny. There will be ample time for that, when we hold Yand in strength.")

("You could be dooming all your men if you go ashore on Yand thinking so. The Ax came up from the sea to Yand in the belly of a whale. From that day to this, the High Beast Wizard and certain of his trusted comrades have always known how to wield it against the Beasts.")

("Then—") Arlor's mind was again working with its normal swiftness, forming gruesome visions that promptly stopped his thoughts as they would have stopped his lips in normal speech.

("Yes. The High Wizard can unleash the Beasts against you, trusting the Ax to drive them back into the Caves when they have done their work.")

("But—the Beasts will destroy everything in their path, without—")

("They will. But you go against men who will become desperate beyond all reason when they see you and know what you seek. If you have forgotten what such desperate men may be prepared to do, perhaps you have forgotten so much that you are not fit to be a captain in war.")

("Sire, I have not forgotten all that you taught me.")

("Good. I put a considerable part of myself into teaching you. The gods forbid it should all be wasted. Go to Yand, Arlor. Go to Yand, and from the moment the first man takes his first step on the shore, seek the Ax of Yevoda. Seek it, take it from the Beast Wizards, give it to Wandor, have him wield it, or face your deaths. Expect no help, hope for none, trust to nothing but your own strength. Nothing. *Nothing*.")

The voice faded from Arlor's mind, and he was alone on the wall, facing into a cold wind suddenly blowing from the sea.

CHAPTER 17

The servant finished oiling Mykto's sword and handed it to him. Mykto ran his thumbnail lightly along the edge, then nodded and thrust it into the scabbard belted on over his robes. He drew the peaked hood up over his head, straightened the pearl-studded crest, and stepped to the door.

The wind had risen since nightfall and a gust jerked the door out of his grip as he opened it. Four servants followed him out, all armed. The wind sent his robes whipping about his ankles and forced him to hold his hood in place with one hand. He counted the men gathered around him. All were present, except those so unfit for fighting that they'd already been sent out to the ships, and the eight Warriors who'd gone ahead to the prison longhouse. Those eight were to have Wandor and Gwynna securely bound before Mykto arrived. He did not trust the guards at the prison to do the job properly, for they were HaroiLina who might be giving an ear to the Hearth Mothers.

Mykto did not trust any of the HaroiLina in anything tonight. So every man and every valuable article in his charge would be aboard the ships for Yand when they sailed. This night could hardly pass without bloodied swords. When the dawn came, the peace between the HaroiLina and the Beast Cult might be a fragile one indeed, if it still existed at all. He would leave none of his people ashore, to face the fury of the HaroiLina that might be unleashed. It would be dishonorable to leave men who'd trusted him, and foolish to leave men who might be tortured into revealing secrets.

If the peace survived, the Beast Cult would return to the shores of Stohra Bay. Meanwhile, wisdom lay in expecting the worst.

It was time to go. Mykto ran swiftly to the head of the line. He stepped into place, raised his free hand to signal, and led his men off into the mile of darkness that lay between them and the prison.

The wind was from the north, and it seemed to Galkor that it blew more strongly with every minute. He was ready to offer complete shrines and any lawful sacrifice to any god who would keep that wind blowing for a few more hours.

It would be hard rowing ashore against the wind, but no one would easily hear them coming. When the time came to return to the ships, the wind would be astern of the boats, speeding them on their way. Then they could make a run to the open sea, where no small boat could catch the fleet and no seal ship could easily close a greatship to board.

From alongside came thuds and bangs as the wind swung the boats against the ship's hull. Galkor looked over the railing. Fifty armed men and the sailors to steer and row packed the three boats from stem to stern. They were beginning to pitch and roll as the water roughened under the breath of the wind, and their masts swayed.

Galkor promised a respectable offering to Mother Yeza, if she would keep his stomach in order this night. Then he swung himself over the railing and climbed down the rope ladder into the largest of the boats.

Daraun had chosen the place several days before. The trees grew thick. Rank secondary growth and a tangle of underbrush provided ample cover for men hiding or fleeing and many barriers to men pursuing. It also lay about equally distant from the two boat landings that served *Kym-Thass*. There were two paths from the prison to the shore, and Mykto might be leading his captives down either one of them. Both paths ended at the boat landings, so Wandor and Gwynna would be passing by one of those landings some time tonight.

If this was the night. Certainly the Keeper had said it was, although she admitted she and her sisters had not been able to explore as deeply as they wished. Mykto was too skilled to make that safe. Certainly there had been a mighty scurrying and confusion around the camp of the Beast Wizards, as though they had some large undertaking planned for tonight. Daraun could not imagine anything so large except getting their prize sacrifices aboard ship.

If only he could have sent some word to Wandor and Gwynna! To have them alert, ready to fight at his side from the first moment—!

It could not be. The guards of the prison were servants of the *Kym* of Captains and therefore sworn to stand aside from what they would doubtless consider a private feud. They were also the personal choices of the Captain of the *Kym* House, a gray-haired, gray-tempered man who hated the Hearth Mothers as much as Foyn did and had far more of his wits about him. What the guards of the prison learned or were told, the Captain of the *Kym* House would learn far too quickly.

A branch cracked close beside Daraun's ear and a whisper came out of the darkness. "The Beast Wizard's men are on the march, and boats are coming in from the ships as well."

"How many in the boats?"

"As many as are on the land, perhaps more."

That meant his fifty men would be outnumbered, and the last faint hope of overawing Mykto without a fight was fast vanishing. So be it. He would strike here on the shore, where he could hope to wield all of his men like a single weapon and then be free to retreat swiftly, bearing Wandor and Gwynna with him.

"You have done well," he said to the voice in the darkness. The man mumbled some formula of thanks, turned, then cursed as his robe caught on a branch. A moment's struggle, the sound of tearing cloth, and he was free again. All Daraun's men tonight wore brown robes made to look like those of the Beast Wizard's servants, at least in the darkness. Some had cursed at taking even a disguise from the Beast Cult, but all had seen the sense of it and obeyed. Robed, they could move into the attack with their enemies confused for a few precious moments.

Haro be merciful, thought Daraun, *and let those moments be enough*. Then he set his will firmly against more praying. He'd been weak too long. Whatever else he did tonight, he would put it beyond any man to call Daraun Son of Hymok weak again.

Wandor was awake when Mykto's Warriors came, but that did him little good. They must have been at the door to the chamber before he heard them. Certainly they were in through the door before he could move.

There were eight of them, in the dim light they all looked as big as King Nond, and they seemed to move as swiftly as Count Arlor. Two came at Wandor. He rolled out of their path and leaped to his feet. He wanted to get his back against the wall, then see what came next. This might be the best—if not the only—chance to resist.

One of the two men charged Wandor head-on, putting everything into his attack. There are few enough ways for even someone as skilled as Wandor to meet an opponent who comes on without fear of death or injury. Wandor had no time for any of them, and the collision knocked him off his feet. As he went down, the Warrior landed on top of him, elbows and knees churning as if he was trying to drive Wandor into the floor.

Wandor heaved the man off and was promptly grappled again. He got an arm free and struggled to reach the man's eyes—a tactic for a tavern brawler rather than a Duelist, but this fight seemed to be at the level of a tavern brawl. Another Warrior caught Wandor's reaching hand and twisted the wrist, while a third clutched him by the feet. Tough cord tightened around his ankles. He twisted to try freeing both wrists and ankles, then found his first attacker dropping on his back like a slab of granite. Wandor's chin hit the floor so hard that he felt teeth loosen as his jaw slammed shut. Then someone was tying his wrists firmly, and several others were rolling him over as unceremoniously as if he'd been a barrel of cheap ale.

After that they made him sit up, in time to see more Warriors finish binding Gwynna. One of the eight had stood apart from the scuffle. Now he came toward Gwynna, unhooking from his belt what looked like a fish bladder filled with liquid. It had a carved bone stopper and cryptic signs in blue around the middle.

Gwynna's eyes widened as she saw the Warrior approaching with the bladder. She flicked a brief glance at Wandor, and he got a message of subdued anger and a strong DON'T MOVE A MUSCLE. Then Gwynna shook her head at the man.

"No. We shall not come before the Beasts as we must if you give us the *suurd*. What we have learned has worked in our bodies so that the *suurd* may kill. Certainly it will make us sick for long months, too sick to be fit for the Beasts."

The Warrior stopped and frowned. Wandor held his breath. What was the *suurd*? A drug, to render prisoners helpless or at least harmless? Probably. Now Gwynna had thrown in the man's face the one possible argument against forcing them to take it. He might think she was lying, but as long as he didn't know he would have to be wary. Whatever might come of not drugging them, what would come of killing them would be worse. Gwynna had bought them clear heads and unslowed limbs, at no higher price than a simple lie. The next advantage they needed might not come so cheap.

Wandor could not keep that bleak thought entirely out of his mind as the men unbound his and Gwynna's ankles and dragged them to their feet. The prison guards stood politely to one side as the Warriors led their captives out of the chamber.

Baron Galkor looked back over his shoulder as he climbed the hill toward the prison. Mykto's men were struggling badly, so that their line now stretched out to half again its original length. Most of the Beast Wizard's armed men were servants and Initiates, who had barely seen enough trained soldiers to do even a good imitation. Mykto seemed to have with him no more than fifteen men who'd be really useful in a fight, apart from the Warriors who'd gone on ahead to take Wandor and Gwynna from the prison.

A line of Galkor's men tramped along on either side of Mykto's. They looked more like bundles of poorly done bed linen than servants of the Beast Wizards, but they all had swords or maces belted on over their robes, or bills and pikes on their shoulders.

The marching men came out of the shelter of the trees for a moment and the wind drowned the thud of feet on the hard-packed earth of the path. They passed two white wooden posts, painted with the rune for the *Kym* of Captains. Now they were in an area under its protection, and for the moment safe from attack. The road swung sharply to the left, and then fifty paces ahead Galkor saw the prison longhouse.

A cluster of dark figures was already at the door facing down the hill. One of them held a torch, and by its light Galkor saw a blaze of red hair in the middle of the cluster. The Sea Folk guards stepped aside as Mykto's warriors led their charges toward Galkor.

The Baron felt almost lightheaded with delight. Now he had *both* Wandor and Gwynna in his hands. Actually they were in Mykto's hands, but that could be changed within a few hours. They were not drugged and they were on their feet, but they were one man and one woman against more than seventy armed guards. They could hardly do enough to get free, only go down on the ground to lie in their blood. Then there could be complete and final victory, with no one able to blame Galkor for anything.

The captives shuffled forward, matching their guards step for step. The Warriors led them into place behind Galkor, just ahead of Mykto. The lines of men turned about and tramped away down the path toward the other *Kym* House boat landing. Galkor would not follow the same route twice, regardless of the enemy.

He looked up at the treetops, vague wraith-shapes dancing in the darkness. The wind was holding strong, but it should not drive the boats away from the landing.

"They come," was the new whisper from the darkness into Daraun's ear.

"We advance," he said, loudly enough to be heard by the men on either side of him. He could hear the order being passed along the line of crouching men as he rose and pushed through the bushes toward the open shore.

Daraun was the first to step from soft fallen needles on to hard gravel. One by one his men drifted out of the trees, to reform their line on either side of him. He counted them as they came, then counted again when they stopped coming and cursed under his breath.

He'd taken all fifty into the trees, but fewer than forty had come out. A dozen men he'd sworn to this task preferred to be forsworn rather than risk whatever fate awaited them for doing their duty. Daraun cursed again and almost forgot his promise to ask the gods for no more favors. If Haro would send those cowards cold hearths and cold loins and a cold wet death—!

At least they hadn't turned traitor, to warn the Beast Wizard of the ambush. The enemy were coming down the path from the prison and on to the shore. As they passed in front of the *Kym* House, the torches burning there silhouetted them. They seemed like a hundred men, and all those Daraun could see were armed. He could also see a fire-glint of red hair among the darker shapes of the fighting men.

It was time. No one had noticed his men. The robes had done their work as he'd hoped. Daraun drew his sword and swung it three times in a circle above his head. Then he ran at the enemy and his men ran with him.

CHAPTER 18

Wandor saw the robed men running out of the darkness with their weapons raised and heard their feet on the gravel. In his mind a warning chimed like a bell— Friends, or enemies of your enemies. He kept his face a mask and forced his feet into the next step, to give no hints to the men around him. He didn't even risk the quickest of glances at Gwynna.

No warning chimed in the minds of the men around Wandor. They saw the robes, and for a few moments they saw nothing else. The new men were coming on in a long line, and the leaders were almost within sword-reach now. Then Mykto let out a screech like a scalded cat and drew his sword. A wordless roar that might have been Galkor echoed him. The oncoming men reached striking distance. Wandor heard the faint hiss of sword blades slicing air, and clangs and cries that weren't faint at all.

The attackers struck Galkor's men close to Wandor and Gwynna. They cut down two who had no time even to raise a weapon and drove back four more who had no chance to brace themselves or strike. One of those men stumbled as he backed away, flourished arms and legs in a fight for balance, and crashed into Wandor.

Both went down. Wandor landed underneath and drove both knees up into the small of the man's back. His breath *whuffed* out. Wandor rolled clear and started to rise. A sword whistled down past the back of his head and bit into the ropes binding his wrists. One gave, the other two held. The man behind Wandor worried at the other two, jabbing his sword into Wandor several times. Fortunately the swords of the Sea Folk were slashing weapons, without sharp points.

At last the ropes fell away and Wandor sprang to his feet with a shout that mixed relief, joy, defiance, and the will to do battle. Men flinched away from him, then flinched again as Gwynna screamed out her own battle-cry. Wandor saw that she was free, with three men protecting her. He bent to pick up a fallen sword, and someone strong enough to handle him like a child jerked him upright again. He whirled, hands raised, to face Daraun.

"We must run!" the Captain snapped.

Everything so far had happened in the time a strong man would need to walk ten paces, too little time for any of the captors to understand clearly what was going on. Daraun slammed a hand into Wandor's back, pushing him forward. The three men around Gwynna nearly snatched her off her feet in their eagerness to get her moving. Daraun led five men against the other line of Galkor's force, sword whirling. A flurry of clanging steel, the howl of a man who'd taken his death wound, a whimpering gasp, and suddenly there were four of Galkor's men and two of Daraun's lying where the line had been. Wandor, Gwynna, and their rescuers burst out into the open.

By now the captors knew that something was happening, if not exactly what. Galkor was bellowing orders and his men were obeying all the ones they could hear and understand. Some ran back to the path to block it off, while others ran along the shore to protect the boat landing.

One of the Warriors saw clearly what was happening. He shrieked, "They're getting away!" and charged Daraun. Daraun's sword cut through the man's spear with one slash and cut off an arm with a second. The man held out the shaft of his spear and stayed on his feet until Daraun's sword split his skull. But the man's shout had alerted comrades, and they came at Daraun. The Captain found a ring of enemies sprouting around him, cut down one, saw two more charge into the ring, and shouted for aid. The man beside Wandor and the three with Gwynna heard their Captain's call and turned back to fight beside him.

Wandor and Gwynna suddenly found themselves alone, with neither captors nor rescuers close at hand, no weapons and no idea of where they were supposed to go. Wandor saw that the path and the shore were blocked off by Galkor's men. There was no retreat for them except up the path to the *Kym* House. The *Kym* House had guards, and those guards would have weapons that might be taken. Wandor clutched Gwynna's hand and broke into a run.

They went up the path so fast that they were passing the white rune-posts before Gwynna realized where they were going. "Bertan, we can't enter the—!"

"We can and we will!" Wandor said without missing a step.

Then they were coming up to the immense carved wooden doors, twice as high as the guard standing in the gap between them. He stood frozen with surprise for a moment, unable to decide whether to shout for help, run for his life, or draw his sword. Before he could make up his mind, Wandor shoved him violently to one side. He slammed into the edge of the door and Wandor held him there while Gwynna drew the sword from the man's scabbard and the dagger from his left boot.

"Hold the door," said Wandor, and darted inside. Oil lamps hung from iron books on each of the eight carved pillars that supported the roof of the eight-sided *Kym* House. They gave enough yellowish light to reveal any man or weapon in the House.

Wandor saw neither. There were no more guards, and the House was as bare of weapons as a temple of Yeza. He clattered down the wooden steps toward the circle of packed earth in the center, vaguely hoping to find some piece of timber he could wrench loose. He wondered how the Sea Folk would greet this violation of the *Kym* House even by one who wished them no real harm. He was also quite certain that he had to be out of here before Galkor and the Beast Wizard finished rallying their men or the Captain of the *Kym* House arrived with more guards.

He reached the central circle of earth, and for the first time noticed the railing on the back of the square platform in the middle of the circle. The railing was a seven-foot Sea Folk spear, the wood of the shaft dark with age, resting on two forked bronze posts.

Wandor's thoughts suddenly took solid shape, like molten metal dropped into cold water. Words spoken from the flames beneath Mount Pendwyr roared in his mind.

"Go and seek these—the Helm of Jagnar, the Ax of Yevoda, the Spear of Valkath..."

The Spear of Valkath. He hadn't sought it. He'd entered the *Kym* House searching for a weapon. The Spear of Valkath was—a weapon, and for the moment that was all it could be. It had to be that, if he didn't want to go back out and face his enemies with his bare hands.

He crossed to the platform and sprang up on it. He gripped the Spear with both hands and snatched it from its support, whirled it around his head and thrust out with it to test its balance. It might have been no more than the sign of the Speakers of the *Kym* of Captains in all the centuries since Valkath laid it down. But it was also a superb weapon, one which seemed to follow the commands of Wandor's muscles as though it were a part of his own body. The head flashed silvery sparks as it caught the light. Was this brightness the result of renewal, devoted care, or a metal that never aged? Wandor didn't know. He only knew that the point drew blood from his thumb and the edges sliced cleanly through the greasy leather of his jerkin.

He had his weapon, and he would consider what the Spear meant for his quest of the Five Crowns when there was no more need for it as a weapon. He turned and retraced his path to the door. He reached the door as Gwynna finished buckling on the belt taken from the unconscious guard. She stared at the Spear, and for a moment the woman of Power and terrible knowledge looked out of her eyes. Then the warrior flowed back into them, and she grinned in a way that made Wandor very glad he wasn't an enemy.

He raised the Spear and held it crosswise with both hands, like a quarterstaff. He noted that the butt end was a cylinder of hammered bronze, with runes chiseled in it. Wandor recognized them—they spelled out JUSTICE. Well, perhaps there was a rough and bloody justice in what he was about to do with the Spear.

Wandor looked at Gwynna again, then thrust the Spear of Valkath through the leather loop on one door and heaved. The door creaked on its iron hinges, then swung smoothly open in the face of a dozen enemies.

CHAPTER 19

The dozen enemies were crowded together on the upper steps, where there was fighting room for no more than half of them. Wandor and Gwynna went straight into the attack, giving their opponents no time to reform or retreat.

Wandor thrust at a man on the left who twisted to avoid the thrust, slashed at the Spear's shaft, lost his balance, and crashed over backward. Wandor sprang down into the gap, swinging the Spear overhead so that the bronze-weighted butt crashed down on the next man's skull. He fell back against two of his comrades and all three went down together.

An opponent grappled Wandor, getting in under the Spear and throwing an arm around his neck while groping for a knife with the other hand. Wandor pulled the Spear hard against the base of the man's skull, until he gasped and loosened his grip. Gwynna closed from behind, drove a swordsman back to a safe distance with three quick slashes, then drove her dagger through the neck of the man grappling Wandor. Someone swung a bill and it sank into one of the fallen men. His scream still hung in the air as Wandor and Gwynna attacked the man with the bill. Wandor thrust deep into the man's thigh, while Gwynna opened his face from ear to nose. Then suddenly they had a clear path to the bottom of the stairs.

They took the stairs three at a time, with enemies clattering down after them and others running to catch them at the foot. Behind the enemies on the ground came Daraun and some of his men, while others drew more of Galkor's men off along the shore.

As Wandor and Gwynna reached the bottom of the stairs, Daraun's men saw what Wandor was carrying. They stopped, mouths opened to shout war cries staying open in amazement, weapons raised to strike sagging like broken branches. With the heightened awareness that came to him in battle, Wandor could sense the almost physical impact on Daraun's men of the sight of the Spear of Valkath with blood dripping from both point and butt.

It was different with Galkor's men. Most of them were solid veterans who'd seen many years of service and many battles. They worshipped only Staz the Warrior, if they worshipped anything besides their weapons, their comrades' loyalty, and good wine. They didn't care whether Wandor held in his hands the Spear of Valkath or a log of firewood, except that the Spear was far more dangerous. They knew only that for a moment their enemies were hesitating and Wandor and Gwynna stood alone. A solid wedge of Galkor's men advanced to the attack.

For nearly a year Wandor and Gwynna had been training to fight together, building from Wandor's skills as a Duelist but moving on from there along paths of their own. Now for the first time they could throw that training into battle. Galkor's men came at them, and met one mind controlling two bodies, with four arms, four legs, and three weapons weaving a finely meshed net of steel in a circle that grew and shrank from one second to the next, but never broke.

Wandor thrust with the Spear's butt to shatter a billman's jaw, then thrust down over the top of an axman's shield. The axman threw up his shield and for a moment held the Spear's point between the top of his shield and the rim of his helmet. A swordsman closed to thrust at Wandor. Gwynna ducked under the shaft of the Spear and came up with a dagger for the swordsman's throat. He started to fall, and she guided that fall so that he crashed into the axman. Both went down, Gwynna sprang clear, and Wandor thrust into the axman's face while Gwynna matched sword against sword with two more men until Wandor could turn to flank one of them and thrust him in the leg...

Wandor and Gwynna put seven men out of the fight before Daraun could launch his own attack. As he did, the torches lighting the path to the *Kym* House started going out. It seemed a good idea to many men on both sides to deprive their opponents of light, so all the torches vanished like candles blown out by a giant's sneeze.

Darkness swallowed the battle. Suddenly it was impossible to tell whether the robed figure at the end of one's sword was friend or foe. Wandor and Gwynna stood out by wearing no robes, but Galkor's men had seen that it was death to approach them and had held back.

Daraun had his men better in hand. As the close grapple broke up, he drew them one by one into a compact body, with Wandor and Gwynna in the center. Slowly they moved off, expecting at every moment the new flare of a torch among the enemy, wild shouts, and a scrambling pursuit. Over the wind they could hear the moans of the dying and Galkor's curses as he called in his scattered men. Before they heard anything else, they reached a break in the trees. Daraun slapped Wandor on the shoulder.

"Run!"

Wandor and Gwynna ran, and heard Daraun and the men still with him running after them. They didn't know how many of their rescuers were left, and for the moment didn't care. They ran with total concentration on putting one foot in front of the other, hardly noticing when the slope they were climbing turned into a level crest, then into a gentle downhill run with a narrow but hard-beaten path underfoot. They ran on, until at last Daraun's voice came again.

"We stop here."

Wandor and Gwynna sat down where they were. Gwynna sheathed her dagger and laid her sword across her knees. Wandor held the Spear in one hand as he looked up at Daraun and spoke in the tongue of the Sea Folk.

"My first words must be—thank you, Captain. The next— where do we go from here?"

"We go west about an hour's march, keeping well away from the shore and from villages and houses. Then we come down to the shore again and take boats across the bay, to the Hearth House and the Grove of the Mother. You will be safe there." He stepped back from Wandor. "Are you ready to go on?" His tone was much less polite than his words.

As the party moved on in the darkness, Wandor counted about twenty men besides Daraun. All of them were long-limbed fighting men of the Sea Folk. All of them were also clearly fighting down fear, as if they expected to pay a dreadful price for what they'd done this night.

They could be right. They'd spat in the face not only of Cragor's chief servant but of a formidable sorcerer. Too many of the Sea Folk had already taken Cragor's gold and made his enemies theirs. Galkor would not lack for willing allies if he had time to call for them. And if the Beast Wizard, reached out—

If Mykto reached out, he and Gwynna could probably call Cheloth and the *Red Seers* to their aid. But that would take time and effort, as well as a halt which might not be possible and which Daraun would probably not allow them. Wandor had never seen a rescuer quite so eager to have those he rescued out of his hands.

Wandor fell back until he was walking close enough to Gwynna to reach her with a whisper. "Can we trust the Hearth Mothers?"

A laugh. "I was about to ask you the same thing about Daraun."

"We can trust him and his men to pass us on to the Hearth Mothers as quickly as possible, and defend us on the way. They all seem to have committed their honor to getting us safely out of the hands of Galkor and Mykto. They are good for that much, but no more. Will it be enough?"

"The Hearth Mothers can be trusted, once we're within the Grove of the Mother. The sacred trees for the Hearth grow there, and anyone invading it would be cursed and their sons after them to the ninth generation. No Captain could get his men to follow him there, no matter how much of Cragor's gold he offered or what threats Mykto hurled. Even a common thrall-girl is safe if she can reach the Grove."

"But they will do nothing until we reach the Grove?" "Nothing. The Keepers do not yet have the Powers to face Mykto alone, and they can hardly be sure of our bringing Cheloth and the *Red Seers* to their aid. Mykto may be cautious in the use of his own Powers if he does not wish an open clash with the Hearth Mothers. That is the most I can see happening."

Wandor shook his head. "I don't care for the idea of crossing to the Grove tonight, with Galkor's ships still offshore. He can sail west faster than we can walk, and stands a good chance of cutting us off. We'd do better to turn inland. Galkor hasn't enough men to risk following us there, and we can go to ground long enough to call Cheloth in and put Mykto out of the fight for good."

"Would Daraun protect us that long?"

"We wouldn't need his protection. Remember your own woodscraft. The enemy's not knowing where you are is a better protection than stone walls and sorcery together."

"Perhaps. Should we slip off now?"

Wandor shook his head again. "We'd be breaking with the only certain friend we have here, and doing him an ill-turn for the service he's done us. We're safe enough for the moment."

Wandor spoke as his reason commanded him. To do this he had to ignore his instincts, which told him to forget about Daraun and vanish into the forest, where he and Gwynna would be safe from both the strength of their enemies and the weakness of their friends.

Mykto was still sitting cross-legged and rigid on the beach when Galkor finished gathering and counting his men. He'd lost twenty-two, dead or dying. Wandor and Gwynna were gone into the night with rescuers who'd lost no more than half that many. The baron's face twisted, and he threw his sword halfway to the water's edge. Its clang on the gravel seemed to bring Mykto back to life. He rose with serpentine grace and approached Galkor, brushing his robes smooth as he came.

"You are despairing?" It was as much a statement as a question.

Galkor's hands gripped his sword belt. He could feel the leather beginning to tear before he felt able to speak. "You've lost more than I have, Mykto. They were your sacrifices, your prisoners."

"Ah." The look on the thin, tanned face made Galkor ready to suspect anything but proved nothing. "We have more hope than you think. I have learned this."

Galkor was about to ask, "How?" but the word seemed to twist and turn all up and down his throat until he could hardly breathe. He was reminded, in a way that he had not been since he began dealing with Mykto, that the man was a sorcerer—a man at home in the world beyond the world he himself hated and feared when he couldn't ignore it.

So Mykto knew they had some hope of remaining what they'd lost. He would go on from there. "What should I do with my men and my ships?"

"Go aboard your ships, and my people will go aboard ours. Raise anchor, and we shall sail along the shore toward the west. Have all your men armed and boats trailing alongside ready for them to enter."

So Wandor and Gwynna might be found somewhere along the shore to the west? That made as much sense as anything could this night, and why should Mykto not tell the truth in a matter that meant so much to him as well?

Besides, the Beast Wizard had said he would be going aboard one of his own ships. The farther off Mykto was, the better, as far as Galkor was concerned. His master's interests and his own peace of mind would best be served by Mykto's absence.

Wandor and Gwynna were among the first to come out on the shore and see what had happened to the boats.

Daraun had promised four boats, guarded and waiting to take them across Stohra Bay to the Grove of the Mother. What they saw was four furrows in the gravel of the beach where the keels had dug in, five men lying sprawled beside the furrows, and no boats at all. Only the dark water and the dark empty shore and the chill wind blowing across both.

Daraun seemed unable to move or speak. Wandor and Gwynna slipped forward for a closer look, alert and crouching low. After a moment several of the men followed them.

Three of the boat guards were dead, arrows driven neatly into chests or backs. Wandor pulled out one of the arrows and stared at it. He'd seen pile-head arrows like this before, drawn out of Gwynna's legs. Telek the Fatherless, he thought. He would not trust himself to speak the name out loud. Silently he held the arrow out to Gwynna, and as silently she nodded. There were no words to express what they felt about Telek, and they would not waste breath on futile curses.

Wandor had just discovered that one of the other two guards was alive, when one of Daraun's men shouted, *"Hoaaaa!* Look!"

Wandor shifted his attention to where the man was pointing, and saw one of the boats grounded farther down the beach. Apparently Telek hadn't pushed it far enough for the wind and waves to catch it and carry it out into the bay.

Now the other men also saw the boat. A mad rush nearly knocked Daraun off his feet and left Wandor and Gwynna racing to catch up. They reached the boat to find a circle of men already forming around it, working themselves into an increasingly ugly temper as they listened to Daraun.

"This boat only has room for eight besides myself and Wandor and Gwynna. The rest of you must take to the woods or find refuge with your families."

One man gave an angry bull's snort. "Why should you be in the boat, Daraun?"

"The Keepers will not accept anyone but—"

"Tell us another tale," said the man. His hand was close to the hilt of his sword, and so was Daraun's. Calling a warrior of the Sea Folk a liar to his face was among the deadliest of insults.

Wandor knew he had to speak out. His instinct called even more loudly for him to flee away from all this. But without his presence and support, Daraun's remaining authority would vanish in a moment and his life would not last much longer. Wandor did not care to face Berek and tell him that he'd left the man's uncle to die at the hands of his mutinous followers.

Besides, fleeing inland might no longer be wise. Now that Telek Son of a Hundred Fathers had taken a hand, word of what Daraun was doing would quickly reach those Captains deep in Cragor's pay. Their men would be joining the search before morning, perhaps within an hour or two. Wandor took a deep breath. "All of you—be silent! Listen to your Captain, and listen to me. Berek Strong-Ax, son of the brother of Daraun, has sworn to me the Oath of the Drunk Blood. I will not let Daraun be slain while I live. But neither will I cast you to the wind like a gull's feather, not after you have put your lives in danger for me."

He lifted the Spear. "I swear by the Five Gods of my own people, by Haro Sea Father, and by this the Spear of Valkath which I have used in battle, that I will have the blood of anyone who lifts a weapon against any of you. I cannot promise you safety tonight, but I can promise that all in this land will know of my oath tomorrow. I will have vengeance against those who do you harm if I live, and Berek Strong-Ax will have it if I do not."

"I stand beside him in this oath," said Gwynna.

The prospect of having Wandor and Gwynna fighting against them if they attacked Daraun and for them if they obeyed him was enough for the men. The circle broke up, and Daraun quickly counted off eight men. Gwynna climbed into the boat, and Wandor after her. He laid the Spear of Valkath in the bottom of the boat and lashed it to one of the ribs. It would be out of the way there, and safe until they reached the Grove and he could turn it over to the Keepers. Then the crew pushed the boat off the gravel and climbed aboard, one by one. By the time Daraun took his place at the steering oar, the men left behind were vanishing into the night.

With the rowers hard at work and the wind behind them, the shore faded away quickly. Two or three lights shone dimly at some unguessable distance in the blackness, then they vanished too. Wandor held Gwynna's hand. He wanted to believe they were safe, but he wouldn't until the gates of the Grove of the Mother closed behind them. Nor would he think of what they'd accomplished tonight until he was sure they'd accomplished it.

As the boat crept out into open water, the waves began to toss it, at first playfully, then with an erratic but steadily increasing strength. The rowers kept at their work, Daraun tightened his grip on the steering oar, and Wandor and Gwynna hunched lower in the boat. With eleven people aboard, the boat was so packed that no one could move from his place without danger of capsizing it. With the wind above and the cold water below, that would almost certainly mean the end for all of them. The water would sap their strength and swallow them long before they could fight through the waves to either shore of the bay.

They rowed on. Daraun seemed fixed in his place in the stern like part of the boat itself. The rowers squeezed their eyes half shut against the wind that blew spray from the wave crests into their face, and seldom missed a stroke. The superbly buoyant Sea Folk boat took each wave as gracefully as the mood of the sea allowed it.

Wandor was beginning to think of asking Daraun how far they'd come, when far across the water to port lights suddenly glowed. At first there seemed to be solid masses of orange flame, as if fire were being carried toward them by an army of spirits walking across the water. Then he saw the flames were only torches in the bows of three large boats. The torchlight showed hunched figures and the glint of weapons and armor. Each boat had a square sail spread on a stubby mast amidships, and all three grew larger even as Wandor stared.

Daraun now had only one hand on the steering oar. The other gripped his sword. The rowers were doing the same. They couldn't hope to stay clear of the three oncoming boats long enough to do any good. It was better to fight now, while they still had the strength to give a good account of themselves. Wandor found himself sorry he'd doubted the courage of these men of the Sea Folk. They might be slow to stand against their customs and beliefs, but not slow to stand against enemies outnumbering them at least three-to-one.

The boats came on, as implacable as sharks. Before long

Wandor could recognize Galkor in the bow of the one farthest to the right. He hoped luck would bring that boat close enough for a grapple. He was not sure he could hope to do much more against Cragor except cut down the Black Duke's best servant before he himself went down and Gwynna with him. At least they would not go to Yand to be torn apart by the Beasts, and perhaps some among the Sea Folk...

Then there was no time to think of the future or whether there was to be any. There was no time to think of untying the Spear of Valkath and hurling it across the water at Galkor. There were only the three boats growing out of the night, a wild cry as one of Daraun's men hurled himself into the sea, a wilder rocking of the boat before Daraun steadied it to meet the attack—then the attack itself.

The boats to the left and right passed around the bow and stern of their prey, while the middle boat swept down to ram. Daraun roared an order, oars thrashed, and his boat clawed backward, trying to escape the ramming. The loss of a rower threw off the stroke too much. The high bluff bow of the enemy's boat filled Wandor's vision, drove in, rode up over the bow of his own boat, and trampled it down into the side of a wave.

Cold water churned around Wandor's ankles, then around his knees. A flailing oar crashed into his thigh, knocking him sideways. Sword and shield overbalanced him and he sprawled on top of one of the rowers, nearly impaling himself on the man's spear. Gwynna beat down a clumsily swung oar with her sword, hacked at another, and left herself open to a third. It grazed Wandor's hair and came up under Gwynna's right arm, lifting her over the side of the boat.

She came to the surface spitting out water and curses. A boathook stabbed down like a harpoon, snagging the back of her jerkin. The tough leather held long enough for a second man to grab the boathook. Both heaved with all their strength. Gwynna shrieked as she felt herself drawn helplessly toward the enemy's boat. The two men fell over backward and their boat rocked wildly, but one of them held on to the boathook. Three pairs of hands clutched Gwynna by the hair and one arm as the boathook ripped free, and she was dragged in over the oars. One of Daraun's men struck with an ax and a hand clutching Gwynna's hair fell from a spouting stump into the water. A harsh scream sounded, then a squishy crunch as a bill lifted off the top of the axman's skull.

The boat slid out from under Wandor and he found himself swimming, as the enemy's boat drifted past. It swung around as the rowers on the far side kept working while those on the near side held their oars out toward Wandor like pikes. He dropped his shield, clutched at an oar blade with his left hand, gripped it as if a chasm yawned beneath him, then heaved. The oar splashed into the water and the rower went with it. Wandor gripped the side of the boat and pulled himself out of the water with one hand while he slashed with his sword to widen the clear space in front of him.

Gwynna shrieked again. "No, you fool! Don't come—!" then muffled and meaningless noises as someone clamped a hand over her mouth. Wandor heard a wonderfully satisfying bowl of agony that could only be a man with his hand bitten to the bone, then "Save your—!", breaking off in choking sounds that told him far too much.

The man at the tiller unshipped it and swung at Wandor. He

caught the blow on one shoulder, rode with it as he sliced off the head of a lunging pike, turned, and chopped sideways at the steersman's throat with the edge of his left hand. The steersman dropped the tiller. Wandor grabbed the man by one wrist and whipped him forward, to knock down two of his comrades, then closed in. Two quick slashes kept the fallen men from rising, a third slash shattered one's jaw, a fourth opened the other's thigh. Now Wandor held the stern of the boat.

Then another boat closed in from the port side—Galkor's boat, with the Baron standing fully armed in the bow beside the torchbearer. The two boats ran together, planks cracked like whiplashes, both torchbearers flew overboard, and in the darkness a crossbow went *snik*.

A bolt that should have drilled Wandor's forehead tore his right ear. It felt like a red-hot poker laid across his temple. An oar battered at his ribs and another at his cheekbone, and his head felt as if it was coming loose from his shoulders. He threw himself backward with all the strength he had left. He could do nothing for Gwynna if he let himself be clubbed down like a seal asleep on a rock. The heel of his boot caught the gunwale but didn't hold him. He plunged down, kicking with both feet, flailing with both arms, determined to surface far away or not surface at all. He sensed that both hands were free—his sword was gone. His chest tightened and the darkness around him began to creep within. He rose, and the blackness within rose nearly as fast. Flame filled his lungs, then his head broke the surface and he gulped in an enormous breath of damp air.

He swam with only his head above the water, and that only when the waves lifted him instead of rolling over him. Distant torches lit up a pinnace hove to, with Galkor's three boats alongside it. They looked like piglets nuzzling up to their sow. Figures twisted by distance and shadows were clambering up from the boats. He was still in danger if they made a thorough search for him, but they didn't look as if they'd be making one.

The pain was fading from his lungs and growing in other parts of his body. For better or worse, the cold water would soon numb that pain. He ducked under to unlace his boots and kick them off. Then he turned on his back and began to swim with slow, controlled strokes. He could go on swimming like this for hours, or as long as the water did not leech away his strength, and thoughts of Gwynna as Baron Galkor's prisoner did not leech away his will.

The seven ships—his own four and the three from Yand—were already well down the bay when Galkor came on deck. There were dry clothes on his body, hot spiced wine in his belly, and bricks heated by the cookfire warming his bed. There were a few more orders to give, then he could sleep until the weather changed.

If the weather changed for the better...well, one did not spit at good weather on the Ocean. If it changed for the worse, on the other hand, there could be a veil of storm, behind which his squadron could hope to slip away from Mykto's ships and make for Benzos.

Galkor pulled his cloak about him and walked forward. It had been a good night's work. Gwynna lay safely locked below, chained, drugged, and beyond hope of any escape other than to the House of Shadows. Wandor had gone overboard, probably wounded, certainly into water that would chill the life out of him before he could reach the shore or a boat could reach him.

A good night indeed, after its bad beginning. Now all that remained was to slip Gwynna out of Mykto's grasp and into the hands of Cragor's executioners, and with luck—

Galkor stopped, and after a moment he sighed and put away some of his hopes for good luck. Sitting on the deck abreast of the foremast was a familiar robed figure, one Galkor had thought safely aboard one of the Yand ships. To slip away for Benzos now would throw down the gauntlet to the Beast Wizards of Yand with an open breach of faith, not to mention carrying off Mykto himself. That would be less than wise, particularly when there were five hundred of Galkor's men still on Yand—men who might be in peril if he broke faith with Mykto, but a second line of defense if he carried Gwynna straight to Yand. There would be other dark nights, other disguises his men could use, and other chances to please Cragor without offending Mykto.

He would think more on this—but at another time and somewhere else. There was Mykto to deceive--and now Galkor saw and recognized the hooded man perched on the edge of the fo'c'sle, thin legs dangling like those of a small boy on a branch. How Telek the Fatherless had come here, Galkor did not even care to guess. Still less did he care to think of Telek and Mykto working hand in hand. The Beast Wizard's purposes were not Galkor's, but at least the Baron could understand them. Telek was another matter. For the first time in his life Galkor found a sorcerer less fearsome and mysterious than a human being without Powers.

He was close enough to Mykto that some polite formula of greeting seemed called for. He opened his mouth to speak, then looked again at the sorcerer and let the words die on the wind. Mykto sat apart from the world around him, eyes blank and unfocused, his mouth drawn tight with concentration or perhaps pain. Galkor suspected those blank eyes were focused inward, on the work of another's Power.

Whose? Not Gwynna, certainly. Perhaps the Hearth Mothers. Perhaps Cheloth. Or perhaps someone or something Galkor could not even imagine.

The Baron turned and strode aft. Suddenly he found the warmed bed more appealing than ever.

There was a smaller, dense darkness forming out of the great darkness ahead. Now Wandor had a goal for the first time. He swam toward the smaller darkness and saw it grow, until it became the upturned bottom of Daraun's boat, floating on air trapped within. The clinker construction gave Wandor a precarious handhold. He wormed his way up on to the bottom, at each lurch of the boat expecting it to sink under him.

Finally he lay motionless, fingers locked and toes dug in. Often the waves rolled high and he tasted salt water. Always he felt a chill in his hands and his feet.

At first the chill was a vague presence, something he sensed clearly only when he paid attention to it. Then it crept higher and he could drive it away only by thinking of Gwynna. Finally the chill was creeping in even past the warmth of those thoughts. He knew the next stage would turn the world to cold and blackness. Then it would not matter that he'd found the boat and climbed out of the water, because his end would be the same.

How close he came to that end he never knew. He only knew that out of the blackness came light and voices, the sound of oars and the splash of water at a boat's prow. Hands drew him into the boat, faces looked down at him, but neither hands nor faces seemed to have bodies joined to them.

But then why should they, when his own body was floating away?

CHAPTER 20

Wandor awoke in a bed with furs piled thickly upon him, in a chamber where a fire devoured what seemed to be half a year's supply of logs. A serious-looking, gray-robed woman just short of middle age was sitting on a bench by the fire. When she saw he was awake she took a steaming jug from atop a panful of coals on the hearth and poured some of the liquid into a wooden cup.

"Drink this," she said, holding out the cup.

Wandor obeyed without a word. He seemed to have no will left in his mind or strength left in his limbs, only dull weariness, throbbing pains, and a blank spot that might conceal Gwynna. If it did, it was a merciful gift.

Perhaps it was the weariness, or perhaps there was a drug in the hot cup. Wandor slept again, and this time when he awoke he found his thoughts coming clearly. He still felt the pains, and when the woman let him look at himself in a bronze mirror he understood why. One ear was wrapped in bandages, and so were half his ribs. His lip was split and one side of his face was purple-black.

The woman went out, and came back with another woman, whose hair was the same color as her robe. It was this woman who told Wandor what had happened during the night and the day and the second night that he lay in this chamber in the guest house of the Grove of the Mother.

The escape and the running battle along the shore and across the water were only the beginning, and of all that had happened, they were the easiest to understand. Or so the old woman said. After hearing her, Wandor had to agree.

When Valkath sailed on his last voyage he left his Spear behind to serve as the sign of the Speaker of the *Kym* of Captains. He left behind no other word or warning about it. It was a thousand years of custom and tradition that held the Spear inviolate and stunned those of the HaroiLina who saw Wandor wielding it in battle.

"There were no legends about what would happen if the Spear was blooded again?" asked Wandor.

"None," said the woman.

Wandor smiled, although it hurt his face to do so. "Then I suppose we shall just have to invent a few."

The woman's lips also curled into a faint smile, but her eyes told Wandor that the matter was not one for cynical jests. He decided to guard his tongue and listen. As he listened, he came to understand the look in the woman's eyes.

Valkath had promised nothing; but on the night of the escape, and the night after that, he came forth from the House of Shadows and walked through the lands of the HaroiLina and along the shores of Stohra Bay. A hundred men and women saw him in as many different places—at the *Kym* House, at the very Hearth of the Mother, in the Grove only a score of paces from where Wandor lay, in the longhouses of Captains who'd taken Cragor's gold, in the longhouses of Captains who'd held as firm for the old ways as they dared when the others grew strong, and on the decks of ships drawn up on the shore or beating homeward against the wind.

It was Valkath, with his beard in the same two plaits, the belt with the serpent's-head buckle, the boots with the silver metalwork. His eyes were all shining gold, and some said there was another figure walking with him. That second figure was a great bulky man, tall and stout, clad in a dark robe, and his eyes also burned like molten gold.

Nond. Wandor let the name echo in his mind but kept it from his lips and went on listening.

Valkath spoke as he walked, and everyone who saw him with their eyes heard him in their minds. Those who'd held back from Cragor and the Beast Wizards heard his blessing. Those who'd raided the Viceroyalty and no more heard his warning. Those who'd carried sacrifices to the Beasts of Yand and done honor to the Beast Wizards heard his curse.

"Your arms will wither," said Valkath. "Your swords will break, your loins will become dry as bone, your women will be barren, your sons will spit in your faces, and your daughters will turn whore. Your hearths will grow cold, your crops will rot in the fields, your houses will fall down upon your heads. Everyone and everything that is yours will utterly fail and betray you."

The curse put fear into those who'd served the Beast Wizards, and their eyes turned toward their ships and the Ocean. On the second night more than curses came upon them. Three Captains and four strong warriors who'd gone often and willingly to Yand were found dead. It was as though white-hot pincers had closed on their throats, leaving only blackened bone and charred scraps of flesh. None who saw the bodies could bear to look at them for long.

There had been fear before. Now there was panic. Every captain, every warrior weak or strong, every ship's boy and harlot who'd ever put their hopes in the Beast Wizards of Yand was fighting for a place aboard an outbound ship. A dozen ships and more than five hundred people were already driving madly out to sea. Twice as many again were preparing for the voyage.

There was also fighting for more than places aboard ships to Yand. It was easy to think of those whom Valkath had cursed as outlaws. After thinking that, it became easy to also think of raiding their herds, their fields, their houses and ships. Men lay dead in a score of places all up and down the shores of Stohra Bay, and the darkness was pocked with the glow of burning buildings.

"The HaroiLina have been smitten by the hand of the Sea Father, and I do not think the smiting is yet finished. I am a Keeper of the Hearth of the Mother, and Foyn Son of Thadul is my own brother. I am a Keeper, and I should rejoice that so much is being done against our enemies."

"Yes," said Wandor. "It saves the Keepers further labor. It also means you need not fear any punishment for your aid and counsel to Captain Daraun, or your part in my escape."

The Keeper flushed. "You might say that. I—no, I admit that you shall say it, and have justice on your side. Had we been bolder..."

Wandor did not want to speak or think of what might have happened if the Hearth Mothers had spoken out sooner. In time he would have the strength to face his fears for Gwynna and beat them down, but not yet.

"What is done is done. You could not be sure that what has happened would happen. Without it, perhaps you would be in as much danger as you feared."

"Those are kind words. Are you sure we deserve them?"

"I am sure of very little at this moment, good Keeper. No, I am sure that I am hungry. Is there any food to be had?"

The Keeper smiled. "That will be easy enough."

The Keeper came back with the younger woman, bearing a platter of food, and also with a barrel-chested man who introduced himself as Captain Reyget Son of Kurt, friend to Daraun Son of Hymok. He sat silently by the hearth while Wandor ate, thrusting his damp boots almost into the fire and oiling the blade of his battleax.

When Wandor finished eating, the Keeper poured herself and Reyget some ale and stared at Wandor for a long time. She seemed to be having trouble finding the right words or perhaps even the will to speak.

Finally she said, "I will not say that you may do with the HaroiLina as you wish—"

"That is as well," said Reyget. "It would be tempting Haro's wrath to promise too much."

"We would be promising it to a man blessed by Haro through Valkath the First Speaker," said the Keeper sharply. "How can that tempt the Sea Father?"

"His wrath will fall upon those who make fools of themselves, however good their intentions," said Reyget. He looked apologetically at Wandor and poured himself more ale. "Of course I do not speak for the Captains in this, but I speak as one who knows the mind of many of them. They will carry out no promises of the Hearth Mothers unless those promises show some wisdom in war."

The curse of Valkath and the burning hands of King Nond had made the Sea Folk willing to turn away from Duke Cragor and toward Wandor. They had not made the Captains and the Hearth Mothers embrace each other in friendship, and perhaps there was nothing that could do so. Wandor suspected he would have to teach the Captains some wisdom that had nothing to do with war, and Zakonta—or Gwynna—and Cheloth would have to do the same with the Hearth Mothers.

But that was for another time and place. Here and now he said, "I have three things to ask. One is that you end this bickering and casting of doubts on each other's wisdom and honor. You sound like a whore and her pimp arguing over the night's earnings." The words were not soft, and neither was Wandor's mood. Both Reyget and the Keeper started.

"The second thing I ask is a good, well-manned ship to take me south to the Viceroyalty. I must return to Fors and take matters in hand for an expedition to Yand. That ship must be ready as soon as possible.

"The third thing I ask is all the ships and fighting men you can spare, to sail to Yand and sweep it clear of both your enemies and mine. I trust you know better than I how many ships and men that will be. All must be prepared and sent as swiftly as possible."

Both the Keeper and the Captain bowed their heads stiffly. They looked at each other, then at Wandor, and Reyget nodded.

"Certainly we can do these things. The ship to take you south will be easy. I will offer my own, and I think we may even find more than one ship ready to sail. As for sailing to Yand—that also can be done, but not so quickly."

"I did not think so," said Wandor. "I would like to know how long, though."

Reyget frowned. "That I cannot say. I fear there will be a good deal of work for fighting men here at home before we can think of sailing to Yand."

"What sort of work?" said Wandor. "Stealing the sheep and the thrall-women of those who've fled?" He did not even want to keep the bitterness out of his voice.

"There will be much of that," said Reyget. "Haro may not bless it, but I certainly cannot stop it. There is also this, Lord Wandor. Those who sail to Yand for you will be leaving behind their women, their children, everything. They will want to be sure they leave no enemies behind them as well, to strike for the Black Duke or the Beast

Wizards."

"There is some wisdom in that," said the Keeper. "But they will leave fewer enemies behind them if they stop the slaughter and the burning now. The Hearth Mothers will give no blessing for the slaying of those not in arms for Cragor and the Beast Wizards."

"The Captains will know whom to strike down without the advice of the Hearth Mothers," said Reyget. He might have said more, but Wandor fixed both of them with a look which would have stretched them both dead on the floor if his eyes had been crossbows.

"The deadliest enemies of us all are on Yand," said Wandor. "Give that word to the Captains, Reyget, and start readying your ship. Good Keeper, how soon may I leave here?"

"You may go on this blessed voyage whenever you choose," said the Keeper. "We cannot hold you back."

"No," said Wandor, throwing back the furs. "You cannot." He gasped at the pain in his ribs, then stood up. His eyes searched the chamber. "Now—my clothes, or at least some that will fit me, and weapons."

The sharpness of his voice seemed to push both the Keeper and Reyget out of the chamber. It struck Wandor that if he could go on giving orders this way, perhaps he could keep both Captains and Hearth Mothers too busy to quarrel until the fighting was over.

Reyget had his seal ship manned, provisioned, and ready for sea in two days. So did six other Captains, whose lands and families lay far enough from any likely enemies to be safe. They were joined by a good many men who followed no Captain at all. Seven ships in all would be sailing south with Wandor, and aboard them more than four hundred fighting men of the HaroiLina.

Wandor had expected to be leaving quickly on the voyage south. He had not expected to be taking with him an important addition to the attack on Yand. Indeed the squadron with him would be strong enough to take Galkor's ships if he could catch them. It would almost be strong enough for an attempt against Yand itself, if he could reach it before the fleeing Sea Folk did.

Sadly, Wandor realized he could do neither. Galkor had too

much of a head start, unless the weather turned against him in a way that was beyond all reasonable hope. Nearly a thousand armed Sea Folk in some thirty seal ships were also on their way to Yand. They would have joined Galkor's strength long before Wandor could hope to reach the island.

He would have to wait until he could strike with all his own strength, and meanwhile Gwynna would have to rely on the favor of the gods and her own wits and endurance. Neither was to be despised—but curse it, he would *not* see his world end under a stone inscribed:

HERE LIES GWYNNA DELVORA, THE BELOVED
OF BERTAN WANDOR AND AN EASY PREY TO
NO MAN

He wanted her lying nowhere except in his arms.

His orders to the Captains were strict. "No man must sail for Yand until I send word through the Keepers of the Hearth that you should all do so. If a few of you arrive before the rest, it will be your own death, at the hands of Galkor's men or the outlaws of the HaroiLina. It may also mean death for those who come after you. If Galkor is warned of what we plan, he may send word to Benzos. Cragor has enough fighting men there to array them shoulder to shoulder around the shores of Yand."

Not that the Duke could spare that many, but certainly he could send another two or three thousand. That would mean a long struggle for Yand, instead of a quick decisive stroke, and a certain death for Gwynna. She would die from the Beasts, under Cragor's tortures, by steel from Galkor's assassins, or by her own hand if she saw she had no way of avoiding one of the other fates. She would die, and leave Wandor to plod along after his destiny in the spirit of a pack mule who accepts the burden bound upon his back.

On the third day the waters of Stohra Bay gave up the body of Captain Daraun. Wandor saw him borne up from the shore and laid before the pillars of his own longhouse. Outside, men were piling the logs for his pyre.

In the evening they laid Daraun on the pyre and cast a torch into the oil-soaked straw packed beneath the wood. The flames rose around him, and Wandor stood watching beside the bronze urn that would hold the ashes when they were laid in the grave-barrow.

"He never had a War Name, did he?" Wandor asked of no one in particular.

No one in particular answered. Several men shook their heads. One Captain shrugged. "You know as much of his qualities as any of us. Was such a man likely to gain the Sea Father's great blessing of a War Name?"

Wandor would not disagree, but neither would he openly speak ill of a dead man who had certainly done his best. "Daraun had a good heart, and was filled with good intentions. That is certain."

The Captain who'd spoken nodded. "Then he should have the War Name of Daraun *Hutar Gona*—Daraun of Good Intent."

Wandor nodded in turn. He looked at the rising flames for a moment longer, then turned away. The pyre was still burning far off in the darkness when he boarded Reyget's seal ship.

CHAPTER 21

Wandor's voyage south was swift, with the men ready to break out the oars whenever the wind failed. Wandor held Mind Speech briefly with Cheloth, telling him what had happened and giving warning of his return. Cheloth had already learned much from the Keepers, but was glad to learn more from Wandor himself. He was not glad enough to admit this openly, but Wandor now had some skill in reading meanings lurking behind the words in Cheloth's Mind Speech.

There were three ships off the mouth of Fors Bay to greet the Sea Folk the day they sailed in from the Ocean. There was no panic this time, although there were no cheering crowds either. The people of Fors were not quite ready to believe that any of the Sea Folk could become friends. They were also busily at work on their own ships and weapons for the expedition to Yand.

Count Arlor was aboard one of the welcoming ships, but he and Wandor had no chance for private words until late that night. First there were the ceremonies of greeting, giving the Captains bread and salt, wine and flowers, the cautious thanks of the Civic Council of Fors and the still more cautious kisses of carefully selected young women, Then there was a parade through the streets to the castle, with men picked by Master Besz marching ahead, behind, and on either side, acting as guards as well as escorts.

After that there was a meeting of the full Council of the Viceroyalty, the first one in many months. Wandor let Arlor conduct it, and the Count was brisk and unsympathetic to those who allowed themselves to be carried away by the occasion—delivering orations instead of telling Wandor what he needed to know. Wandor found most of what he heard informative, and some of it even interesting. But all of it was exceedingly public, and his patience wore thin before the meeting ended and he could at last speak to Count Arlor alone.

Both men had much to say and some trouble in choosing words to say it. There was good news—the ships would be ready weeks earlier than expected. There was also bad news—Cheloth's warning of an awakening Power in the sea (which did not greatly surprise Wandor) and King Nond's warning that they must seek out the Ax of Yevoda on Yand.

"The Ax surprises me," said Wandor. "King Nond does not. I think we can rely on his aid in seeking the Ax." He told Arlor those details of what had happened among the Sea Folk that he hadn't seen fit to give in the open Council.

Whether the news was good or bad, one thought hung over both men and everything they said. Gwynna. The knowledge that she was a prisoner had not thrown the people of the Viceroyalty into despair. It had spread a furious determination to snatch her away from Beasts, Black Dukes, stubborn barons, and every other imaginable menace. A great deal could be done with that determination, if there were good planning behind it.

Wandor and Arlor called for food and wine and settled down to that planning.

Men called it Yand Island, but in fact it was four islands and assorted piles of rocks that were reefs at high tide and islands at low. Three of the four islands were of concern only to sailors who had to avoid them, and to the handful of fishermen and bird hunters who lived on each of them.

The fourth island was Yand itself, stretching a long day's ride on a good horse from north to south. Inland it was a tangle of coarse pasture, stunted trees, and fissured gray hills. Deep water lay close into shore on all sides, but there were only two landing places where a substantial fleet could anchor with some hope of safety. The voyage of Wandor's fleet would have to end, and the march of his army begin, at one of those two landing places.

From Berek's prisoners and from what the Sea Folk who'd heard Galkor had told Wandor, they had a good notion of how Yand would be defended. Galkor's men were all in the southern part of the island, where the only town and four of the five villages lay. The High Wizard allowed eighty of Galkor's men at a time as far north as the Beast Caves and the pit, to join his Warriors in guarding them. None were allowed north of the humped peak that sheltered the men and shrines of the Beast Cult.

Galkor's main camp lay just north of the principal town, and one landing place lay just south of the town. The beach there lay on the inward side of a peninsula forming the western shore of a bay. Across the neck of the peninsula, Galkor had raised a wall. It was nothing to stand a real siege, but more than enough to let even a mob of islanders and Sea Folk fugitives hold off an attacker until Galkor's men could reach the scene.

But even after the wall was passed, the only route north from it lay through the town. There the islanders could fight from cover they knew well, and they would be fighting for their homes. Even the least skilled of fighting men can be formidable when they have to be rooted out of cover and killed one by one. Long before Wandor's men could fight their way into the open, the Beast Wizards would be warned and Gwynna would be dead.

So much for the south. To land in the north meant landing farther from the heart of the cult and facing a longer march over more rugged land. But that land was virtually uninhabited, and there was some chance that the northern bay would be undefended. Time lost on the march could be more than regained by not having to fight their way off the beach. They might even come down on the shrines and the pit by surprise, and then some sort of victory would be inevitable. The Warriors of the Beast Cult could fight well, but they would be too badly outnumbered.

"If we can do nothing else then, we can free Gwynna," said Wandor. "I want to do much more, but that *must* be done. I will not be too cautious until it is done."

Arlor nodded. Anyone who looked at Wandor's face and still argued the matter deserved to be thrown into Fors Bay with a stone tied to his neck as too stupid to live.

Would the northern bay be undefended? Galkor would hardly divide his men to send a strong force that far north, even if the Beast Wizards allowed it. The fighting men of Yand had flocks and fields and fishing boats to care for. Few of them would readily go so far from their villages and camp in the wild.

That left the Sea Folk who'd fled to Yand in fear of Valkath's curse, of the fiery clutch of Nond, and of the wrath or greed of their neighbors. Unless Galkor contrived to get more men from Benzos the Sea Folk would be the most numerous force the invaders would face. They would not be the strongest, and there lay hope for the invaders.

Galkor's men would fight, and fight well, because he ordered them to do so. The people of Yand would fight bravely, for their lives and homes (which Wandor would spare if he could) and perhaps for the Beast Cult (which Wandor would cast down if he could). What would drive the Sea Folk into battle?

A leader? They had none whom all would follow. Foyn was among them, of course, but at the thought of his taking command both Wandor and Arlor laughed as though they'd heard a coarse jest. Homes and families? They'd already abandoned those. Even if by some chance they were allowed to return to their homeland they would be kinless, friendless, landless—hardly better than thralls. Yand Island? There'd been little love lost between the villagers and even those of the Sea Folk who worshipped the Beasts. More than a thousand wretched fugitives thrown down to devour the already scanty fish and mutton of Yand would not improve matters. Cragor? They'd taken his gold, but Cragor was not a man to be generous to those who could give him no further service. If the fugitives didn't know that already, Baron Galkor would be telling them now. Their lives? Yes, the fugitives would certainly fight for their lives, and they might be as desperate and dangerous in that fight as cornered bears. Suppose their lives were not put in danger?

"I want three things done on Yand," said Wander. "Gwynna rescued, the Beast Cult cast down so that it may never again be used against us, and Yand forever cleared of our enemies. I do not care whether those enemies die in battle, cast themselves off the cliffs along the shore, or board their ships and flee across the Ocean to the end of the world. Certainly I will not mind giving those we face a chance to save their lives if they will leave the island in our hands."

If the Sea Folk were in the south along with the rest of Yand's defenders, the fugitives would have a clear path to their ships and the open Ocean. Even if they were in the north, a promise of their lives and freedom if they would not fight might do the trick. Certainly Wandor would make that promise, and he would hold everyone who followed him to it.

"What about some of the Sea Folk who now follow us?" said Arlor. "They seem to feel they are at blood-feud with those who fled."

"They will have to lay aside their feud for the moment," said Wandor. "That will be my order."

"It will not be a popular order."

"No. But how much is the Spear of Valkath worth, if it cannot get obedience for my unpopular orders as well as the others?"

So they decided. They would be taking sixteen hundred fighting men to Yand. They would go ashore in the north, clear a path by promises or by the sword, and march south to the heart of the Beast Cult. They would land at dawn, leave the ships to the sailors, and move on the Caves and the shrines fast enough to reach them by mid-afternoon. They would have several hours of daylight left, to do whatever fighting might be needed against whomever they might face.

And then? Wandor shrugged. "This is a battle that will be coming at us in pieces. We can do nothing but take each piece as it comes, and meanwhile keep our men together. This will not be a battle with much room for subtlety or any skill except hard, close fighting."

Arlor was not so sure of that. He did not know what the search for the Ax of Yevoda might demand, or when. He also knew there was no reason to speak more of the Ax. Wandor did not care to be reminded that he was hardly more than a stone, kicked along the path of his quest by forces above and beyond the world. He had already made a clear-headed war plan that would allow everything that unaided men could do to be done against the Beasts and their Wizards. Perhaps Cheloth or Nond or the Guardian of the Mountain or all three of them knew what more would be needed. But a man learned what such as those three knew only when they chose to tell it, and so far they had held their peace. Arlor would do the same.

He still did not care for this fumbling forward in misty ignorance, since he knew too well what it might mean. It might mean that in the hour when they came to the shrine, they would find—Arlor forced himself not to flinch from the picture—nothing but the bloody shreds that were all the Beasts had left of Gwynna.

Then the man would be torn out of Wandor, like the entrails from a butchered animal, though the king and the war leader might remain. There were times when Arlor was glad to be spared such a vulnerable spot, into which his enemies could so easily thrust a weapon. More often he envied Wandor the soaring joy that came along with the vulnerability. He would have given honor and fortune and twenty years off his life for there to be between him and Queen Anya what there was between Wandor and Gwynna.

CHAPTER 21

In Benzos it was the time when men began to sense the approach of autumn, scouting out the land for winter. They thought less of fighting or fleeing, more of firewood and patching the cracks in the roofs of huts where they might hope to pass the winter.

Captain Tagor was happy, seeing an easing of his burdens with the coming of foul weather. Because he was happy, Jaira was well-fed, well-clothed, warm, unbruised, and almost content with her situation.

Count Ferjor was hard at work, finding safe routes for messengers and safe men to follow those routes. He had to make sure that word could pass from one hand of Cragor's enemies to another even when the snow lay thickest.

Kaldmor the Dark came down out of the Hills, with the *limar* of Nem of Toshak riding beside him. The sorcerer rode with a warm glow inside him from triumph and from strong wine. He had given the *limar* every possible quality of a living man. Now it could use his own Powers where it stood and hold Mind Speech with him.

In Benzos, Duke Cragor considered Galkor's message asking for another two thousand men to hold Yand and supplies to feed them through the winter. His men and treasure were not endless. What of the harm Wandor could do if he took Yand?

Part of it was already done. The Sea Folk were turned away from him, toward Wandor, and this would not change whether he sent one man or ten thousand to Yand.

On the other hand, Gwynna was doomed. She would not see

winter, and more men for Galkor would not change this either. All Galkor could do with a stronger force was to defy openly the Beast Wizards by snatching Gwynna away from them and carrying her off to a more elaborate and fitting death in Benzos.

This was not worth two thousand men and all they would need. This was even less worthwhile when it would arouse the anger of the Beast Wizards at the loss of their grand sacrifice. With the friendship of the Beast Wizards, on the other hand, Cragor had as firm a grip on Yand Island as he could hope for. With Kaldmor's aid the Beast Cult would hold Yand more securely than any number of fighting men that could be spared from Benzos.

The Duke decided he would not send the men. He would sent Kaldmor and the *limar*, as soon as possible, and also give Galkor a free hand with those men he already had. No questions would be asked of the Baron as long as Wandor never again embraced anything but Gwynna's bloody corpse and the Beast Wizards remained friendly. If by some chance Galkor still saw a way to snatch Gwynna off to Benzos—well, if he could think of a way to do this without the Beast Wizards suspecting him...

Soberly, Cragor knew there was small hope of that, and mourned the lost pleasure of Gwynna's slow death. But better a lost pleasure than lost allies, when one had to choose.

Galkor sat on his horse, the only one on Yand Island. He'd asked for a hundred more to be sent from Benzos, but he'd be surprised to receive more than a "Do you think horses grow on bushes?" or words that meant the same.

This was true. It was equally true that a hundred horses or even a hundred mules could keep Yand far safer. The island was just too large to hold securely when only one man on it could move faster than his own feet could carry him.

Galkor looked down the slope to the bottom of the ravine. Twenty of the Beast Wizard's Warriors stood in a line across the middle of the ravine. Eighty of his own men were marching up the ravine toward the guards. Beyond the guards eighty more of his men were marching toward them from the opposite direction. Beyond them, at the head of the ravine, rose the mountain of the Beasts.

The Beast Caves and the great pit before them were invisible, around on the eastern slope of the mountain. But Galkor could see every detail of the long, low stone buildings that held storehouses, quarters for the Wizards and their servants, and the stout cells for the sacrificial captives. The Baron's gaze shifted up and down and across the mountainside, taking everything into his memory. By now it would have been easy for him to find his way around the mountainside on the darkest of nights.

He'd been coming here every three days since the Beast Wizards agreed to have his men aid in guarding the mountain and the shrines. Every three days the eighty who'd been on guard marched out and eighty others marched in. The Beast Wizards insisted on that, and Galkor didn't mind in the least. Day after day, week after week, every one of his men was learning his way around the home of the Beast Wizards. A time might come when their knowledge would lead them swiftly to Gwynna's cell, to add terribly to Wandor's defeat or at least tear away some part of his victory.

He would not do this if the Beast Wizards went about their sacrifices as planned, and on the appointed day cast Gwynna down into the pit and into the claws and teeth of the Beasts. He would not do it even if some of the Beast Wizards found some reason or whim to delay the sacrifice as long as a proper "accident" could be arranged to do the work of the Beasts. He would only do it if there were no other way of seeing Gwynna dead before he himself left Yand, whether for Benzos or for the House of Shadows.

Galkor shook himself like a wet dog. He was not being quite wise, thinking such thoughts. They had the ring of Cragor's grim obsession with seeing Gwynna die by torture. They also might reach the awareness of Mykto or some of the other Beast Wizards. Ever the High Wizard, old as he was, seemed to have gifts far better not tested.

Of course, Mykto might be on his side. The younger Wizard seemed to be bored and not afraid to show it when the High Wizard rambled on at tedious length about the proper time for the sacrifice. But seemings were not certainties. Mykto might not be giving his superior total obedience, but that didn't mean he would give Galkor any useful aid.

Even if Mykto had notions that might make him an ally, there was still Telek the Fatherless. He played no man's game except his own, followed nothing except his own whims, and was most often found in places where he was least wanted. Beyond going where he wanted to and seeing what he wanted to see, Telek did not take much advantage of the awe and fear most people felt toward him. Even that was enough to make him a grim and ever-present menace to any plans that required secrecy for their success.

If death came to Telek some night—? Yes, but who had the courage or skill to match against Telek's? He could make the attempt himself, of course. But what if he failed, to die and leave his men leaderless amid uncertain friends and likely to be facing certain enemies?

The two parties of his men had passed each other now. Galkor turned his horse and rode down the slope, to join the departing men and ride south with them.

Gwynna sat cross-legged on the floor of her cell, wrapped in a light blue robe. She remained motionless except for slow, regular breathing, until she heard the sound of footsteps in the passage outside her cell door. Then she stood up, dropped her robe to the floor, and began doing a complex series of exercises.

One movement, one posture flowed smoothly into the next. At every possible moment she held herself so that her body seemed to breathe a warm sensuality. She did not have to do this merely to keep her muscles firm and her limbs supple and skilled. She did it in the hope of doing something to the men watching from the passage outside.

The Beast Wizards and their servants were supposed to be celibate. Most of the Initiates and some of the servants were young men, for whom no amount of dedication could make such self-denial easy. Galkor's soldiers were not celibate, but they had few women for their use. Watching Gwynna exercise, her body a glorious chant of praise to what they were denied, could hardly leave Beast Wizards or soldiers with their peace of mind completely intact.

Perhaps this would sow a little confusion among her enemies, or at least give Baron Galkor one more problem to face. The more confusion among her enemies, the better. Yet if all that happened was a few nights of disturbed sleep for those who saw her, it was still worthwhile. Even to hope that she was chipping away at her enemies' peace of mind did much to give her a firmer grasp on her own. She needed all the calm she could achieve, and modesty was a very small thing to set against that need.

She was almost healed of the small wounds she'd taken the night of the escape and the battle. The food and the healing skills of the Beast Wizards took care of that. She could use no spells to slow her healing and keep herself too flawed for sacrifice. The Powers that Mykto and others could bring against her would be too great. She was cut off from Mind Speech and outside aid by those same Powers, and also by something she sensed hanging over the Ocean, like a mist that somehow held life, rising from deep within the water.

She was alone, with the day of the sacrifice drawing closer and closer. There was nothing in the cell she could use to choose another death. Every surface was padded, she was given no tableware, the window was too high to reach, and the robe that was her only garment was too light to make a rope. As for her Powers, Mykto could strike them down long before she could use them to plunge into the House of Shadows.

She was alone, and she would be alone on the day of her death. She could imagine far too clearly everything that would happen to her and every sensation she would feel on that day. At times those imaginings made her whimper and bite at her robe, in fear that was no longer that of a warrior but that of a child who sees monsters lurking in the darkness about her.

CHAPTER 23

Twenty-five ships drifted sluggishly on the Ocean, like bits of meat on the surface of a simmering pot of soup. Seventeen were sailing ships, ranging from a North Ocean whale hunter up through *Red Pearl* to *Silver Crown*, bearing the name of a royal greatship and nearly as large as one. She also bore Bertan Wandor. The eight others' were seal ships of the Sea Folk, including Berek's *Fire of Elya*, Captain Reyget's *Horned Snake*, and six more. All drifted as though they had neither plan nor purpose nor place to go in all the world, their sails hanging limply from the yards, their crews sprawled as limply in boredom and weariness on the decks.

By themselves the seal ship crews might have broken out their oars and crept off toward Yand. But they could hardly row all the way to Yand without exhausting themselves. Nor could they afford to leave behind the sailing ships that carried most of the fighting men, and there was no way they could tow the sailing ships for more than a day or two. Wandor's fleet needed a wind.

They'd come north along the coast of the Viceroyalty, beating their way against the northwest wind. In time Captain Thargor saw from the land to starboard and the sun overhead that they had only to sail due west and they would probably fetch Yand Island. The ships came about, and in that very hour the northwester died. Puffs of wind blew from other quarters for a few more hours, then they died also. The fleet lay to, the coast of the Viceroyalty still visible astern.

Now they'd been drifting for six days, and if hope was not yet dying it was at least sickly. Certainly something was dying inside Bertan Wandor. He ate little, slept less, and spent the greater part of his waking hours pacing the deck of *Silver Crown* until the soles of his boots began to wear thin. There was no reason for him to do anything else. The ship captains and the sailors knew their work. Master Besz, Sir Gilas Lanor, and Berek would not let the fighting men grow slack. Jos-Pran would see to the horses, and Cheloth and Zakonta would do all they dared to hold Mind Speech with the Keepers far to the north. It was not worth bothering any of these people, to give useless orders merely to deafen his own ears to the mad voices whispering insistently that Gwynna was already dead.

The voices grew louder. Wandor's face grew gaunt with the effort not to listen to them and his body began to lose more flesh than it could spare. From the foredeck of *Fire of Elya* a hundred paces astern, Berek and Sir Gilas could see Wandor change almost from one morning to the next. They saw it; they talked of it in low tones; they heard the whispering voices themselves; and they felt as helpless as Wandor. Like his Master, Berek took to pacing the deck of his ship. Sir Gilas would have joined him, except that Berek prevented it. The Knight had walked aboard *Fire of Elya* with a dozen fighting men of his own household, but he had no strength yet to throw away on anything except the battle which would come when they reached Yand.

If they reached Yand. The voices began to whisper that also, not only to Wandor but to everyone with an ear to listen. There was only so much food and water aboard the ships. With good luck they might eke out their supplies with fish and rainwater, but what wise man would now rely on good luck? Sooner or later they would have to put in to shore for water and fresh food. By the time they put to sea again, Gwynna would long since have been nothing but fragments of stained bone in the Beast Caves. Certainly also Galkor would have enough word of their coming to be ready for them. Perhaps he would even have enough men and ships on hand to hold Yand against any attack the fleet could deliver.

Then what? Return home, no doubt, and join with the ships that would be coming south from the lands of the Sea Folk. By then it would be too late in the year to strike at Yand. Wait until spring? Yes, and leave Galkor with a whole winter to tighten his grip on the island.

What would face them in the spring?

Would the duel over Yand go on, with each side gathering more and more ships to carry more and more men to the island, until the sheer weight of fighting men and weapons made it sink below the waves of the Ocean? The voices did not whisper this last nightmare, they shouted it out like Chongan auctioneers in the Brass Market of Old Dyroka.

On the morning of the ninth day Wandor came on deck to find no more wind than on the previous eight. He could wet a finger and hold it up without being able to feel one side growing cooler than another.

He could no longer believe that this calm was anything natural. Captain Thargor had already plainly said as much and other captains who did not know Wandor so well murmured it when they thought he was out of hearing. Those who murmured would be calling this fleet accursed before another week passed. In a week after that they would be saying that the curse was upon Wandor and his cause.

Wandor did not let the murmurings worry him. He could not feel real anger against men who saw themselves as dolls the gods might rend apart at a whim, not when his own feelings were so often like theirs. What did matter was the shrinking chance of saving Gwynna.

Wandor knew that chance still existed, because he knew Gwynna was not dead. She lived, and because he was sure of this he could now ignore those voices that whispered or shouted otherwise. To save his life he could not have said how he knew this. There was no Mind Speech with her, not as long as the Ocean and what it held was between them, and the Beast Wizards were watching on Yand. Yet in Wandor's mind and body there was the certainty that he would feel the moment when Gwynna's life was torn from her. He had not felt it, so it had not come. Gwynna still lived, and if they reached Yand soon enough she might go on living.

The winds were being held back. Wandor wanted them released. That meant calling Cheloth. It also meant all the usual dangers which came from the working of great sorcery and many more besides. Wandor hoped he would not have to listen once more to Cheloth explaining those dangers. He'd already done so often enough.

He called a messenger and ordered the man into a boat, to row across to Cheloth's ship and bring the sorcerer back to *Silver Crown*. By Cheloth's wish, they used no Mind Speech out here on the Ocean, for fear of attracting from that which lay in the water more attention than it had already given them.

Wandor paced for an hour before the boat returned with Cheloth and the three Khindi—a Tree Sister and two warriors—who accompanied him everywhere. Like a young sailor racing to the masthead on a wager the sorcerer darted up *Silver Crown*'s side and came aft to stand before Wandor. From the way Cheloth held his silver-encased head and green-clad body, Wandor could almost believe the sorcerer was ready to receive commands and do his bidding. Yet that was imagining that Cheloth had become human, at least in spirit, something altogether against nature.

They spoke together in the extreme stem of the ship, while the Khindi and Count Arlor held the crew safely beyond earshot.

"Cheloth, we need wind."

"You need wind. Is that not a better way of saying it?"

No, Cheloth had not become human. Would he understand what must be done, in spite of that?

"This fleet must come to Yand quickly, whether Gwynna lives to await us there or not. Otherwise nothing will come of all the work that went into getting us to sea. Gwynna is part of my...purpose." He could use no stronger word to the blank, shimmering silver helmet, although pain shrieked within him. "This fleet is part of your purposes as well, and you have never cast them aside."

"Indeed, I have not," said Cheloth. "I have also told you that I may find what I can do here upon the Ocean flawed, or leading in strange directions I cannot even guess. I have said that which is in the water should not be given cause to pay us more attention than it has already." He made a sweeping gesture that took in the whole seascape and the fleet frozen upon the water.

"You have said all these things," Wandor said, nodding. "I have heard them and understand them." His voice had the quality of a blacksmith's hammer and chisel at work, with each word sliced off like a length of red-hot iron.

"I don't care about any of them!" he shouted. Every man on

the ship heard the cry and jumped as if stung. "I don't care. I want Gwynna back. Bring her back to me, Cheloth. Don't let her die. Don't—" He turned away and wept.

After a time he heard Cheloth's footsteps receding. After another, longer time, he felt a hand on his shoulder, turned, and faced Arlor. Together they walked forward. Cheloth had already gone down into his boat, and it was well on its way back to his own ship. Wandor stood looking after it for a moment, then went below to his cabin.

As soon as he returned to his own ship, Cheloth also went below, vanishing into the depths of the hold. The two carpenters repairing barrels shot up the ladder to the safety of the open deck. The Tree Sister and the two Khind warriors pulled the hatch closed and sat upon it. The fleet settled down to wait for Cheloth to begin his work.

They never knew exactly when he began it, but they certainly knew when it began to take effect. Over the distant shore to the east the sky began to darken. First it was no more than a small cloud, rising unnaturally straight from a valley like a volcano's first up-spewings. Slowly it spread along the horizon, creeping over one crest after another in both directions and down into one valley after another,

"He's forming it over the land," Wandor murmured. "He's forming it over the land, so he can draw on all the Earth Power he has before it strikes the water. Bring it fast, Cheloth, bring it fast." He was aware of Count Arlor listening to the murmured words, then walking across the deck to stand at the far railing.

The darkness now stretched all along the eastern horizon and rose steadily higher into the sky. It was black and green, shot through at random moments with a shimmering blue fire that made Wandor choke with the pain of recognizing it. Once he'd known that shimmering blueness as witch-fire. It danced across the hills north of Castle Delvor the night that he and Gwynna first came together as man and woman. Now it played among the green and black of the dark wall Cheloth's Powers were calling up. The wall rolled forward across the land from which Cheloth had drawn it, toward the Ocean where Cheloth himself had only as much Power as that which lay in the water allowed him. Wandor prayed that he had done nothing to make the

Ocean's master unwilling to let Cheloth carry the fleet to Yand. He prayed, hoping that in his pain and fear for Gwynna he promised nothing he had no right to give.

The darkness passed from the land to the water, and suddenly it was everywhere. The only way to tell sky from sea was that in the sky there was more green than black, and in the sea there was more black than green. In his mind Wandor heard Cheloth cry out. There was anguish in that cry and Wandor feared that Cheloth himself had all at once sunk to the level of a toy for the gods. For the first time a fear swept through him that was strong enough to overpower his fear for Gwynna. Then Wandor no longer heard the cries in his mind. He felt a puff of wind on his cheek.

It came again, and then a third time. Wandor looked over the side as he felt a fourth puff, and watched the water ripple. Then he felt the wind begin to blow steadily.

The breeze was gentle at first, but grew rapidly stronger. Before long it was not a breeze at all, but a wind that raised the sea into waves. The sails overhead bellied out, filling with sharp cracks. Wandor heard the clatter of blocks and the *tunnnng* and groaning as rigging came taut. From below came more clattering, as sailors threw the tiller over to bring *Silver Crown* on to her course. The deck heeled sharply. Wandor tightened his grip on the railing and watched the other ships of the fleet. They were all doing the same as *Silver Crown*. Like a pack of vast, clumsy hounds turning on to the trail of a new scent, the ships turned their bows to the west. Tiny figures scuttled about their decks, furiously doing the hundred-and-one things necessary to make sure that the wind which could drive them to Yand would not instead drive them to the bottom of the Ocean.

Wandor heard Cheloth again. This time the sorcerer's pain was unmistakable. It was swiftly drowned out by Wandor's joy, roaring as loudly in his mind as the wind roared in his ears. The fleet was on the move again, the wind astern, bows toward Yand, course set, sails swollen round and hard. The fleet was on the move again, and Wandor had a moment's vision of a gigantic hand reaching out across the Ocean to close protectively around Gwynna and snatch her from the Beasts.

The wind grew stronger, until sailors had to scramble aloft to reef the mainsail. The waves grew higher, until black water rose above the level of the railing amidships and spray blew into Wandor's face. The deck under his feet was in ceaseless movement now, and his hands were growing numb from their grip on the railing.

The wind rose until the fore topsail blew out with a crack like a tree going down. Wandor could see that several other ships also flew rags of canvas where sails had been. Then the wind held steady, although Wandor heard an order—not meant for his ears, he suspected—to have the hold sounded.

Still, ships could drive onward before wind and waves like this for days on end. Wandor knew of several which had done so while fleeing from Benzos to the Viceroyalty. Surely this was just as desperate a voyage, with the same need to keep the sails spread and the sailors at their posts until the last possible moment?

Every hour for the rest of the day and on through the night, Wandor asked himself that question. Every time he had to shout the yes louder, to drown out the howl of the wind, the creaking of the ship's timbers—and by midnight, the distant *bunk-bunk-bunk* of the pumps at work keeping the water down in the hold. *Silver Crown* was a stout ship, stronger than most of the fleet. The lighter seal ships could ride the waves in a way the greatships could not, but even they—

No. No doubts or questions. Not until morning.

Morning came, and there was fear on the wind and the sea and in the eyes of the sailors. *Silver Crown* was driving under topsails only. The main course was furled and the fore course stripped clean from its yard.

"I would no order men aloft," said the sailing master. "They went themselves, and two went o'er side. After that..." He shrugged, and nervously pulled at both ends of his beard in turn. "I think, lord, ye'd best ask Master Cheloth to be puttin' some o' the wind back where he took it."

Count Arlor came up in time to hear the master's last words and glare at him. Wandor ignored both men and looked across the water. Three ships were in sight, a greatship, a seal ship, and the North Ocean whaler. The first drove under fore topsail only, the second under bare poles, the third had lost her bowsprit and seemed sluggish in rising to the waves.

At noon there was only a grim twilight upon the sea and the battered ships that drove before the storm. An hour into the afternoon the wind rose again. *Silver Crown*'s mizzen yard split, and by luck, or the mercy of whatever gods still held power here, it went overboard.

"If it come down through the deck..." the master said, and shrugged wearily. "The pumps do enough now, but more water comin' in..." Another shrug.

Now the seal ship alone seemed to ride easily. The greatship fought her way through waves that rose as high as her fo'c'sle, with not a hand's breadth of canvas showing. The whaler had lost her main topmast, and sometimes Wandor could see solid water sweeping across her waist. Once he saw a black figure go overboard with the water, arms and legs flailing.

This was not a storm sent by nature or by any sane gods. This was a storm risen out of the Ocean itself, filled with the Powers of what lay in the water, made to rise at Cheloth's call to show the truth of the sorcerer's warnings. What lay in the water could give the law to all else in the world if it chose. Cheloth's call for the wind had made it choose, and now the storm was blowing the fleet madly across the Ocean while it lay back and laughed. Wandor heard that laughter as clearly as he heard the madman's shriek of the wind. He wanted to shriek himself. Instead he clung more tightly to the railing. By now saltwater sores were forming on both hands.

Two hours into the afternoon, and the North Ocean whaler went down. She went down with Wandor's eyes upon her, diving into one side of a wave and not coming out the other. For a moment the foretop jutted above the white crest, then it too was gone. For another moment Wandor fancied he heard the screams of drowning men in his ears, and he was certain he heard the wordless call of Cheloth in his own mind.

He could do only one thing now, and that swiftly, while Cheloth was reaching out to him.

"Stop it," he said, the words forming on salt-caked lips as well as in his mind. "Stop the storm, Cheloth. Beg its pardon, for me, for you, for all of us. Stop the storm, and let the fleet live."

If the storm did not ease, the whaler would be only the first among the fleet to go down. Half of it might follow her, and not a man or a ship would reach Yand fit for battle. The hand would not reach out across the Ocean and snatch Gwynna from the Beasts. It could not—at least not without its strength withering from the storm as it reached out.

This is what it comes to when you rule and lead, thought Wandor. It comes to saving your men and your hopes for a greater victory, even though you must cast Gwynna down to the Beasts to do it.

It also came to a feeling that his soul was a desolate plain of black rock and cinder, with an icy wind blowing across it. He tried to say, "Forgive me, Gwynna." Neither his lips nor his mind obeyed. At last he went below and locked himself in his cabin. He had more than tears to hide from Arlor and the men of *Silver Crown*.

The wind died swiftly, before any more ships went down. For the rest of the day and all that night the fleet wallowed on the great swells, counting up the leaks, the smashed gear, the sprung spars, and the men swept overboard, bending on new sails and putting fresh men to the pumps.

Then the morning came, and with it a clean fresh breeze which seemed a messenger from gods a man could worship and honor, instead of cringing or groveling at the very thought of them. The wind filled sails and drove the fleet on toward the west, it dried decks and clothes, it blew fear from the sailors' minds and despair from Bertan Wandor's. It blew away everything from his mind except the gifts as a warrior and leader, given by generous gods and sharpened like one of his own swords by years of use. He drew out the maps of Yand and the sheets of notes on its shores, its land, and its defenders. He called for food and wine. Then he sat down to finish planning the battle which would lie at the end of this voyage.

Certainly the northern bay would be defended by now, and probably by more than Sea Folk. Galkor's men or the men of Yand would fight. How to deal with them so that they could do nothing to delay the march south? Apart from Gwynna, there were other reasons to get south as fast as possible. There seemed to be a number of places suitable for ambushes or delaying actions on the route from the northern bay to the Beast Cult's shrines. He would have to get his men past these places before he could be sure of fighting a battle in the open, where their training and weight of numbers could tell.

There were also the shrines and Caves themselves. Whatever the Wizards might choose to do with the Beasts and the Ax of Yevoda, it would probably take time. If they were surprised and given no time, would they be able to unleash their Powers?

Wandor refused to indulge himself in wild hopes. He studied the map instead. To the west of the bay, at the very northernmost tip of Yand, lay a small cove. Its entrance was narrow, so that only a seal ship under oars could get in safely. But men going ashore there could sweep south, into the rear of anyone holding the main bay. How many men? Enough to fight a pitched battle against the defenders of the bay. several times more than any one ship carried now. But...in the lee of one of the lesser islands to the north of Yand itself, the sea would be calm enough for small boats.

Yes. Send to the cove the largest of the seal ships, with Berek and Sir Gilas leading every man who could be crammed aboard her for a day and a night. It would be the best opening move they could make and the swiftest, when every hour gained was worth more than a chest of rubies.

CHAPTER 24

Foyn stepped out the door of the hut into mist and a hint of light which a hopeful man could have called dawn. Behind him he heard the soft padding of Telek the Fatherless in his *mungan's* shoes. It was remarkable how much Telek on the move sounded like a prowling wolf.

Foyn walked briskly along the path in spite of the mist. He'd walked it fifty times before, making his rounds of the camp, on the shore of the bay whose name none of Haro's children could ever hope to pronounce. He and his two hundred men had taken to calling it North Bay.

He slowed as he came to the place where the path turned toward the bluff and dropped sharply downward for a hundred paces to the camp of Galkor's sixty men. That path was full of twists and turns, loose stones to turn an ankle, and little drops to break one. It was also guarded by Galkor's men, who were more dangerous to the careless than ten loose stones and twenty unexpected turns. Very ready with their swords, they were, and not too ready to apologize for the kind of little affairs that already had two men of the HaroiLina dead and nine more being healed of their wounds. Ever since the High Wizard let Galkor's men into the north, they'd behaved as if they were the only true and chosen friends of the Beast Cult. Those of the HaroiLina who'd fled their homes because of their faith in the Beast Wizards would not endure this much longer.

Foyn reached the edge of the bluff, and Telek came forward to take the lead. In that moment it seemed that all the swirls in the mist and all the boulders on the ground transformed themselves into armed men. The men were all around him, in the garb and weapons of the HaroiLina, of mercenary soldiers, of the royal troops of Benzos. All wore white sashes across their chests.

They'd come in silence like hunting beasts. Now they had their prey in their grip. All the men Foyn could see and more who were invisible in the mist shouted war cries matching their garbs and stormed forward. They went down the path like logs hurtling down a mountain stream, seeming to skim over loose stones, leap down their own height without breaking stride, brandish swords and axes and pikes with more arms than men ought to have. Foyn whimpered. They weren't men. They were something Valkath had sent, to carry his curse across the water against those who'd served the Beast Cult.

The men swarmed past Foyn as if he and Telek were not there. Foyn turned as he drew his sword, to discover that Telek was indeed gone. His whimper of fear turned into a scream of rage, and his sword leaped out. He caught a passing shape in one arm, and a man of the HaroiLina turned to fight, ax against sword. Foyn drove down the man's guard and slashed him in the shoulder, slashed him again across the stomach, saw him go down, stepped forward to finish him—

A shape three times too large to be human stepped forward out of the mist and seemed to snatch the wounded man clear of Foyn's cut with one hand. Then it raised an ax as tall as a man and Foyn knew he faced Berek Strong-Ax and Thunderstone. Foyn's sword swung and the ax swept it out of his hands as if it had been a feather. The sword clattered on the rocks far down the slope. In the same moment the ax took Foyn in the right hip. It was the back of the ax head that struck Foyn, not the edge, so the stroke did not cut him in two. It merely smashed him to the ground, hip shattered, writhing, gasping, voiding bowels and bladder in fear and shock.

Berek loomed over him, then stepped aside. A thin figure stepped forward, the badge of Benzos' Order of Knights on his chest, sword raised.

"He is yours, brother," said Berek.

"My thanks," said the thin Knight. Now Foyn recognized him as the one who'd ridden so furiously after the raiders as they bore off

Wandor and Gwynna. Sir Gilas...Sir Gilas...

Then the pain struck. Foyn stopped thinking and began to scream. He did not scream long. Sir Gilas Lanor's sword came down, and Foyn Son of Thadul passed beyond the reach of all fortune, good or bad.

By the time the main fleet entered the bay and dropped anchor, a sea breeze had blown away the mist and day had come to the land. It was a half-hearted, dreary day, with low clouds that made one wonder what they might conceal; nonetheless, a day which would serve well enough for fighting.

Wandor came ashore, to find a pike stuck firmly between two rocks just above high-tide mark and Foyn's head stuck on the end of that pike. Along the black gravel beach the dead were laid out, a score from Berek's landing party and over a hundred of the enemy's. Galkor's men had asked for no quarter and had been given none. The Sea Folk had been spared when possible. More than a hundred and fifty of them had survived to sit wretchedly on the gravel, guarded by Berek and a circle of his men who seemed to be practicing grim and forbidding expressions.

Wandor led Count Arlor and Captain Thargor up to the prisoners. Berek bowed to Wandor and reported.

"Sir Gilas has gone forward with a hundred men to hold the pass from the bay. A message came from him an hour ago. There is no enemy in sight."

"Did anyone get away from here?" asked Wandor.

"It is certain that none of Galkor's men did," said Berek. "Of the HaroiLina, it is not known. Certainly no more than a handful can have reached the hills."

"And they won't have enough of a lead to reach the shrines before we're clear of the last pass," said Wandor. "Well done, Berek. As for these—" He swept a chill stare across the prisoners, and watched them cringe. Then he turned to face them, raised his voice, and also raised in both hands the Spear of Valkath.

"Children forsaken by Haro and cursed by Valkath, hear me. I grant you your lives, the clothes you bear on your backs, and, in time, a safe passage to some other land. I have no great quarrel with fools who have already been punished and may yet be punished more by gods not so forgiving as I am." He turned his back on them before any could speak or even attempt to meet his eyes and walked away.

A few score paces off, Wandor turned. "Captain Thargor."

"My lord Viceroy?"

"Have those prisoners taken out to the ships as fast as the boats return from landing the soldiers. Divide them among three or four seal ships. Berek!"

"Master?"

"Take command of the ships with the prisoners aboard. As soon as we've marched out of sight, weigh anchor and turn south. Steer inshore just north of Gsed Point—they won't be able to see you from the fort or the town on South Bay. Set the prisoners ashore there."

"Master!"

"Berek, we have no time to argue the matter of your right to accompany me into battle. Think what will happen when these fools come running up to their comrades, crying that Wandor has come to Yand but will spare all the HaroiLina who do not stand against him?"

Berek's mouth snapped shut on any further protest. He threw back his head, to give a great shout that mixed joy and laughter and vengeful triumph. Then he bowed again. "As you wish, Master."

Cheloth touched Wandor's mind.

("For now, my work is done. No spells that any Beast Wizard can cast will reveal your men. But do not think that because of this you need not make haste.")

Wandor ignored the note of strained temper. In so far as Cheloth had a physical body, it was for the moment a sadly weakened one. To raise and then lay the winds in the face of that which was in the water had pushed Cheloth close to the limits of even his Powers and resources. The sorcerer could hardly admit this, of course, but the veiled phrases and the bite in every word told Wandor all he needed to know.

("We will make haste. Have you sought out any messages from the shrine?") That meant from Gwynna.

("I listen. There is Beast Magic at work there, but do not yet ask for the names of the spells or what they mean.") If Cheloth could not answer those questions, he doubtless had sufficient reasons, though perhaps unpleasant ones.

("Listen well, Cheloth. We will do our part.")

("One may hope so. You are part of my purposes, and those purposes are very far from accomplished yet.")

When Cheloth spoke like that, it was wise to break off the Mind Speech. Wandor did so, and turned to the matter of getting his fighting men ashore.

Galkor's servants took great care to dress him more carefully than usual, in spite of the curses spraying about their ears. The Baron's head throbbed from last night's wine. The continuous *pum-pum-pum* of ceremonial drums and the occasional harsh horn calls didn't ease the throbbing in the slightest.

At last he felt himself fit to do the Beast Wizards proper honor at today's sacrifice. His head still ached, his mouth still felt sour and wool-packed, and doubtless this showed. The High Wizard would probably consider that Galkor was not in a truly proper state of purity to watch the sacrifice. Mykto would speak up for him in this matter, however; so let sea snakes bite the High Wizard on his bony behind!

Today Gwynna would be cast down to the Beasts, and the taste of that victory would surpass any wine that any man or god had ever tasted. He had waited long enough, and done much more than wait. Today the waiting and the struggle would end. It would not end in a way entirely pleasing to Duke Cragor, who would see a great pleasure snatched away from him for all time. But Cragor would also have to admit that Gwynna sent swiftly down into the House of Shadows was better than Gwynna returned to Wandor's side.

The victory was even more satisfactory, in that no shadow of blame could fall on Galkor for not snatching Gwynna from the Beast Wizards before the sacrifice. Galkor would have done his best in the matter, given half a chance, but the Wizards had given him none at all. Five days before, the High Wizard suddenly ordered Galkor's men from the shrine's precincts, out to well beyond easy striking distance of the mountain either by day or by night. Only Galkor himself, one chosen captain, and four men were permitted on the slopes of the mountain now, and they without armor and with no weapons but swords. Someone among the Beast Wizards had a shrewd eye for other men's possible intrigues. Was it the High Wizard or, perhaps, Mykto? Probably Mykto—the High Wizard seemed to have no attention for anything except the condition of Gwynna (who was in considerably better health than Galkor) and the proper conduct of the sacrifice (which would mean some nine hours of standing for the baron today).

Galkor stepped out the door and winced as the massed horns blew a particularly raucous blast. With the best possible combination of haste and dignity he trotted down the stone stairs, his cloak flowing behind him. The sky overhead was sullen and sunless. Let it stay that way, thought Galkor. The sun need not smile on the sacrifice, or so the High Wizard says, and I'd rather not stand on a bare slab of rock in the full sun for nine hours with neither food nor drink nor any other comfort or convenience.

Yet he knew that he would have been there to watch the sacrifice even if he'd had to stand on a plate of hot iron in his bare feet. He hadn't felt such delighted anticipation since he was fifteen and paying his first visit to a brothel nor such triumph since he'd been made a baron for good service to the Kingdom of Benzos. (In truth, it had been for service to Duke Cragor, but Letters Patent could lie almost as glibly as whoremongers or Chongan moneylenders.)

At the bottom of the slope the procession was forming—all the people who would stand by the lip of the pit before the Beast Caves that day, to conduct the sacrifice in which Gwynna would die. There was the High Beast Wizard, there was Mykto, and there were three other Beast Wizards who were no more than faces to Galkor. There were nine Warriors of the Cult and four unarmed Initiates. The Warriors had helmets on their heads and swords and daggers belted on over their robes. Three carried spears.

Gwynna herself lay on a litter of polished driftwood. She wore a robe of blue Chongan silk that covered her from her throat to ankles. The ankles and the wrists were both firmly bound with silvered cord. Her head was free, but as motionless as if it too were bound in place.

Had fear at last gripped her? Perhaps. One reason the Beast Wizards did not drug the sacrifices was that they were more often than not too stricken with fear to move.

Galkor stepped closer, and Gwynna's eyes met his. It was like a sword meeting a shield and cutting halfway through it at one blow. Some of Galkor's sense of triumph crumbled to dust and blew away in the breeze that rippled the skirt and sleeves of Gwynna's robe.

It was not fear—not in those eyes or in the body and mind behind them. It was something else—many things that Galkor could not have named even if he'd thought it wise to try. Her attention was certainly not on the world around her, but neither was it on the death this day would bring her.

She could not cast spells, not with all the Beast Wizards around—or so Galkor wanted to believe. Furtively, so that the High Wizard would not see him, he made the conventional gesture of aversion from the rites of the Five Gods. Perhaps Beast Wizards did not matter, in the face of a will like Gwynna's. If she could put her witcheries to no other use, she would at least see that the Beast which ate her died of a stomach ache!

Let her. It would be worth every Beast on Yand, and all the Beast Wizards and Beast Wizards' Warriors and servants as well, to have Gwynna safely dead. It would be worth Yand Island and everything on it—save perhaps Galkor's own men and the ships to take them home—to have Wandor bound on another litter beside Gwynna.

Homs blared again from high on the mountain. The four Initiates picked up the litter, and the procession began to move.

Wandor saw a man riding back toward him with another report from the mounted scouts. Then he felt the fumbling touch of someone trying to form a Mind Speech link with him. It was so weak that he could not recognize it. Was the source feeble, the distance impossibly great, or were the Beast Wizards doing too much to interfere? He reined in his horse and sat motionless in the saddle, controlling his breathing, closing his eyes, shutting everything else out of his awareness in order to make his mind more receptive.

Far away at the other end of the link someone sensed Wandor's receptiveness. In one moment the link was like a flame suddenly roaring up, strong that Wandor cried out with the pain. In the next moment it faded almost out of existence, as if the flame had been blown out. Then the link became strong and solid again, and now it poured its message into Wandor's mind. He cried out again, but now there was more than pain in his cry.

It was Gwynna reaching out to him. He was not and could not be mistaken. Gwynna's mind and his struck sparks like flint and steel when there was Mind Speech between them—sparks which took their heat from shared images, shared memories, shared feelings good and bad, shared passion.

It was Gwynna reaching out to him, her message completely clear although coming in flaring images without words. She was alive; she was healthy in mind and body; but death was only a few hours away, and she could not lift a finger or work a single spell to save herself. She showed Wandor the pit that yawned beyond her feet, the mouth of the Beast Caves on the far side of the pit, the Beast Wizards, Warriors, and Baron Galkor standing around her. She made him hear the chanting, the solemn incantations, the distant thunder-rumble of the aroused Beasts.

Then the link dissolved. Wandor caught the faint hint of someone trying to hear what was no longer there to be heard, then his mind was empty until roaring exaltation filled it. Gwynna lived! The exaltation roared on for a moment, then fear tightened itself on his chest and stomach like a great snake. Gwynna lived, but she was also to be sacrificed today. With desperate strength and control he drove both exaltation and fear from his mind and looked back along the line of marching men.

There were a dozen races and kinds of fighting men in the line, and a dozen different paces. By now they stretched away along the valley: thin here, clumped together elsewhere, the rear far out of Wandor's sight. All were stepping along at the fastest pace they could keep up over this kind of ground.

If he ordered his little army to plunge forward even faster, they might race up to the pit in time to save Gwynna. They might also break apart into scattered handfuls of exhausted stragglers, easy prey for the Warriors of the Beast Cult, let alone Galkor's men or the Beasts themselves.

He wanted to cry out wildly and see the army hurling itself forward. He wanted it with a physical passion, wanted it and knew he could not have it. In this moment his first duty was not to Gwynna, one woman, but to his army, fourteen hundred fighting men. Not one of them was holding back. It was his duty to hold his peace and hold them together.

Then Cheloth was in his mind.

("She reached you?")

("She did. Did anyone hear us?")

("As far as I can tell, no one.")

("How far can you tell, Cheloth?")

Silence.

("Can you stay linked with her?")

("Not now. They would take warning too soon. Certainly Mykto and therefore Galkor, perhaps others. Then you would face the Beasts.")

("What will you do?")

("Wait. When your men are climbing the mountain to the pit, the Beast Wizards will not be keeping such a careful watch. If Gwynna goes to work then, I can aid her.")

("And if she can still do nothing?")

Silence.

The silence went on until Wandor realized there would be no answer. He broke the link and turned his mind to guiding his horse over a particularly rough patch of ground.

Patches of thin cloud toward the west showed fading sunlight. The day was wearing on. It was only a few hours to darkness. It was still fewer, thank all the gods twenty times over, to the end of the sacrifice and Gwynna's death. For the hundredth time Galkor shifted his weight from one aching foot to the other. For the hundredth time he tried to shut out the foul smells rising from the pit, and failed. For the hundredth time he ran his hands around his sword belt and wished he had his sword hanging from it, for his own peace of mind if nothing else.

He might do all of these things a hundred times more, and with as little effect as the first hundred times. The rites would go on in the proper fashion, hour after hour, though the sky might threaten to fall down on Yand. The smells from the pit would get no better, and they could not get worse. His sword would remain in the hands of one of the Warriors, and not Duke Cragor nor even Staz the Warrior could put it back in the scabbard on Galkor's belt.

He sighed and stared past the Beast Wizards. Mykto was now doing what looked like the dance of a man with bees in his breechclout. No doubt it had some profound meaning. Gwynna lay on her driftwood litter, as motionless and expressionless as ever. She seemed to have withdrawn all her attention from the world around her. Mykto would have noticed if she'd been doing anything with her Powers. He'd shot her one brief glance, about noon, but otherwise, he seemed satisfied that she was passively waiting for death. Galkor hoped the Wizard was right.

Beyond Gwynna the pit gaped, two hundred feet across and fifty deep. On the far side the Beast Caves opened their black maw to the world, exhaling more indescribably putrid odors and the swelling rumble of the Beasts.

On the far side of the pit the mountain rose steeply toward its humped summit. Galkor liked the thought of the steadily thickening layer of solid rock over the Beast Caves. He liked much less the way the slope dropped off steeply to his right. Only a thin rim of rock held the Beasts within the pit on that side.

Nonsense! The "thin rim" was a hundred feet of solid granite, weighing more than all the Beasts put together and beyond any living power to break or move. The Beasts would stay within their pit and do their work. It was his distaste for sorcery and being so close to where it was at work that spoke to him, nothing more. It would never be silent, either, but he would have the strength not to listen to it.

Put an end to it, he thought wearily. Put an end to it and to that cursed flame-haired witch. How does that old bastard's voice last? Mykto's younger, I can understand his lasting out the day, but—

Then his eyes stopped their casual search of the land to see the north beyond the pit. Between two of the gray hills he could see movement that should not have been there. He saw the familiar crawling dots that were marching men shrunk by distance, and out in front of them horsemen.

Horsemen.

Enemy!

The distant figures might have shouted the word in Galkor's ear, and echoes seemed to roll around the mountainside. He swallowed. So far none of the Beast Cult people seemed to have noticed anything. He took a step forward, to be stopped by a glare from one of the Warriors. Sacrifice her, he thought. End this nonsense and sacrifice her. Can't you see? Can't you understand? His lips moved, but no sound came out. His hands clutched futilely where his sword would have been.

Hours that were only minutes crept by. The High Wizard was now intoning a high-pitched walling song that sounded like a chorus of starving infants. To Galkor it was like an executioner pouring hot wax into his ears.

Sacrifice her, he thought again. Sacrifice her; sacrifice her; for the love or the fear or the honor of all the gods anyone believes in, *sacrifice her*! He would have liked to scream the words out loud, but didn't dare. There were three Warriors staring at him already. To draw more attention from them could only make things still worse.

Yet how could they become worse, if Gywnna were to escape? How—

Now a Warrior, silent but frantically waving his arms, was running up the path toward the Wizards. He caught Mykto's eye. Mykto stepped away from the pit to meet him. They spoke a few low-voiced words, none of which Galkor understood.

"*Doiiii-ya!*" Mykto's shout made Galkor start. It made the High Wizard quiver all over and break off his song to glare at Mykto. Then the words poured off the younger man's lips. Galkor ignored the Warriors to step as close as he dared, staring at the two Wizards. He watched the furious play of emotions across their faces—the thin wrinkled one and the thin tanned one—listening to their words without real understanding in the hope of learning something...anything.

Three times in rapid succession Galkor heard a word which sounded like "Yovawdah." Four times he heard what he knew was the Yandish word for "Beast." Twice the High Wizard shook his head, then a third time he nodded—very slowly, with his eyes squeezed shut and one hand gripping his beard as if he feared his head would fall off if he let go.

"Doiii-ya!" Mykto shouted again. He drew his staff from its hole in the rock and handed it to the High Wizard. Then he whirled, waved his arms at all the Warriors, and dashed away up the slope toward the entrance to the underground shrines. The Warriors followed him, almost falling over each other in their haste, drawing their swords as they ran. In moments they were gone, leaving behind the High Wizard with the two staves, the four Initiates, Gwynna on her litter, and Galkor with the knowledge of what was happening dawning terrifyingly in his mind.

Yevoda Slayer of Beasts was truth, not tale. He had slain Beasts with his spell-sown Ax, and that Ax still existed. Because it still existed, the High Wizard was going to release the Beasts, to slaughter Wandor's approaching army. Meanwhile, Mykto had gone to fetch the Ax of Yevoda from its hiding place, and when the Beasts had finished their work he would use it to drive them back to the Caves—or if all else failed, slay them. Faced with complete destruction, the Beast Wizards of Yand were making a complete response.

Galkor had neither time for prayers nor any hope they'd be answered. Instead his mind leaped to Gwynna. What would happen to her? Would the Beast Wizards think to put her in a place where she would certainly die long before Wandor could reach her? Galkor laughed aloud at the idea of the Wizards being so helpful. The High Wizard didn't notice him.

Galkor looked about him. There was no longer anyone on hand who looked capable of resisting him. Gwynna was bound and helpless. He had no sword; he could see no loose stones large enough to crush her skull; and he knew that strangling would be slow and uncertain against such a woman. But there was a fifty-foot drop only a few paces away. After that, the claws, teeth, and trampling feet of the Beasts would finish the job.

Galkor plunged forward. He bent, hands closing on one end of Gwynna's litter. He heaved with a strength that would have unseated a boulder or pulled a small tree up by the roots. The litter flew through the air and vanished over the edge of the pit. Gwynna screamed, the High Wizard howled a curse, and Galkor let out a roar of triumph. Then the litter struck with a soggy thump. The High Wizard drove both staves down against the rock with all his strength, and Galkor ran.

He'd won footraces as a boy, and now he ran even faster. He ran down the path, his heart going like the hammer of a mad blacksmith with fear and triumph and furious effort all together. Behind him he heard the roaring of the Beasts—and then another roaring, as rock crumbled and fell, opening a way for the Beasts out of their pit.

That had to do for the witch, if she wasn't already dead.

CHAPTER 25

Fear tore the scream from Gwynna, but she went on fighting even in the time of her fall to the bottom of the pit. She managed to land nearly flat instead of on her head, and on her back, with the litter under her, instead of on her face. She landed in a reeking muck of blood, mud, decaying flesh, the dung of the Beasts, reeds and rushes gone spongy with rot—a muck that could have suffocated her horribly if she'd landed face down. Instead the knee-deep blackness broke the worst of her fall.

The crossbar under her head smashed into the back of her skull like a club. Pain turned the world fire-shot gray for a moment, but she distinctly heard the wood of the litter crack. She waited only the brief moment needed to clear her head, then tensed all her muscles and heaved shoulders and legs upward. Cords bit into her wrists, but she also heard wood crack again. Another heave and the litter split apart. She could move and even stand, though awkwardly, with lengths of wood still bound to her wrists and ankles.

As she stood, the earth quivered under her and the walls of the pit did a stately dance. For a moment she thought they were about to come down on top of her. Instead only one part of the wall fell, and that was halfway around the pit from her.

For thirty paces the gray rock cracked apart into jagged chunks and slabs; the chunks and slabs settled down upon each other and crumbled into smaller pieces; and the smaller pieces became gravel and even dust, as though monstrous hammers were pounding them. A wall of dust swept across the pit, half choking Gwynna, and spreading a layer of gray over the black muck. Out of the dust cloud, chunks of rock fell around her splattering filth on her robe as she untied the last pieces of wood from wrists and ankles. She sensed the powerful spell that had gone to make the rock crumble, and desperately wanted the feel of the solid granite of Yand behind her. She backed away toward the wall of the pit.

Then the dust fell like the rock. Gwynna saw a ragged, new-made ravine floored with gravel, dust, and chunks of rock, leading out of the pit on to the lower slope of the mountain. Knowledge of what was coming struck her, and fear struck just behind it. She crammed a dusty fist into her mouth to keep from screaming, and for a moment her legs would barely support her, let alone carry her toward the wall. She stumbled as the spell-bound gate across the mouth of the Beast Caves slid down with a squeal and a crash. The wall was close enough to keep her from falling into the muck. She took the last two steps, turned, braced herself against the rock, and saw the Beasts of Yand come forth from their Caves.

It was said of the first High Wizard that he'd made the Beasts from the rock of the island itself. Gwynna could believe this. If the rock of Yand had been formed into things as long as a large fishing boat and as high as two tall men, and those things given life, breath, glaring yellow eyes, mouths that flowed with fuming green drool, teeth a foot long, scaled legs as thick as barrels and ending in claws—

Gwynna stopped trying to reduce what was coming at her to a list, for fear that her mind would crumble like the rocks of Yand and she would die whimpering, with nothing more that was human left in her than in the Beast that killed her.

The first Beast was now clear of the Caves, the second was emerging, a third was visible behind. How many would there be in all? Less than a dozen now, or so the tales ran. But they were tales. Here was the truth—living hills of flesh filled with hunger and rage and the spells of the Beast Wizards—coming out of the Caves toward her.

Now one of them had noticed her. The head dipped, the massive feet squelched into the mud, the tail that ended in a spiked club of bone rose as high as the mast of a small ship. Jaws opened, a rumble came out and turned into a hiss. Carrion-laden breath made her gag.

It would come at her in another moment, but before it did she would make one more effort to defend herself. She stripped off the robe and threw it down. She stood with her hands at her side, feet wide apart, forcing herself to breathe slowly and regularly, forcing herself not to clench her fists, letting her eyes drift shut as if she were falling asleep. She would take no attention, no strength away from the spells she was trying to work.

In the next moment she was gripped with sudden awesome strength in both mind and body. She felt herself bent backward until her head touched the wall and her spine seemed about to snap. She ignored dimly-sensed pain that should have been agony; ignored the fact that she was not falling into the muck as she should have been; ignored all the logic of the world around her. Like a Plains blizzard, Power raged through her, and she forced herself to be nothing except the best possible channel for that Power to come into the pit against the Beasts.

Cheloth was there as part of the Power, but he was no more than one bee in a swarm or a single voice in the shouting of an angry mob. Then he was not there at all. She forced her eyes open, drew herself straight, saw from the dim reflections around her that her hair was glowing, saw the Beast take another step toward her, then another. As though they had a will of their own, her arms rose. She spread out all ten fingers, then pointed them at the Beast.

Go back. Go back. *Go back!* She could not ignore the pain now, but the message was still there, and so were the Beasts. The pain was the least important thing in all the world for Gwynna.

Go back. Go back. *Go back!*

Wandor had already dismounted and started up the mountain when Cheloth reached out to him.

("The High Wizard has let loose the Beasts. Mykto has gone to bring the Ax of Yevoda from the main shrine. Seek him out.")

("Gwynna?")

("Gwynna is in the pit, facing the Beasts. She—")

A wordless cry of agony.

("Listen!"—It would have been a shout in physical speech—"Gwynna is working a spell to ward off the Beasts, with Powers that I do not clearly understand how she can use. I must aid her, or she may die as surely from what she is doing as from what the Beasts may do to her.")

("Help her, Cheloth. Help her—save her.")

No reply. Cheloth was gone, and Wandor ran on. Little pains began to flare in his chest and his legs. He ignored them. He could not ignore the *luor* of unchecked sorcery, a dozen spells all together, that was spreading across the island like lava oozing from a volcano. He could not ignore it, although he was normally one of the least sensitive of men to the presence of sorcery. What must it feel like for Cheloth and Gwynna, or even Zakonta and the Tree Sisters?

He stormed up the mountain. A Beast Cult servant ran at him, eyes wide and staring. He slowed to cut the man down with his sword, then saw that he'd been unarmed, fleeing in terror rather than coming out to fight. The pause gave Count Arlor and Sir Gilas Lanor time to catch up with Wandor. The Count's long legs seemed ready to carry him all the way to the southern end of the island. Sir Gilas was already panting and chalk-faced, but moving as fast as Arlor.

Behind him Wandor heard Master Besz's bull-roars, every word as clear as a trumpet's note in spite of this. "There are men of Galkor down that valley to our left. Men of Hushga, Dodor—take them! Yhangi, Khindi, royals—follow the Viceroy!"

Wandor didn't slow to watch his men divide. No one would disobey Besz. He ran on, and Sir Gilas and Count Arlor ran with him.

There was pain in every part of Gwynna's body, from the ends of every hair on her head down to the toes which were sinking deeper and deeper into the black muck. She could not have felt more pain if the jaws of a Beast had closed on her, and perhaps she would have felt less. But pain or not, her body was intact. She could feel that too, and she could see through the pain-haze that the Beasts were keeping their distance. Whatever she was doing and whoever was helping her do it, her "Go back" was reaching them and they were obeying it.

There were ten of the Beasts visible when a shudder went

through the whole mass of flesh. Then the Beast nearest the ravine leading to the mountainside took a ponderous step forward, a second, then two more in rapid succession. Suddenly it was running—or rather lumbering—covering ground as fast as a fleet-footed man in spite of its bulk. It lumbered through the ravine, crunching rocks underfoot and raising a trail of dust. The other nine turned slowly, butting against each other, hissing and growling, and snapping their jaws with the sound of iron-bound doors closing. Then they were following the leader out of the pit and out on to the mountainside.

Finally, they were gone, and for Gwynna only the pain remained. Her arms fell and she sobbed out loud. She felt tears on her cheek and the salt taste of blood from deep-bitten lips. She felt her knees turn to liquid, and she fell forward. At the last moment she was able to turn so that her face was out of the muck. She lay for a moment, wondering vaguely what the Beasts would do out on the mountainside. Then the pain and everything else went away.

Wandor's men were upon the mountain now, and they numbered at least five to one against the Warriors of the Beast Cult. The Warriors were brave and skilled, but not brave enough or skilled enough to stand against such odds. None of them fled. Most of them died quickly. A few of the unarmed servants tried to flee, but they did not get far. Wandor's men swarmed up and down the narrow alleys between the houses, through the cellars and across the roofs of the houses themselves, out on to the mountainside beyond. They had no plan or purpose except to kill every living thing that served or might serve the Beast Cult. No other plan was needed.

Even if they had needed one, Wandor could not have given it to them. With Arlor and Sir Gilas on either side of him, he was far below the surface of the mountain, in the deeper twilight of the tunnels and caves twisting downward toward the central shrines of the Beast Cult. This was where Mykto had gone for the Ax of Yevoda, or so Cheloth and Wandor's own instincts told him. He would not think of what might happen if both were wrong.

In the tunnel between the seventh and eighth caves the last Warriors of the Beast Cult were waiting. In the narrow passage only three men could fight on each side, and no three Beast Cult Warriors were a match for three such masters of the sword as Wandor, Arlor, and Sir Gilas. But the Warriors could sell their lives slowly, winning time as they died. Wandor could spare his own blood far better than time. He drove in with reckless fury, and twice Count Arlor had to save him from thrusts or slashes which would have brought him down. The second time, Arlor himself was wounded. He fought on, but there were still seven of the Warriors standing across the path to the shrines and to Mykto.

Then the rearmost man rose into the air, as if an invisible net had lifted him. He rose more than his own height, then suddenly seemed to lie at full length on the empty air. His swollen eyes showed nothing but white, and his gaping mouth showed a tongue flapping like a dying fish. Then smoke swirled up from his throat, as the flesh there turned black, crumbling into ashes, falling away to expose bare bones that in turn became black. Life went out of the man in a cloud of greasy smoke, and the body crashed to the floor.

The other Warriors forgot the enemy to their front and turned to gape at what was striking their rear. A second man rose into the air. Wandor cut down another. Then the remaining four broke and ran.

Wandor and his companions strode forward. For a moment it seemed that golden light washed about them and two immense, golden eyes looked at them from all directions at once. Then they were running. They ran through two more caves, and burst into the chamber which held the Beast Cult's central shrines.

On the far side of the domed chamber stood an image of one of the Beasts, white whale ivory set with sea jade, rising on a black marble pedestal. From a hole in the base of the pedestal Mykto was drawing a two-handed ax, with a double-edged head of blued iron.

Mykto whirled as the three men burst upon him, then ran toward a niche in the wall of the chamber. From a hole in the top of the niche gushed a stream of silver-green water, falling soundlessly out of sight below the bottom of the niche.

Wandor realized what Mykto hoped to do. That water fell down into a shaft of unguessable depth. If Mykto cast the Ax down there it would be past easy recovery. He could no longer hope for victory, but he could hope to drag his conquerors down with him.

Wandor had no throwing knife, but he did have his Duelist's sword, and he knew everything there was to know about that weapon and what could be done with it. He tossed it, caught it by the blade, and hurled it. The weighted hilt caught Mykto in the temple, a glancing blow that was still enough to make him miss a step on the damp floor and go down. Before he could rise or hurl the Ax toward the niche Wandor was on him.

Mykto screamed, froth on his lips, and struck at Wandor with a dagger and a hand twisted into an animal's claw. Wandor gripped the dagger by wrist and elbow and snapped it. Then he chopped the edge of one hand down across Mykto's throat. Before the Beast Wizard stopped writhing, Wandor was on his feet again, the Ax of Yevoda in his hands.

It was no heavier and no lighter, no sharper nor blunter, no better-balanced nor clumsier than any other such ax in the style of the Sea Folk. There was no need for it to be otherwise. The spells that slept within it were as weight-less as the smoke from a fire. The work it was meant to do would be done by those spells. The Ax only held them like a casket holding jewels.

Wandor took a firm grip and swung the Ax in the widest circle he could make. It hissed in the heavy air of the chamber. He would need to strike the Beasts from as far away as possible, to keep clear of the teeth and claws and lashing tails, and he would need to strike as hard as possible. He did not know how quickly the Ax-spells would work on the Beasts he struck; and as a Duelist, he knew too many tales of dying men who still slew their enemies.

He retrieved his sword, thrust it into his scabbard, and swung the Ax up on one shoulder. "Take care of the men while I go to Gwynna."

"But—the Beasts?" said Arlor.

"Gwynna," said Wandor. He knew he would neither think nor act to any good purpose now until he had with his own hands taken a living Gwynna from the pit and seen her safe.

The tunnels and caves seemed to have shrunk between their coming in and their going out. It seemed to Wandor that he and his companions took no more than fifty steps before they were climbing the last stairs amid a crowd of their men. Wandor brushed past them as if they'd been ghosts.

He plunged down the mountain toward the pit. Behind him Arlor and Sir Gilas did their best to keep up. It seemed to them that men stepped from Wandor's path before they could see him. If a building had been in his path, he would have gone through it without harm; or it would have sunk into the earth rather than delay him.

They came to the edge of the pit, to find the High Wizard standing there, hands clasped on his chest, head bowed, lips moving in an incantation. He turned as Wandor ran up, and his arms flopped bonelessly as he saw the Ax of Yevoda in Wandor's hands.

"Aiiya!" he said. It seemed to Wandor that the High Wizard had called up all the despair in the world and put it into the one sound. Then the old man took two steps forward, and a third out into the empty air. He landed only a few paces from the pale, sprawled form of Gwynna.

Wandor dropped the Ax and reached out with his mind as he ran toward the ravine leading to the pit, listening for some sign of life from Gwynna. He sensed nothing. He found a place where the wall of the ravine would let him pass and plunged down the treacherous surface in leaping strides.

He came up to Gwynna and called her name. She did not answer. He knelt beside her, laid a hand on her breast and another on her lips. Then, high above, Arlor and Sir Gilas started at the wild cry that echoed around the pit.

"She lives!" He lifted her in his arms. "She lives," he said more softly, kissing a cheek black with bruises where it wasn't black with caked muck.

He didn't have to wonder about the High Wizard. The old man lay with his head at an impossible angle to his shoulders. Both his luck and his bones had been more fragile than Gwynna's. Wandor lifted Gwynna and turned back toward the ravine.

Zakonta rode up on Jos-Pran's horse as Wandor carried Gwynna out of the ravine. She sprang down from the saddle, pulling off her cloak as she came. "Leave her with me," she said. "The Beasts are among the men, and the Ax is needed." Wandor saw red fire in the wide gray eyes and heard steel in her voice. "Go! You cannot heal her, and your men are dying."

So perhaps is Gwynna, he thought. He would not ask, though. He didn't want to know, at least until he'd finished the rest of the work he'd come to Yand to do.

Wandor walked back up the mountain to where he'd left the Ax. He took it up from the ground and once more swung it up on one shoulder. Then he ran back down the slope, sprang into the saddle of Jos-Pran's horse, and rode off to finish the work begun so long before by Yevoda Slayer of Beasts.

In time the Beasts would have killed many of Wandor's men, perhaps all of them. They had slain more than a hundred, but this was no great number considering their strength and speed and hunger, Master Besz and Jos-Pran led the battle against the Beasts with skill, and made certain that their men heard more than their own fear and the roars of the Beasts coming at them out of the twilight.

They gathered the men into squares which could, move almost as fast as a Beast. They kept arrows and swords, pikes and axes, ready for the Beasts, and struck or shot when a Beast came too dose. They said that Wandor would certainly come soon, and meanwhile they must do their best to help him by keeping the Beasts in play.

The Beasts were invulnerable to normal weapons, and even to pain. But they could tell difficult prey when they met it, and think sluggishly about seeking easier prey elsewhere.

They found it in those men who listened to their fear rather than to their captains, broke from the squares, and ran. Most of them died in the Beasts' jaws or under their feet. So did some of the men who drifted down from the mountain when there was nothing more to be killed in the stone houses and tunnels. Then at last Wandor came down upon the Beasts with the Ax of Yevoda in his hands.

He rode up to a Beast and struck at one of the tree-thick hind limbs, to slow it. The Ax bit into the ridged hide, and it was as if a piece of the sun had fallen down to the earth. Men screamed and clapped their hands over dazzled eyes. They did not see a dim, yellow glow burning in the wound made by the Ax. They did not see the glow spread, eating away at the leg from within until suddenly the Beast was struggling along on three legs and a sack of skin. Then the skin itself dissolved into a dark powder like the finest sand; and the glow ate its way out of sight into the Beast's body. By then the men could see again, and they saw the whole Beast slowly crumble away into powder until there was nothing left of it but a dark stain on the darkening ground. They could also see Wandor, riding on to the next Beast.

Wandor rode with a clear mind and eyes that saw. One of the spells in the Ax made the searing, yellow glare of its strokes invisible to the man who wielded it. He rode from Beast to Beast, striking swiftly and riding on. He rode and struck with neither hatred nor rage, nor anger, nor joy, nor anything else that he'd expected to feel in this moment. He wanted at least to feel triumph at ridding the world of these relics of ancient and unclean sorcery; but he remembered the High Wizard's despair and his twisted body, and he could not even feel that.

It took Wandor a good while to finish off the last of the Beasts. It was growing dark, he was weary and the horse wearier still, the ground underfoot was treacherous, and the Beasts were scattering far and wide. They were not very intelligent, the Beasts of Yand, but they could still understand when there was something it was wise to avoid and do their best to avoid it.

Their best was not good enough, however. In the time it would have taken to serve three courses of a banquet, the last of the Beasts of Yand was dead. Only the dark stains on the ground remained, and even those were nearly invisible in the twilight.

Wandor had barely reined in his horse after finishing off the last Beast when the earth heaved under him. The horse squealed in raw fear. As he gentled it, he heard a swelling rumble, and saw the whole mountain of the Beast Cult collapse into itself.

The collapse started at the top, with house-sized rocks dropping out of sight as if some vast mouth were swallowing them. It worked its way down the slope, a rising cloud of dust behind it, and reached the buildings of the Cult. They vanished, long cracks ran across the mountainside, smoke poured up from where the pit had been, and the roar swelled until the sound was like a mace battering at Wandor. He put his hands over his ears and opened his mouth wide, but the sound came to him through the ground until he wondered if he and the horse and every living thing here would be shaken into a jelly.

Slowly the roar died away and the dust cloud settled. Where the mountain of the Beast Cult had stood was a gaping chasm, miles long and wide, deeper than Wandor cared to imagine. Where all the rock in the mountain had gone, he didn't know and wouldn't try to guess. He did know that the very earth had, for reasons of its own, seen fit to swallow the last trace of the Beast Cult of Yand.

Fear thrust into Wandor for a moment, as he remembered the men who'd been up on the mountain. Then he saw a long, straggling line of dust-grayed figures making their way along the edge of the chasm toward him. He rode over to meet them. Count Arlor was in the lead. Behind him came an enormous pikeman, carrying Sir Gilas Lanor in his arms like a child fallen asleep after too long a day's playing.

"We felt the first quiverings up on the mountain," said Arlor. "So I brought the men down. Zakonta carried Gwynna clear."

"Well done," said Wandor. Before he could say anything more, Cheloth broke in.

("So you have your victory?")

("I can't answer that until I know how Gwynna is.")

Cheloth ignored the implied question. ("I did nothing to make the earth move, that is certain. I think I know how it came about, but—")

("The Guardian of the Mountain?")

("—but I will not try to explain it to you now, for you would not understand it.")

("Oh, be quiet, you faceless—!") Wandor knew he was tired beyond reason, or he would have been rude to Cheloth in a somewhat more elegant fashion.

Now Master Besz was marching briskly up to report on the battle. "I regret that Baron Galkor seems to have made off with his men. It was my mistake to bring back those I had sent against him, and—"

Wandor waved a hand, dismissing the matter. "Leave it be, Master Besz. Baron Galkor can do nothing against us tonight."

"But—"

"I said, enough! Make camp, see to the wounded, and set out a double guard."

"Yes, my lord." Besz turned away and Wandor slid out of the saddle. If he'd stayed on the horse another minute he would have fallen.

CHAPTER 26

Baron Galkor's men fled south through the darkness, with fear lengthening their strides. The Baron had his doubts about the future, but he was far from despairing yet. He still had nearly four hundred men of his own. The people of Yand could turn out at least five hundred, and perhaps as many as half the Sea Folk could be trusted to fight. He would have enough to give Wandor's army a good fight when it came south.

He tramped into the town at the head of his men just as the sky began to hint at dawn. Then he learned the truth about his position. It would have made him weep if he'd had the strength.

Berek's ships had done their work, setting their prisoners inshore and slipping away. The prisoners came to the camp of the Sea Folk and told their comrades of Wandor's promise, and the frayed courage of the fugitives snapped entirely. In furious haste they swarmed down to the harbor and began boarding their ships.

"You—you let them go?" said Galkor.

"Yes," said his chief captain. "They outnumbered us two to one. They might not fight against Wandor, but they'd most certainly fight against us if we tried to stop them. Besides, there were the islanders to worry about."

That was the second chapter of the sorry tale. Except for a few honorable or stubborn men, the Sea Folk were all gone by nightfall. It was then that the elders of Yand came to the Captain. They would not lead their people against Wandor, they said, and indeed they might not be able to keep them from striking at Galkor's men.

The people of Yand had no heart left for fighting. The Beast Cult which had been part of their lives for so many centuries was gone, never to rise again. They were lost, alone, not knowing what to do. They only knew that they did not want to die in a futile battle against the man and the army which had cast down the Beast Wizards and slain the Beasts.

When Galkor heard this, he did weep—with rage. For a short time he seriously thought of sending his men out to burn every house and slaughter every man, woman, and child within reach. Then the rage passed. If he did that, he would still be fighting in the streets of the town when Wandor's army and fleet came down upon him.

It was over. He'd fought long and hard, and he had reason to hope he'd slain Gwynna. There was nothing more to do, except try to give back to Duke Cragor all the men and ships which still remained.

So Galkor's men went aboard their ships, and by dawn the sea around Yand was bare except for Wandor's fleet.

About noon of that day Wandor rode into the main town of Yand. A hundred men marched on either side of him, and behind him marched Berek, the Ax of Yevoda on one shoulder. Now that the last of the Beasts was dead, so were all the spells in the Ax. Any man could carry it and wield it without harm. Since Yevoda seemed to have been nearly Berek's size, Berek seemed the best man to bear and wield the Ax as a normal weapon.

The streets and shore were deserted, and in most of the houses and huts the sheepskins which served for shutters and doors were tied snugly in place. Here and there Wandor saw a face peering out as the new masters of Yand marched past. There was fear and doubt written across all those faces, particularly in the eyes. At least the eyes were not staring sightlessly upward from a corpse-strewn battlefield at the sky and the wheeling gulls.

It would be well to meet with the elders as soon as possible, since the life of Yand had to go on. It would be enough work to feed the men he would be leaving here, without having starving islanders as well. Yand would need at least two thousand fighting men to keep it safe, a quarter of them mounted. That meant fodder as well as salt provisions and drink.

Sir Gilas Lanor rode up.as Wandor reached the waterfront end of the street.

"How is it with our men?" Wandor asked.

"Master Besz is sending four columns to search the island."

Wandor knew he'd have to watch Besz. In his desire to make up for letting Galkor escape, the mercenary Captain was perfectly capable of having his men look under every stone on the whole island of Yand and then starting to look on the other islands if he could find ships to carry him to them.

"No one seems to have seen or heard anything of Telek the Fatherless," the Knight continued. "It is certain that he was with Foyn in the north. He fled during the fighting, and since then...nothing."

With a *mungan's* training and two dark nights on his side, this was not surprising. Wandor was about to say this aloud, when he sensed Mind Speech. Then he knew it was Gwynna, and he was no longer a part of the world around him.

("You?...") Thoughts formed themselves with difficulty. In his mind was fog and confusion equal to a great lump in his throat.

("Alive and healing, Bertan. Zakonta and Cheloth have both worked on me until they are sicker than I. A week in bed, and then...") There were no more coherent thoughts from Gwynna's end, which was just as well, for Wandor was in no state to receive them.

At last they broke the link. It had done all that was needed for the moment. There were still a thousand questions to be asked, but other and better times to ask them. Wandor raised his face to the sky and let the sun dry the tears on his cheeks.

A seal ship came gliding in to the shore. The splash of her oars and the grinding as she took the ground startled the gulls on the beach. They whirled up in a cloud, and their white wings seemed to glow in the sun.

CHAPTER 27

Galkor's men sailed back to Benzos without harm. A week out from Yand they met the ships bearing Kaldmor the Dark and the vitalized *limar* of Nem of Toshak toward the island. Galkor told him of what had happened, and he turned his ships about to follow in the Baron's wake.

The next day Kaldmor hailed Galkor's ship. He had probed Yand, he said, and he was sorry to report that Gwynna Firehair still lived. Not only did she still live, but she had wrought changes in her own Powers that he did not fully understand. Baron Galkor heard the sorcerer in silence, went below, and locked himself in his cabin until the fleet reached Avarmouth.

Somewhat to Galkor's surprise, he was not at once dragged off to the nearest prison by Duke Cragor. In fact, he was praised for his faithful service and given three thousand gold crowns, four suits of armor, and two large manor farms.

The Black Duke was shaken by the defeat and by thoughts of what might come of it, but he would not cast Galkor down. He could not afford to cast down one of the few men who would be loyal to him to the last. That would be foolish, for it would look capricious. When men began to think he was capricious, they could also begin to think that Wandor would be a better, or at least safer, master for them and ruler for Benzos. He could hardly afford to have anyone think that, with the Ocean now open to Wandor's ships, wherever and whenever he might care to send them.

* * *

The HaroiLina had neither crowns nor kings. They did have the wisdom to see that a man who had wielded the Spear of Valkath in battle and slain the Beasts of Yand with the Ax of Yevoda was a man the HaroiLina should honor and obey. So the *Kym* of Captains and the *Kym* of Hearth Mothers met, and they declared that Bertan Wandor should bear the new title of *KymDurd*, or *Kym* Master. He could call on the obedience of all the HaroiLina. That meant, among other things, a good twelve thousand warriors and nearly two hundred seal ships fit to cross the Ocean.

They also made for him a bronze circlet, with jewels from the treasures of both *Kyms* set in it. That was as good a crown as any.

Winter came down on the Ocean and on the lands around it. Snow swirled across the sullen rock of Yand, and the sentries of the garrison stamped their feet and thought of hot wine and hot fish stew. It swirled down on the forests of Benzos, where there was no more thought of ambush and raid, only of keeping warm and fed. It piled itself as high as a man around the shiphouses in the lands of the HaroiLina. Shipwrights were hard at work inside those houses, preparing the fleet of the Children of Haro for the war that would come in the spring.

It also swirled past the window of the chamber in Fors Castle where Wandor and Gwynna lay in bed, as close as man and woman can be.

"We still know nothing of what has happened to Telek, do we?"

Wandor shook his head. "I doubt if we will, either, until the next time he appears. If he doesn't appear for ten years, then I'll assume he's dead. Not before."

"Sir Gilas may have a long wait," said Gwynna.

"Yes. And if he does meet Telek, I'm not sure I'm going to let him kill the man. At least not until I ask Telek a few questions."

"Why in the name of any god do you want to—?"

He ran his fingers over her lips to silence her. "It's against my instincts too. But I've thought over all that Telek did, and I wonder about him. Was he our enemy, or was he simply trying to make as much trouble as he could for everybody?"

"But why?"

"To see how each man and each side would respond."

Gwynna was silent for a moment, then slowly nodded. "I can almost believe it. The *mungans* had some reputation for playing such games, a few centuries ago. They've decayed since then, though."

"Precisely. They've decayed so that they can now send only one man to play such games, instead of a score."

"You think the *mungans* sent Telek?"

"Let's say that I want to ask him about it, before he dies."

A long silence intervened, with the warm fog of fresh memories of shared pleasure swallowing any wish to speak. Then:

"Gwynna, do you know now what's happened to your Powers?"

"I don't know that anything has happened directly to mine. It was Earth Power I used against the Beasts, almost pure and simple. It came from elsewhere, through me, but it was not mine. This happened once before, when I was crossing the Silver Mountains to be taught by Zakonta. I was fourteen, but when danger came I found there was the Power of a full *Red Seer* passing through me. It was much more difficult this time. I could direct the Power against the Beasts, but that was all."

"I see. So you've become a better...a better passage, for other Powers than yours?"

"I think so."

"Like the *limar* of Nem of Toshak?" He had to force himself to make the comparison, and for a moment his flesh tried to shrink away from hers.

"Yes. That is a very good comparison. You're learning much more about sorcery than I expected you would."

"I have a good teacher." His thoughts ran on. Why should she be bothered by the comparison? All forms of sorcery share common techniques, laws, and inner logic. That the *limar* is a creation of Toshakan sorcery, and Gwynna is all she is to me, makes no difference when the casting of spells begins.

Let it not begin again soon, he asked. He did not know or care whom he was asking. He would accept the favor from anyone or anything which could grant it.

"Of course, I must have changed a good deal, or I could not have controlled and directed that much of any Power. If I am changing, perhaps I can hope for more Power that is mine alone. That is always easier and safer for a sorcerer to use."

"Safe?" No, there was nothing deserving that word to be found anywhere along the path they'd been called on to walk. But as long as they could walk it together!...

The thought made Wandor tighten his embrace, and in a short while the embrace brought new desire to both of them.

THE END

Continued in the next Wandor adventure: *WANDOR'S FLIGHT*

LOOKING FOR ACTION AND ADVENTURE
AUTHOR ALAN CAILLOU
NOVELS DELIVER!
WWW.CALIBERCOMICS.COM

AVAILABLE IN PAPERBACK OR EBOOK

DON'T MISS ANY OF MICHAEL KASNER'S HARD HITTING MILITARY NOVEL SERIES

BLACK OPS

Formed by an elite cadre of government officials, the Black OPS team goes where the law can't - to seek retribution for acts of terror directed against Americans anywhere in the world.

3 BOOK SERIES

Armed with all the tactical advantages of modern technology, battle hard and ready when the free world is threatened - the Peacekeepers are the baddest grunts on the planet.

4 BOOK SERIES

CHOPPER COPS

America is being torn apart as criminal cartels terrorize our cities, dealing drugs and death wholesale. Local police are outgunned, so the President unleashes the U.S. TACTICAL POLICE FORCE. An elite army of super cops with ammo to burn, they swoop down on the hot spots in sleek high-tech attack choppers to win the dirty war and take back America!

4 BOOK SERIES

FROM CALIBER BOOKS

www.calibercomics.com

DON'T MISS ANY OF NEIL HUNTER'S NOVELS FROM CALIBER BOOKS

Reporter Les Mason is completing an expose on the Long Point Nuclear Plant. But before he can finish he dies an agonizing death. The doctors are baffled—and there are similar cases to follow...Chris Lane, his girlfriend, and organizer of the Long Point Protestors, discovers Mason's notes, and decides to find out for herself what the plant has to hide.

2 BOOK SERIES

In middle of the 21st century America – over-populated decaying cities are ruled by hi-tech gangs pushing every vice and wastelands are controlled by bands of mutants. Ordinary citizens are oppressed and face a hopeless future. But Marshal T.J. Cade is a new breed of law enforcer. Teamed with his cyborg partner, Janek, Cade takes on these criminals and works in the gray areas of the law to get the job done.

3 BOOK SERIES

The village of Shepthorne England wasn't being gripped, but strangled by a winter's blanket of heavy snow and Arctic temperatures. The trouble began innocently enough with a massive pile-up of autos on frozen roads leading to and from the village. Then, from the sky, a military transport plane with its top secret cargo of devastation crashed down towards the center of the village. Hell was just beginning to touch Shepthorne and its unsuspecting citizens...

FROM CALIBER BOOKS

www.calibercomics.com

CALIBER COMICS GOES TO WAR!
HISTORICAL AND MILITARY THEMED GRAPHIC NOVELS

WORLD WAR ONE: MO MAN'S LAND

ISBN: 9781635298123

A look at World War 1 from the French trenches as they faced the Imperial German Army.

CORTEZ AND THE FALL OF THE AZTECS

ISBN: 9781635299779

Cortez battles the Aztecs while in search of Inca gold.

TROY: AN EMPIRE UNDER SIEGE

ISBN: 9781635298635

Homer's famous The Iliad and the Trojan War is given a unique human perspective rather than from the God's.

WITNESS TO WAR

ISBN: 9781635299700

WW2's Battle of the Bulge is seen up close by an embedded female war reporter.

THE LINCOLN BRIGADE

ISBN: 9781635298222

American volunteers head to Spain in the 1930s to fight in their civil war against the fascist regime.

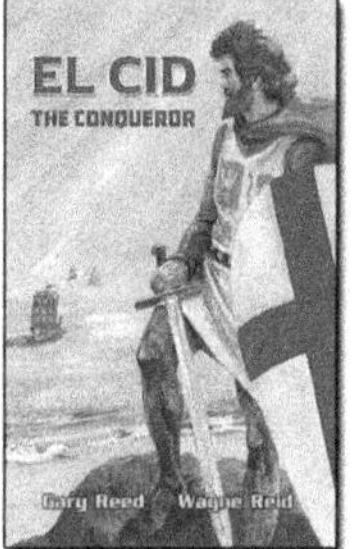

EL CID: THE CONQUEROR

ISBN: 9780982654996

Europe's greatest warrior attempts to unify Spain against invading foreign and domestic armies.

WINTER WAR

ISBN: 9780985749392

At the outbreak of WW2 Finland fights against an invading Soviet army.

ZULUNATION: END OF EMPIRE

ISBN: 9780941613415

The global British Empire and far-reaching influence is threatened by a Zulu uprising in southern Africa.

AIR WARRIORS: WORLD WAR ONE #V1 - V4   *Take to the skys of WW1 as various fighter aces tell their harrowing stories.*
ISBN: 9781635297973 (V1), 9781635297980 (V2), 9781635297997 (V3), 9781635298000 (V4)

CALIBER COMICS GOES TO THE EDGE!
Science Fiction and Horror themed graphic novels

DEADWORLD
ISBN: 9781942351245

RENFIELD
ISBN: 9781942351825

NOSFERATU
ISBN: 9781942351931

**LOVECRAFT:
THE EARLY STORIES**
ISBN: 9781942351634

**THE WAR OF THE WORLDS:
INFESTATION**
ISBN: 9781942351962

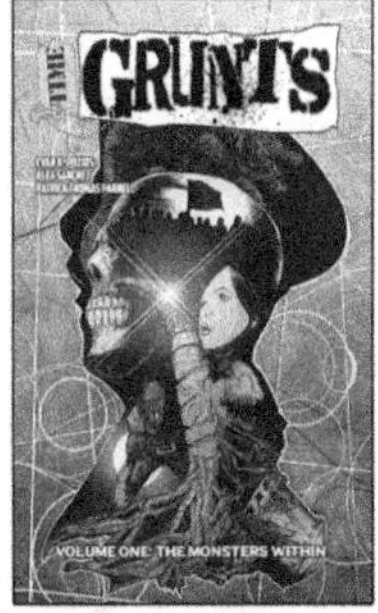

TIME GRUNTS
ISBN: 9781635299472

DRACULA
ISBN: 9780996030649

**DRACULA:
THE SUICIDE CLUB**
ISBN: 9781635299571

**JACK THE RIPPER
ILLUSTRATED**
ISBN: 9781942351917

THE SEARCHERS
ISBN: 9781942351979

A.A.I. WARS
ISBN: 9781635299168

**AUTUMN: TERROR IN THE
LONDON UNDERGROUND**
ISBN: 9781544624020

www.calibercomics.com

www.ingramcontent.com/pod-product-compliance
Lightning Source LLC
Chambersburg PA
CBHW070528100726
47907CB00004B/1034